STRIKE FORCE BLACK

KORTH CHRONICLES BOOK 2

C.T. GLATTE

For my Family. Thank you for your trust and support.

1

Captain Vannt stood on the bridge of his colony ship and looked down upon what the humans called, Western Europe. There were no windows, he saw a holographic representation. His XO, Commander Vox, stood behind him a step, his four arms crossed. His head was flat and dark, a sign he was unhappy. Captain Vannt's mouth clicked and hummed, "You still think we should exterminate the humans, despite the TRs blessings. Why?"

Commander Vox uncrossed his arms and took a step forward to stand beside his Captain. He pointed at the planet, perched on the edge of the atmosphere. "We landed here 11 earth years ago. If we'd started exterminating them immediately we'd be done by..."

Vannt interrupted, his head deflating slightly in displeasure. "That didn't happen. I'm asking why you *still* want that path."

Commander Vox's head went back to flat and his clear eyelids compressed over his eyes like a camera shutter snapping a picture. "Without them we could drill much faster. We are near the earth's core, but with the rudimentary metals we're forced to use, even with the alloy processes, the last bit will be cumbersome. If we lifted the radiation containment field, we'd have more power to finish the project quickly and ahead of schedule."

"I know all this, however you know as well as I do the humans would have no other choice but to attack us once they realized what was happening. Without our system's core operational, we're vulnerable to their weapons. Indeed, we've lost Korth in North America already. Their weapons are rudimentary, but they are able to kill us. The containment is necessary to keep them ignorant."

"I understand that. Of course. I just don't like having these vermin around. I'm sick of seeing them. I want to get off this cursed, small, ugly planet. I want to watch them burn."

Vannt's head expanded in mirth. "You are a warrior. You want to kill the enemy in front of you. Is it not enough to watch them battle amongst themselves? I find it wholly entertaining."

Vox's head expanded too and the crimson lightened, "I do enjoy it, but it's only a game and I'm tired of games."

"A dangerous game for some," Vannt thought of the 10 warriors he'd lost so far in the Russian ranks. His head flattened. "Perhaps it would please you to put our warriors on the front line in more than an advisory role?"

Vox didn't answer at first. Finally he said, "It would do them good...they grow tired of this occupation."

Vannt crossed his arms. "The Germans and Scandinavians are ready to attack the United States' East Coast. Perhaps some of your warriors would enjoy the fight?"

Vox's head expanded, "Yes they would, Captain. Thank you, sir." He bowed and Vannt bent slightly at the waist.

————

CAPTAIN VANNT and Commander Vox stood at the head of the massive wooden table. The human heads of states were all seated in their over-large chairs; chairs built for the eight-foot tall Korth.

It pleased Vannt to see the humans looking and feeling small and insignificant, like snot-nosed children. He eyed each man, keeping his gaze steady and his senses tense and connected to their neural cores. General Mao Ze Dong was to his left. Vannt found the man's visage almost impossible to decipher, but he knew his mind and it twisted and squirmed like all the others. He was simply better at hiding it.

Next was Josef Stalin. He stared straight ahead, not wanting to make eye contact. Vannt could feel fear coursing through him, making his mind a morass of darkness. His attack into North America's north had initially been a great success but soon stalled as the Americans and Canadians were finally able to stop his advance. Heavy fighting continued, but the harsh winter and the stalwart enemy made each yard gained, bloody.

He'd lost a carrier group in the Pacific, which assured he wouldn't be able to break the stalemate anytime soon. Stalin thought he'd be punished as his other Generals had been and Vannt wanted him to continue to think he was on thin ice. The truth was, Vannt didn't give a Stellantian Worm's ass who won, as long as they continued to fight each other.

He released him from his gaze and found the next man, Field Marshall Rommel, staring back at him with his chin raised. His straight nose was like a runway and his thin, slicked back hair was immaculate. He'd lost much of his hair since he first elevated him to the role of Western European Premier over a decade before.

It was disgusting how these humans aged in such odd ways. Vannt searched his mind, he was more stable than the other leaders, more calculating, due no doubt, to his lifetime devotion to military service. He allowed Rommel to continue his gaze for another second then plucked the back of his mind like a string, making him wince and divert his eyes.

The man beside Rommel, President Quisling, didn't try to look Vannt in the eyes. His mind was simple. He simply wanted to keep fucking his mistresses and drinking his Aquavit. Vannt gave him little notice, he was always the same; uncomfortable and driven by sex. Pairing him with Rommel, a consummate professional, was like pairing an infant with an adult and calling them equal.

Quisling's self-esteem was low, he knew he was a minor player and he always thought the next moment would be his last. He was good at keeping his rather uppity people in order however, and that was something Vannt found valuable.

The last man was President Vorster. Vannt gave his mind a quick overview, knowing what he'd find. He was a brutal man and he took great pleasure in exuding his power and his viciousness by killing his own people in cruel and surprising ways. He didn't think Vannt knew about his secret killings, but nothing could be further from the truth.

For some reason the people of Africa thought they were far enough away from the mother ship to be able to get away with things. At first, Vannt punished them with public and brutal executions, but he soon found if he left Vorster to his own devices, he'd do the work for him. There was no justice involved, but the randomness kept the population cowed and obedient.

Vannt pulled hard on his line and Vorster's thin mouth opened and his bloodshot eyes widened in excruciating pain. Hatred flared, but was quickly extinguished. Vannt knew some innocent South African citizen would pay that very night.

Vannt raised his hands, extending all 12 fingers. They glistened with thick snail-like goo. "Friends, welcome." His embedded translator device glowed slightly in his neck, turning his clicks and hums into language each could understand. In turn, the gathered leader's red translators glowed. They all nodded and answered in greetings. Even with the translator, Vannt was always irritated with their nasal tones. He glanced at Vox whose head reddened in irritation.

"It is time to take pressure off the valiant forces of the Russian Army. As you all know, they've been stopped by the North Americans outside Anchorage Alaska. The fighting is fierce and I'm sure Stalin's men are performing valiantly but nonetheless, they are in a stalemate."

Stalin's thick mustache moved on his lip like a centipede in a bird's beak. He stammered, "That's right you're…"

His voice broke and he gagged as pain crossed his face, "No one speaks until asked to speak!" Vannt slammed a hand down on the table and it cracked like a rifle shot. The men flinched and cringed and the room went completely silent. Seconds passed, Vannt stood to his full height and his head transformed from deep crimson back to just red.

He continued, "Stalin has failed to advance his Army, but he has succeeded in pulling many American troops north. Now it is time to strike them again." He looked at each man. They gazed back and he could tell each man, except Quisling was hoping he'd be called on to attack. Vannt glanced at Vox, *they are so bloodthirsty.* Vox's head expanded slightly, agreeing.

Vannt leaned forward and centered his gaze on Field Marshall Romell. "Field Marshall. You and Quisling will have the honor and privilege of attacking the United States' East Coast." He surveyed each man. Quisling was smiling but his thoughts were wondering if he'd really have to do anything or if he could leave it all to Rommel. Rommel, on the other hand was already sifting through which units he'd send, how many and when. "I trust your men and ships are ready to move?" He already knew the answer but wanted Rommel to speak.

Rommel shot to his feet, clicked his boot heels and nodded. "Jawohl. With your blessing I will release my Wolfpack from their berths in the British Isles and commence attacks on North American shipping. We'll block their harbors with sunken ships then pick off any remaining vessels at our leisure."

He was going to continue but Vannt flicked his brain ever so slightly and Rommel instantly stopped talking. "I'm sure your plan is a good one Field Marshall. No need to give me the details. A weekly update of your progress will be sufficient." Rommel nodded and fidgeted, wanting to leave immediately to set his long-awaited plan into motion.

Vannt looked at Moa and Vorster. "In a few months I will release your troops as well and you can sweep south and east, taking the rest of the island chains including Australia and Hawaii. You must be ready at a moment's notice, in case I need an earlier attack. Is that clear?"

They both stood and Mao barked, "Clear, Excellency. We are ready now and will be whenever you give the order." Vorster frowned wanting to be the first to speak. He satisfied himself with a deep bow instead.

Vannt looked to Vox then back to the assembled despots. "Dismissed."

The leaders hustled out the heavy double doors leaving Vannt and Vox alone. Vannt asked, "Which legion will you send?"

Vox's head expanded, "The most deserving are the Allegios. They've been the most involved with keeping order amongst the humans. They would relish a chance to dole out some real punishment."

Vannt nodded, "A good choice. They'll have plenty of opportunities."

Commander Vox nodded his agreement. "I'll wait until the humans have invaded the mainland, no need to risk our warriors in the first wave."

"Just remember, we are *not* trying to win this war, only to keep it going until we have what we need. Use the battle for training. Inevitably some warriors will be lost, but I agree it will be good for them to do some killing."

2

First Lieutenant MaryAnn Larkin strode into the ready room and took her seat beside Captain Elizabeth Perkins, callsign Viper, and Captain Amanda Withers, callsign Snake. Behind her, pilots watched and spoke in hushed, awed tones. She heard the female pilot seated directly behind whisper to her friend, "I hear she's got eight Russian kills and sank their aircraft carrier."

MaryAnn ignored them and greeted her two friends. She reached out and pretended to dust off Amanda's brand-new Captain's bars. "Wow, spiffy. Haven't seen them on you yet. They look magnificent."

Mandy shoved her hand away and looked over her sunglasses to view MaryAnn's shoulders, "Looks like your butter bars turned silver. When did that happen?"

MaryAnn's smile radiated with pride, "Soon after Captain Willis offloaded me onto the mainland."

Mandy looked at her and gave a knowing smile. *"Captain Willis,"* she emphasized his name. "He sounds sexy." MaryAnn's smile changed and her cheeks turned a shade of red. MaryAnn looked at her feet and she shrugged. Mandy put her hand over open mouth, "You didn't."

MaryAnn's head snapped up and she shook it back and forth. "Of course not." She pointed with her thumb over her shoulder at the two gossips behind her, "That's how rumors get started."

The two newbie pilots sat bolt upright and the talkative one stammered, "S - sorry, ma'am, I mean sir. I didn't think you could hear…"

MaryAnn cut her off, "I have four confirmed kills and half a destroyer. I didn't sink their carrier." She pointed to the two captains, "They did. Or at least, they helped." She leaned toward her friends, "Captain Willis helped too."

Captain Perkins shook her head, "You *do* have feelings for him. I knew it."

MaryAnn shrugged again, "He's much older, but he's very handsome and incredibly brave."

Mandy shook her head, "What ever happened to that hometown boy you used to talk about? The Army puke."

A faraway look came over MaryAnn as she realized she hadn't thought about Jimmy Crandall for weeks. She'd heard nothing from him, but figured he was probably fighting somewhere in Alaska with all the other west coast boys. "Jimmy." Saying the name made her suddenly long to see him. "I - well we don't keep in touch. We were neighbors, nothing more. Just friends."

Captain Perkins rubbed her forehead. "You don't know whether you're coming or going, do you?"

MaryAnn scowled, "What do you mean?"

"I mean you've got two men on your mind and you don't have a clue about your true feelings for either one."

MaryAnn shook her head and crossed her arms over her chest. "Until this war's over none of it matters. I don't have time for boys or men, or whatever."

Mandy smiled and slapped Perkin's leg, "That's why she's got more kills than either of us."

Lizzy Perkins guffawed and was about to defend her honor when the door behind the podium opened and in walked Admiral Walter Childreth with two lieutenant commanders on either shoulder. Everyone in the room shot to their feet and braced.

Admiral Childreth smiled and held up his hands. "At ease, ladies. Take your seats." There was scuffling as the women sat. Childreth's broad shoulders and athletic build made the podium look small, like he was standing on a stage where children performed plays.

Before everyone was seated, Mandy leaned toward MaryAnn and whispered, "Now *that's* a sexy man."

MaryAnn had to cover her mouth to keep from laughing out loud. "You're awful," she scolded.

Childreth cleared his throat and addressed the room, "It's an honor to speak with you ladies today." He shook his head, "Scratch that," he grinned. "I never know how to address women like you. You're as tough as the toughest men we have, but you're also knockouts." There was a smattering of laughter, "Forgive an old man. I'm honored to be here today to bestow upon The Fighting 4th a unit citation. This signifies all your many achievements over the last few months in stemming the red tide which has plagued our fine nation and turned our peace to war.

"Your tenacity, your bravery, your grit and unrelenting attacks on the Russian carrier fleet despite suffering terrible losses, shall be remembered as a true highpoint in this terrible conflict." He stopped to gather his thoughts. The room was silent, "I know this citation, though deserved and earned, means little to those of you who lost friends, but let it shine as a remembrance to those brave pilots. And let it be a symbol of your history and your shining future." He pulled something from beneath the podium and held it up. It was a flute of sparkling champagne. "To you, The Fighting 4th. Give 'em hell, ladies!" He lifted the glass and drained it to their raucous cheers.

He slammed the glass down and wiped his mouth with the back of his hand, "I'm sorry we can't serve you, officially you're still on the clock." He grinned, "But know this, that was damned good and I owe each and every one of you a drink." With that he turned and walked out the door, flanked by his two lieutenant commanders who were grinning ear to ear.

———

THE FIGHTING 4TH didn't get any time to celebrate their unit citation. Admiral Childreth wasn't kidding about them being on duty. Two hours after he'd slammed his glass of Champagne back, they were on the flight line getting ready to move north, likely into combat.

MaryAnn's *Tigress* purred like a kitten. Sergeant Callahan and her ground crew worked all night getting the P-51 ready to fly. MaryAnn pushed the plane to the limits every time she tangled with the more powerful Russian fighters. It's why she was still alive and had four confirmed kills and two more probables. She hadn't fought the Russian fighters in weeks, having destroyed the Russian Carrier group the month before, but she'd been put in charge of training replacements and she trained and flew hard.

The month of September had been busy and violent. Half the squadron had been lost, but now their ranks were back to full strength, albeit with raw, green pilots.

They were being moved north, to station themselves closer to the fighting in Alaska and Canada. The Russian advance had been stopped for the moment. Harsh weather along with the arrival of 10 fresh Canadian divisions had been enough to stop their advance, but neither side was able to move forward. They were calling it a stalemate, reminiscent of World War I.

The Fighting 4th was moving to Anchorage to bolster the Canadian Air Force, which had been taking heavy losses. The trip was just over 2,000 miles which they'd break up into three legs. Weather permitting, they'd be landing in Alaska in three days.

The move worried MaryAnn. The mere mention of Alaska brought up harrowing images of heavy combat. They'd be landing on an airfield that was under constant threat of air raids. So far, her war had been brutal and violent, but she knew safety was only a couple hundred miles away, on the mainland. If she were hit, she could limp back to the states, or if she had to bail out, as happened before, she'd at least have a chance of being picked up by friendly forces. In Alaska she'd be under the constant stress of a combat zone and if she went down behind enemy lines...?

Over the radio she heard the tower. "Flight squadron, tower. Cleared for takeoff on three-two. Wind calm, ceiling's 5,000 feet."

MaryAnn heard Captain Perkins' calm voice answer. "Tower, flight lead. Understand cleared for takeoff on three-two."

MaryAnn leaned over and saw the P-51 at the head of long line move forward toward the active runway. Before heading north their planes had gotten new paint jobs to match the winter conditions they'd be fighting in. The white mottled camouflage would make them nearly invisible from above and the grayish-white bottoms invisible from below. Her chest swelled with pride, they looked deadly and beautiful all at once.

She looked over her controls paying close attention to the oil pressure. The increased throb of a nearby Merlin engine caught her attention. Captain Perkins was taking off. MaryAnn looked left and saw the magnificent outline of the P-51 just as it lifted off. She could see her squadron commander's helmeted head through the plexiglass of the bubble canopy, and the faint shimmer of the two red stars signifying kills, beneath her canopy.

Finally, it was MaryAnn's turn. She put in right rudder to compensate for the left torque of the engine and added throttle. She felt *Tigress* leap off the runway. The landing gear slipped into the wings and the thrumming purr of her engine carried her through the moist air of northern Washington State.

She made a lazy right turn, gaining altitude quickly. She leaned over and looked down at the airfield she'd called home for the last few months. She'd miss the tiny town and its citizens who'd been so helpful and kind to her.

She wondered if she'd ever enjoy another bear-claw pastry from the tiny shop on the corner with the fat old man in the filthy apron, who always seemed to be smiling. Even with the rationing, he'd always managed to find her one of the delicious delights, as though it was made just for her.

Soon she pushed through the cloud layer and formed up with the rest of her squadron in the clear sunlight. Below, the layer of clouds spread out like a goose down quilt for as far as she could see.

She looked to her right and left, noticing her flight of four forming up on her wings for the first leg of their long trip north. She was proud how far the new recruits had come in their proficiency. When they first arrived, they'd only had the minimum number of hours required in the P-51 and had been raw and even dangerous.

MaryAnn and the other veteran pilots took their training seriously, drilling them relentlessly, knowing if they didn't, they wouldn't last long against the Russian fighters. In the few short months they had them, they'd turned them into competent fighter pilots. Despite going on countless missions patrolling the west coast, they hadn't seen a Russian fighter since the attack on the carrier group. Now they were heading into the teeth of the Bear. They were as prepared as they could be with the short training time.

She'd tried to distance herself from the recruits, knowing there was good chance they'd die in the coming months, but she couldn't help getting to know them as they trained and struggled together.

She'd been assigned three of the new recruits and they flew off her wing now. Rebecca Knipps, on her right was an Oregon girl, just like her, but from the big city of Portland.

She was older than the others, indeed older than herself at twenty-two, but her maturity level was no better than that of a sixteen-year old. She thought her age would give her some kind of advantage, but she was quickly put in her place by the far superior flying skills MaryAnn and the other veterans.

MaryAnn didn't particularly like the pretty city girl; too full of herself. Whenever there was an opportunity to look in a mirror, she'd take it. Somehow, she still had makeup, a commodity tough to find these days, since the factories that produced such frivolity were now putting out goods for the war effort. MaryAnn had to admit though, she'd shown marked improvement in her flying once she'd gotten her ego out of the way.

Second Lt. Lisa Spencer was the quiet type. She hadn't spoken a word the first few days other than to say, 'yes sir, no sir,' and MaryAnn thought the native Washingtonian must have something wrong with her. Once she got inside the cockpit of a P-51, however, she became a different person. It was as though the plane was a part of her and she'd impressed everyone with her ability to make the airplane perform for her like a master orchestra conductor. She even gave MaryAnn a run for her money during one-on-one mock aerial combat training.

She was tiny, barely tall enough to qualify for flight training. Everything about her was small, but she flew the Mustang as though she were the biggest person in the sky. Despite her obvious prowess, she remained humble. In fact, when the others were boasting about this or that, she barely spoke, just smiling and nodding, knowing she could out-fly them but not needing to crow about it.

The third recruit was an Idaho girl. Second Lt. Misty Flaherty grew up in the northern panhandle of Idaho. She was a cowgirl through and through, having lived on a large, rugged ranch all her life. Her hands were huge and calloused even though she hadn't done ranch work for months. Her harsh features were more man-like than womanly. Despite her obvious athleticism, she struggled with the P-51, trying to force the controls as though it was an actual wild mustang.

The ground crew responsible for servicing the planes complained bitterly about having to replace brake pads due to her heavy-footed taxiing methods. But, like the others, she'd eventually gotten the hang of it and was now a competent Mustang pilot. MaryAnn only hoped she'd live long enough to become a pro.

———

THE DRONING of her fighter and the unchanging view beneath her wings lulled MaryAnn into a near stupor. The squadron was on the final leg, having landed, refueled, eaten and used the restroom. She thought sure she'd piss her pants before landing, but she'd made it in the nick of time and she doubted there had ever been a more satisfying release in her entire life.

But that had been two hours ago and she still had four more hours of droning boredom. All that time made her mind wander. She wondered how her parents were doing. She'd written many letters and received letters back assuring her they were fine and they were proud of her and to be careful.

The letters were full of mundane town news, but they were a slice of the normality she craved. She'd written her final letter the night before they left. She'd told them how they were moving again, trying to keep it vague, knowing the military censors would probably black it out anyway.

She wanted to tell them how scared she was, how it felt to helplessly watch a friend shot out of the sky, arcing toward Mother Earth in a ball of fire before finally impacting. She didn't tell them any of this though. Indeed, she never even told them she'd been shot down. She kept her letters upbeat as though she were at summer camp instead of fighting for her life against a relentless enemy.

She doubted her parents bought the act. They knew her unit had been decorated for valor during the last battle, something you didn't get by not being intimately involved in the killing and carnage.

There was a sudden break in radio silence, pulling her from her thoughts. It was Second Lieutenant Spencer's high squeaky voice. Even though she was using the plane to plane channel, she was still breaking protocol and that made MaryAnn seethe for an instant before she finally understood what she'd heard. 'Bombers at 10' o'clock low.'

She looked out her left window, pressing her helmet against the canopy. The squadron was flying between 15,000 and 20,000 feet, spread out at different levels, but within sight of one another. MaryAnn was in the lowest flight so the only thing that should be below her were clouds.

She immediately saw the dark dots against the white clouds and knew they were Russian bombers. She squeezed her radio against her throat, "Flight lead, number three."

There was a moment when nothing happened and she was sure Captain Perkins was livid for her breaking radio silence. Her curt reply, "Three. This is flight lead, go ahead."

"Flight of six Russian bombers at ten o'clock low moving west at approximately 6,000 feet. Over."

There was a pause as Captain Perkins was no doubt trying to find the bombers. MaryAnn knew Perkins was at 20,000 feet and might not be able to see them. She also knew this was not the mission. The P-51s were flying light, but they all had a full load of .50 caliber bullets for their six machine-guns.

Perkins finally replied, "I don't see them. Any fighters with them?"

MaryAnn had been struggling to spot any escorts but hadn't seen any. She shook her head and replied, "Unless they're in the cloud layer, that's a negative, flight lead."

There was a long pause as Captain Perkins weighed the situation. MaryAnn knew taking on the bombers would mean breaking away from the squadron with little to no chance of catching up with them again. If they engaged, they'd be on their own the rest of the way to Anchorage.

Perkins' voice crackled over the radio, "Let 'em go. I'll radio their location, try to warn whoever they're targeting. Maintain radio silence. Over."

MaryAnn knew it was the correct call, but it still grated on her to see the bombers so sure of themselves they didn't even have an escort. She longed to wing over and break them up, saving whoever was slated to be bombed, but she kept flying level fighting the urge, "Another day, Russkies," she muttered to herself.

Lt. Spencer's voice again over the local radio. "Sir, Lieutenant Knipps."

MaryAnn saw it the same instant. Lt. Knipps' gray mottled fighter was winging over and diving straight at the bombers. *Shit.* She keyed the throat mic "Lieutenant Knipps get back in formation right now. We are not to engage. Over." There was no reply. She either had her radio off or was intentionally disobeying orders. She looked up at the streaking P-51s not wanting to do what she had to do. "Flight lead, Knipps is engaging. I'm going down with her to give her a hand. Over."

There was a stunned silence, but MaryAnn didn't have time to wait. She pulled the stick right and winged over, chasing her wayward pilot. She looked behind, seeing the other two in her flight following. Her radio crackled to life with an irate sounding Captain Perkins, "Dammit. Permission to engage granted. Stick together, we'll see you in Anchorage. If she survives tell Lieutenant Knipps she's in deep shit."

"Roger," MaryAnn replied. She switched to the local channel, "Number four, we're coming with you." She watched the bombers growing larger as they descended upon them, "Four, go after the tail-end-Charlie. Acknowledge."

There was a strained curt reply, "Roger."

"Two and Three, take the next in line. Hit them hard and fast then dive into the cloud and break right to," She quickly scanned her compass. "One-four-zero degrees for 30 seconds. We'll come out of the clouds in front and make one more head-on pass, then reform at 15,000 thousand." She didn't wait for replies. She didn't have time.

She edged closer to Lt. Knipps' tail, then moved right, keeping an eye on the clouds beneath the bombers, hoping she didn't see the flash of a Russian fighter.

Lieutenant Knipps opened fire and MaryAnn cursed inside her oxygen mask, *too soon, dammit*. The bombers hadn't noticed them, but now the streaking tracer fire pinpointed them and instantly the sky was filled with tennis ball-sized tracers spewing from the bombers as though they'd kicked a hornet nest.

MaryAnn saw Knipps' plane slew to the side trying to avoid the tracer rounds. She keyed her mic, "Keep it steady, Knipps keep it steady."

The bomber grew in her sights filling the aiming pipper. She pulled the trigger, hearing and feeling the six machine guns coming to life on her wings. She watched the bomber spark with multiple hits along the wing and one of the bomber's two engines erupted in smoke and fire. As she flashed by, she saw the stricken plane list right and descend but lost sight of it when she entered the white abyss of the clouds.

She pulled out of her dive and angled right until her compass showed one 140 degrees. She started counting in her head while scanning her instruments, making sure her wings were level and her altimeter wasn't showing her climbing or worse—diving.

She glanced outside, immediately wishing she hadn't. Her mind tried to tell her she wasn't flying straight and level and it was all she could do to fight the urge to correct. She brought her head back into the cockpit, *trust your instruments*.

She concentrated on counting and when she hit 30 seconds, she gently pulled up, watching her instruments carefully. She hoped her recruits would come out with her or they'd be on their own the rest of the way to Anchorage.

Suddenly the white-gray world disappeared and she flashed into the bright winter sunlight. Her eyes burned and she squinted trying to keep the tears to a minimum to avoid fogging her goggles.

She looked around frantically for the others. She saw first one, then two P-51s emerge not far behind her. She maintained her course and speed swiveling her head trying to find the missing Mustang. She keyed her mic, "This is number one. Check in. Over."

"Two here."

"Three here."

There was another voice fainter and MaryAnn could hear fear in it. "I'm, I'm lost. Can't get out of this damned cloud."

She recognized Second Lieutenant Knipps's voice. "Fly your instruments Lieutenant. What's your heading and altitude?"

At first there was no response. Finally, the voice again, even fainter. It was full of panic. "I - I can't get out. I can't get out."

"Dammit, Knipps. Get control of yourself and your airplane. I want you to survive so I can kick your ass later. Now, give me your heading. Now!" She yelled the last word, hoping to pull her panicked pilot from the brink.

"One-eight-zero. Oh shit, I'm - I'm diving. Redlining."

"Slow down. Fly the instruments. You're fine, just fly the instruments. Don't look outside your cockpit."

The voice was barely audible now. "Oh my God, I'm gonna die." The radio crackled, there was more, but it was fading and uninterpretable.

MaryAnn mashed the mic. "Rebeccca! Rebecca! Lieutenant Knipps, come in. Answer me, dammit." There was no response.

They flew in silence forgetting about the bombers, only thinking of their lost comrade. MaryAnn knew it would be hopeless to search for her. In the vastness of the sky, without the aid of ground radar, it would be like finding the tip of a needle amongst all the hay in the world.

Lt. Knipps' only hope would be getting control of her airplane and finding a landing strip, or hooking up with another flight, both of which were unlikely. Even if she bailed out, she'd be descending into winter with only the clothing on her back and her sidearm.

She edged her plane upward climbing into the crisp clean air. She leveled off at 15,000 feet and continued on course toward Anchorage. Lt. Spencer and Flaherty never left her wings, clinging like scared puppies. She continued swiveling, hoping to see the flash of Knipps' fighter but all she saw were clouds stretching out to infinity.

3

The weeks following the death of Jimmy's best friend, Hank, on the frontlines outside Anchorage, passed like a thick layer of fog. Jimmy didn't remember his fellow GIs having to yank Hank's body from his grip. He didn't remember being put on a stretcher and hauled into the Anchorage hospital, nor the concerned doctors and nurses buzzing from patient to patient, tending ugly wounds and shattered limbs, all around his bed. He didn't remember staring at the ceiling for hours on end.

In fact, the first thing he remembered was being told his father was dead and he needed to return home to console his mother. The stern officer looming above him looked for an instant like Hank but his mind was playing tricks on him. He focused on the face, "Wh - what did you say?"

The officer put a consoling hand on his shoulder, which Jimmy quickly shrugged off. "I said, you need to go home and be with your mother. The rest would do you good and she needs you right now."

"My father's dead?"

He nodded, "Yes, I'm sorry. He…"

Jimmy interrupted, "How? How'd he die? He's not on the front, he's a desk jockey in the Navy, not even on a ship."

The lieutenant who's nametape said, Yates, hesitated, then shrugged and shook his head. "I don't know the specifics."

Jimmy scowled, noticing the hesitation. "You know more than you're saying. Spill it," he demanded.

The lieutenant's face turned a shade of red. "Don't forget who you're talking to, soldier." He was about to say more but his face softened and he looked around as though concerned he'd be overheard. He leaned in close, "I heard he was — well, there's no easy way to say it — executed." Jimmy's eyes widened in confusion. He stood suddenly. He swayed on his feet, it was the most movement he'd done since entering the hospital. "Whoa there, soldier," said Lt. Yates.

Yates reached out to steady him and Jimmy pleaded. "What? Executed? By who? For what? What the hell's going on?"

Lieutenant Yates was clearly flustered at Crandall's outburst and was desperately trying to calm him as bystanders became interested. "Sit down, soldier. Calm down. Just sit a minute."

Jimmy pushed him away, "Get off me." He looked around the open floor. There were far too many wounded for the main hospital, so they'd expanded into the local high school gymnasium. There were hundreds of beds, each filled with a wounded American or Canadian soldier. He saw the exit on the other side of the room and moved towards it.

He only made it a few feet when two MPs were beside him clutching his arms, holding him in place. He struggled to break free but the big men had little trouble holding Jimmy's wiry frame.

Jimmy stomped the right MP's foot, aiming for the toe-box. Despite his slippered feet, Jimmy's heel smashed down hard and the burly MP gasped and bent over, loosening his grip. Jimmy yanked his arm away then smashed his elbow back into the man's nose. Blood squirted in all directions as the MP's head snapped back and he fell backwards, tripping over his own feet.

"Hey," the second MP yelled and gripped him tighter. He stepped behind Jimmy's back and yanked his left arm up until Jimmy thought his shoulder would dislocate. He stopped struggling, trying to relieve the pressure by standing on the tips of his toes. The MP put his foot in front and pushed. Jimmy fell face first and the heavy MP landed on his lower back with his knee firmly planted. "Stop the bullshit, Crandall," he seethed into his ear. "I oughta break your traitorous arm, you little piece of shit..."

Another booming voice, "At ease soldier."

The pressure on Jimmy's back and shoulder remained but slackened slightly. "Sir, PFC Crandall assaulted Richardson. He's trying to...."

The booming voice interrupted. "I saw the whole thing. Now let him up. Get an ice-pack on that nose, Richardson."

Jimmy heard a muffled reply and felt himself being lifted harshly by the uninjured MP. He gave Jimmy one last push and gripped the handle of his sidearm hanging from his utility belt. "Don't try anything, Crandall."

Jimmy saw raw hatred emanating from his eyes. It could've been because he just beat the crap out of his buddy, but this seemed like something else. "Who you calling a traitor, you no good lousy..."

"At ease! Both of you."

Jimmy looked to the voice and immediately stiffened, seeing major's insignia on the unfamiliar officer's shoulder. He ground his jaw together and faced him. He snapped off a half-assed salute, noticing the worried look on Lieutenant Yate's face.

The major didn't have a nametape. He was tall with an athletic build that only comes with constant hard training. There was nothing about his face that was unusual, in fact if you saw him in a crowd you'd never be able to pick him from a myriad of other faces, except for the eyes. The brown color wasn't unusual, but they had depth. As though they'd gazed upon things no man was supposed to gaze upon. They left Jimmy chilled and instantly put him on his guard, as though he were being scoped by a Russian sniper.

There was no return salute and finally Jimmy dropped his hand back to his side. Without taking his eyes from Jimmy's, he spoke to the MP, "Help Richardson out of here, Sergeant."

"But, sir. He just..."

"Now," the major's voice cut him off making the MP jump. Without another word the MPs sulked off, muttering about tearing Jimmy's head off if their paths crossed again.

Jimmy ignored them and asked, "Who are you, sir?" He wasn't in an Army uniform and the only insignia on his tan shirt was the golden major's leaves. He wondered if he were perhaps a navy man.

The major grinned. "I'll ask the questions, *PFC* Crandall."

Jimmy was slow to put his clothes on. His countless cuts and scrapes, some which still had stitches, made his movements slow. His immobility over the past few weeks didn't help anything. After the brief and violent clash with the MPs, his body was now protesting any and all movement, as though making him pay for the abuse.

The major waited with his arms crossed over his broad chest. He watched him as though he were a stack of especially stinky shit. When Jimmy was lacing his boots he asked, "Were you wounded or just...*resting?*"

Jimmy sat upright and scowled at him. "Seen any combat, *Major?*"

The major ignored the jibe and turned his back on him, "Follow me, Private."

————

The walk from the gymnasium to the idling Jeep was cold. Jimmy looked at the slate gray sky and thought it looked like it might snow any moment. The parking lot was wet with puddles of slush, which he tried and failed to avoid. Despite the unpleasant weather, it felt good to move. Even though the air was cold and hurt his lungs, it was good to be outside in fresh air again. He didn't realize until now, just how stifling the gymnasium air was.

The major took the front seat beside his driver who was dressed similarly in nondescript clothes. It was an Army Jeep, but that and the major's insignia were the only indicators they were in the military. Jimmy wanted to ask the major his name but doubted he'd get an answer. The major would tell him whatever he thought he needed to know and nothing more.

The short ride to the hospital was done in silence. The driver pulled up near the front entrance and Jimmy followed the major past the front desk and into the bowels of the hospital, eventually entering a room filled with the smell of cooking food.

The cafeteria was nearly empty, only a few hospital workers clanging pots and pans. Like every other hospital employee he saw, they were old, everyone under 45 was in the service.

He hadn't seen any damage to the building, and wondered how they'd avoided the air and artillery attacks the town of Anchorage had endured. He doubted the Russians cared one wit about the fact it was a hospital. They'd simply been lucky up to this point. For the first time he realized how vulnerable he'd been cooped up in the school gymnasium. A single 500 pound bomb through the roof would've been disastrous.

The major led him to a two-person table set off in the corner and they both sat. The major took a look around making sure no one could eavesdrop and said, "Your father was executed for treason."

The words hit Jimmy like a sledgehammer to the skull. He stared, unable to formulate anything. Only a moment before, he'd been full of questions but now couldn't remember a single one. He opened his mouth to speak, but nothing came out. The major watched him with a bemused look. It sparked Jimmy's anger and he finally found his voice, "Treason!" It wasn't a question, but a stark statement of disbelief.

"It was a secret military trial. Quick and efficient. Your father was found guilty and executed a week later by firing squad."

Jimmy suddenly felt like he'd puke. He managed to stammer, "That - that's insane. My father's not a...*traitor.*" The word tasted foul on his tongue. The major only stared. "For spying?" Jimmy asked. The major's face didn't change, still with the bemused half-grin. Jimmy shot to his feet and leaned forward ready to strike the conceited shithead.

The major leaned forward and pointed a beefy index finger at Jimmy. "No. For the shit you're about to try." His eyes looked dangerous, like those of a python.

Jimmy thought if he tried to strike him, he'd find himself in the hospital again. "What do ya think I'm about to try?"

"He struck an officer. During wartime—that's a traitorous act."

The news was even harder to take. He looked into the major's dark eyes and shook his head, trying to comprehend what he'd just heard. "You—you killed him for..." He could hardly speak. His face was flushed nearly purple with rage and confusion. "For hitting someone? Was it the fucking President or something?"

The major's eyes turned deadly again and his finger wagged, "Watch your mouth, son. You're already walking a thin line."

The anger subsided, replaced with a deep pit of darkness. Jimmy didn't want to cry, to show weakness in front of this asshole, but the emotions coursing through him were too much. First his best friend, now his father? Why? Why was this happening? He dropped his head, feeling the despair overtake him like a black wave. His body jerked with heavy sobs which made no sound.

He didn't know how long he cried but when he looked up, the major was gone. Jimmy looked around, wanting to ask more questions. He wiped his eyes and saw the arrogant bastard pouring himself a cup of coffee. He watched him walk back to the table, sipping the steaming cup, "You done blubbering?"

"Fuck you, *Major.*"

Instead of ripping his head off, the major grinned showing off perfectly straight white teeth. "I'll give you that one for your loss, but that's your one free pass." Jimmy wanted to say it again, louder, but the major continued. "You and your mother will be flown to Washington DC for the funeral."

"Flown?" Jimmy had never been on a plane.

The major nodded. "You'll take a flight out of here in a few days once the escorts arrive. This airspace is still contested." He grinned again and Jimmy decided he liked his serious face better. "Don't be scared, I'll be right there to hold your hand," he teased.

"You're coming along? Why?" The major didn't answer, just stared straight ahead not showing any emotion. Jimmy shook his head. "Can I at least call you something besides, major?"

The major's mouth turned down slightly as he considered. Then he gave a slight nod, "You can call me, Black. Major Black."

"Is that your real name?" Jimmy asked. Major Black looked at him as though he were the stupidest piece of shit on earth.

———

JIMMY SPENT the next few days trying to get in contact with anyone from his unit. Since being carted off the battlefield, he'd only seen a few soldiers from his unit; wounded men. But he had no idea how the rest of his friends were faring on the battlefield and he felt bad that he was in relative safety while they were in mortal danger every day.

He finally ran into Private Caulkins, a soldier from his company. He'd been wounded in an artillery strike. He was missing his right leg from the knee down but despite that, he was upbeat. "Crandall," he exclaimed loudly when Jimmy approached him. "Is that you?"

Jimmy grinned, and reached his hand out. They shook heartily, "In the flesh. You're the first son-of-a-bitch from the company I've seen in a long time."

"Hell, we all thought you'd gone bonkers."

Jimmy looked down, unable to hide his shame. "Yeah, I uh, well, I..."

Caulkins held up his hands. "Hey, don't worry about it. Hell, there aren't many of us originals left. Nothing to be ashamed of—losing Hank like that." He shook his head, "We all liked him."

Jimmy pointed at the stump of his leg, "Does it hurt?"

Caulkins leaned forward and rubbed just above the stump. He shook his head, "Not bad. It's the damned phantoms that are the worst." Jimmy tilted his head and Caulkins explained. "Even though that part of the leg's gone, it's like my brain doesn't get it. I still *feel* stuff down there. They call them phantom pains and they're a bitch. Like having an itch you can't scratch. Drives me insane. They tell me they'll go away, but I don't know." He looked at Jimmy, his eyes taking on a faraway look. "Still better than being up there." He gestured north, toward the front. "This is like heaven."

Jimmy looked around and dug into his boot where he'd stashed a small flask of whisky. He held it up, "Maybe this'll help."

Caulkins' grin broadened, "Can't hurt." He reached out unscrewed the lid and tilted his head back quickly, then cringed as the alcohol burned its way down his throat. He handed the flask back and uttered, "Thanks."

"What's it like up there now?"

Caulkins' grin disappeared, "It's hell. Hell on Earth. When we first pushed 'em back, it was great. I mean, we were finally advancing, pushing *them* back for a change. We'd march past their burned-out tanks, see their dead instead of ours. It felt like we were finally winning, but when we got to the thick forest, they stopped us cold." He leaned back in bed but stayed on his elbows. "We dug in—they dug in. Now it's trench warfare, just like we read about during World War One. It's cold. You're wet all the time, occasionally dry just cause the wet's frozen on you. There's artillery every day going both ways." He pointed to his stump. "That's what got me. I was in the damned latrine taking a shit. Next thing I knew I was 20 feet away, on my back with a shit-ton of dirt and crap on me. My leg was still attached at that point I guess, but hanging by a thread. They cut it off when I got here."

"Jesus, Caulkins. I'm sorry."

"Don't be. I'll be sent home. My war's over and for that I'm grateful. By the way, you getting lucky with any of these nurses? Haven't seen any beauties but," he gave a sideways grin, "beggars can't be choosy."

Jimmy grinned back and shook his head, "Haven't felt the urge, to tell you the truth."

Caulkins guffawed, "You truly *are* fucked up. Hell, I lost a leg and I'm still horny." Despite the grim circumstances, Jimmy laughed. He didn't remember the last time he had and it felt good. But then he thought of his father and the laughter seemed inappropriate and out of place. An image flashed through his mind of his father tied to a post in a field with riflemen facing him. He wondered if he died with a blindfold on or had he stared into the eyes of his executioners. Caulkins noticed the faraway look and put his hand on Jimmy's shoulder. "Just gotta put it behind you until this is all over. Just stow it away or you'll go insane."

Jimmy looked him in the eye, "They shot my father."

Caulkins' expression changed from concerned to confused. "Your father's KIA too? Jesus, I had no..."

Jimmy interrupted, "Not in combat. They shot him for, for—" he found he couldn't say the word. It felt so wrong. He knew it couldn't be true, knew in his heart it wasn't possible.

There was a sudden roar of multiple engines outside making both men cringe and look at the ceiling of the gymnasium. Caulkins had to yell over the din. "Air raid?" There was fear in his voice.

Jimmy stood, keeping his eyes up and shook his head. "There's no siren. There's usually a warning. Must be the bombers and fighters they're expecting. They must be ours," he said excitedly. He murmured, "Means I'll be leaving soon."

Caulkins put his hand to his ear and leaned forward. "Huh?"

Jimmy didn't want to explain. He thrust his hand out, "I've gotta go. Glad you're gonna make it outta here." Caulkins squeezed his hand and waved as Jimmy trotted toward the exit.

––––––––

JIMMY RUSHED OUTSIDE and looked up as wave after wave of beautiful sleek fighters streamed overhead. They circled in pairs, waiting their turns to land. They were painted off-white with splotches of black smudges and he thought they were well camouflaged for the conditions. As they got lower he noticed they weren't entirely camouflaged. The tail was streaked with a pink slash. He wondered what it signified.

The airport was a half-mile away and before he knew it, he was trotting along the slushy road. He'd been released by the doctors a few days before and he'd tried to exercise, but found it difficult to jog on the icy streets without risking a fall, so he'd stuck to the gym, lifting weights.

Running along the edge of the street, splashing through muck and slush felt good for a change. His new uniform and boots were getting wet and dirty but he didn't give a shit. It felt good to run and he relished it.

By the time he got to the airport gate, most of the aircraft had landed. A soldier with the white lettering of an MP on his helmet stepped out from the one-man shack and held up a hand. He had an M1 carbine slung over his shoulder and looked cold and grim. "Hold it right there, buddy."

Jimmy looked beyond him and pointed, "Just want to watch them land, if that's alright."

"You got business inside?"

"I'm supposed to get a flight out of here on one of those."

The MP sneered, "Oh really? Where's your bag? Your weapon? Hell, you don't even have so much as a coat."

Jimmy's shoulders slumped in defeat. "Come on. I just wanted to watch 'em land for chrissakes. What harm can it do?"

"Get the hell outta here." He put his hands together, blew into them then rubbed them together trying to stay warm.

Jimmy remembered the flask in his boot. "Hey, I've got something that'll make your guard shack warmer." The MP looked back at him suspiciously. Jimmy reached into his boot and pulled out the shiny flask. He shook it and the sloshing told the MP it was half full.

The MP looked around sheepishly but approached. Jimmy unscrewed the lid and the MP smelled the contents. "Whisky," Jimmy said smiling. "You can keep it safe for me while I'm inside." He tilted his head, "Deal?"

The MP took another look around then quickly snatched it out of his hand, took a quick slug and shoved it inside his coat. His face contorted as the whisky did its magic. "Deal," he said.

As Jimmy walked past, the MP stuck his head out and handed him a piece of paper. "If anyone harasses you, give 'em this."

Jimmy took it and held it up as he walked past, "Thanks. I won't be long."

The MP smiled, "Take your time."

Jimmy pushed through the front doors of the Anchorage airport. Before the war it had been a small municipal airport with very little activity, but now it was a bustling hive.

Jimmy looked out over the airfield, it was full of taxiing fighters. He remembered months before, sleeping in the field beyond the main runway on his first night in Alaska. He and Hank had dug a foxhole and watched a Russian air attack on the airfield. He tried to identify which hangar he'd seen take a near miss and realized there were far more hangars and buildings than there used to be. The engineers had been busy.

He noticed a viewing deck on the second level. It had a foot of snow on it, but he pushed the door open and crunched through the crusty top layer until he was at the railing. It was cold and he wished he'd brought a heavier coat, but he could see the action on the airfield much better now.

There were six large concrete hangars, each containing two bombers. He didn't know what kind they were, but they had two engines and looked menacing and proud. He could see a flurry of activity around each one and he guessed they were mechanics and air crewmen fussing over their steeds.

The smaller fighters were tethered to the ground with stout chains along the edges of the runway. They were widely spaced, parked inside concrete walls with only camouflage netting for roofs. Jimmy idly wondered when they'd get around to capping the small structures with proper roofing. One good snowstorm would bury them.

He noticed a group of what could only be pilots walking toward the airport. They were dressed in flight suits with heavy leather coats and white fur up around their necks. They wore white helmets with oxygen masks hanging down. They swaggered toward the terminal with a confidence that only fighter pilots could pull off.

They were almost to the terminal doors when there was another roar of aircraft overhead. The pilots stopped and looked up at the late-comers. Jimmy saw them point and followed their fingers. The clouds were descending quickly and it felt like it would snow. He saw a P-51 suddenly burst through the layer and flash over the airfield. Two more appeared and the planes stayed beneath the layer only a couple hundred feet above the ground and flew north up the valley before turning back.

Jimmy watched in fascination as the first pilot deftly lined up and landed without so much as a bounce and taxied off the runway toward an empty revetment. The next two landed hard, each bouncing a few times before finally steadying. He noticed each plane had the same distinctive flash of pink on their tails.

The first group of pilots entered the main terminal, after watching their fellow pilots land safely. He felt like a kid at a major league baseball game wanting to get a closer look at the ballplayers as he trotted through the tracks he'd left in the snow and re-entered the heated terminal. He stomped his feet, leaving a trail of melting snow leading to the stairs.

He stopped halfway down and stood in shock as the group of pilots took off their helmets. They were all women. The pink slash suddenly made sense and he wondered how he'd not thought of it before. There were many all-female units in the armed forces, but he hadn't actually seen any on the front lines yet.

Despite their loose-fitting flight suits and thick layers of winter clothing, he couldn't help evaluating their womanly features. They stood around just inside the door, their attention focused outside. He heard snippets of hushed conversation that made him think they were worried.

He descended the rest of the way to the ground floor and walked past as nonchalantly as possible. No one gave him a second glance. He took a hardwood seat in the main part of the terminal a few yards from them and pretended to read an old magazine while secretly stealing glances and eavesdropping. He didn't know why he was interested, other than the obvious fact that they were women.

As they warmed, some pilots took off their winter coats and Jimmy noticed the stitched-on ranks of officers adorning their shoulders and lapels. He shook his head, of course they'd be officers, flying a plane took brains. He didn't want anything to do with officers, let alone female officers, so he placed the magazine back where he found it and stood to leave.

At that moment the three late pilots entered and were immediately surrounded by the other pilots. One officer with captain's bars questioned the first officer that entered. The captain was obviously upset. She spoke with her fists firmly planted against her hips. Finally, she allowed the newcomer to speak and her voice made Jimmy stop.

He couldn't put his finger on it, but he recognized that voice from somewhere. He tried to see beyond the gaggle of women but it was hopeless. He only got a glimpse of blonde hair, but not much else. He bee-lined it for the stairway again, determined to find out why the voice was so familiar.

He stopped halfway up and couldn't keep himself from blurting out, "MaryAnn?"

The conversation stopped and every pilot's face turned toward him. He gulped, realizing he'd spoken too loudly. He didn't know what else to do, so he braced and saluted.

MaryAnn's worried face turned a bright shade of red as she recognized him. "Jimmy?" she asked. "Jimmy Crandall? Is it really you?"

He dropped his salute and beamed, "Yeah, it's me. Holy-moly, I can't believe it's actually you?"

The other women couldn't keep from covering their mouths and giggling. The captain became annoyed and turned toward him. "You have business here, soldier?"

He braced again and shook his head. "Uh, not really ma'am, I mean sir." To make it less confusing, the United States military had decided years before to address female officers as 'sir' rather than 'ma'am.' He pointed sheepishly at MaryAnn, "She's — well we were neighbors before all this."

Captain Perkins glared at him, "Neighbors? Well, do you mind if I continue with my debrief *private,* or should I get in line behind you?"

————

AN HOUR LATER, MaryAnn finally emerged and approached Jimmy with a huge smile on her face. She'd changed out of her flight suit and wore heavy wool pants, and a button-down shirt with a wool coat over the top. Perched on her head at a jaunty angle was her peaked officer's hat. Jimmy hadn't seen her since he shipped out and he was shocked how beautiful she was.

As she approached, he remembered his manners and snapped off a crisp salute. She grinned and returned it, then stepped forward so they were face to face. "Jimmy Crandall, it really *is* you."

He grinned, "Guilty," he said.

"What are you doing here?"

His smile faded. "I was—I was wounded." She looked worried but he shook his head. "I'm fine now. Scratches really." He showed her his forearm where the skin was still puckered from stitches.

She was about to touch it, but he pulled his sleeve down and shook his head, "It's nothing. Hank..." his voice broke but he recovered. "Hank didn't make it."

MaryAnn's hand went to her mouth and she gasped. "Oh no," she uttered. "Oh no, not Hank." He couldn't bring himself to speak, just nodded. She gripped his arm and pushed him toward the lobby seats. "Let's sit down and talk."

He didn't resist and allowed her to lead him. He waited until she was seated, then sat beside her, "He died in my arms. Russian grenade." His voice quieted. "He saved my life."

A tear welled in MaryAnn's eyes making them glassy. She put her hand on his and it felt warm and comforting. He shook his head, "I should put it past me, but I can't seem to."

She shook her head, "Put it past you? How? He was your best friend. The pain will subside, but you won't ever put it past you. Believe me."

He looked into her eyes. "You've lost friends." It was a statement.

She nodded and wiped her eyes and looked at the ceiling. "Yes, many."

They held hands without speaking and minutes passed. It wasn't awkward, in fact Jimmy thought he could sit beside her the rest of his life and be happy. He wasn't sure what he was feeling, he just knew he didn't want it to end.

The spell was broken when another female captain approached them. Jimmy wiped his red eyes and fidgeted, trying to get to his feet. The captain, whose name-tape said, Withers stopped him. "At ease, soldier." She was short and cute with curves in all the right places. "Any sign of Lieutenant Knipps?"

MaryAnn shook her head and her eyes were full of pain. Jimmy looked outside. It was pitch dark. The sun had set on the short winter day some time ago without him noticing. "Someone's still out there?"

MaryAnn nodded, "One of my pilots. She dove after a group of bombers. I couldn't let her go it alone so we dove after her. We came out of the clouds and she didn't."

"Jesus, MaryAnn. I'm so sorry." He didn't know what else to say.

Captain Withers tilted her head, "Come on, this place is shutting down. We need to get to the mess hall before they close it." She looked at Jimmy, giving him a look up and down and liking what she saw, "How'd you get here?"

He pointed outside, "Ran here. It's not far."

"Well aren't you the sporting one. You want a ride back or you wanna run back in the dark?"

He gave a sideways glance at MaryAnn then back to Withers, "I'll take a ride if you're offering, sir."

She grinned and held out her hand, "You can call me, Mandy." He looked worried and unsure how to take that. She was a captain, he a PFC. Things didn't work that way. She added. "When we're not around other people."

He shook her petite hand and smiled, "Okay, Captain Mandy."

She shook her head and gestured, "Come on, Jeeps out here."

4

Ensign Harry Park smoked a cigarette. He directed half his attention at his gun crew aboard the battleship USS Watkins and the other half trying to keep the cold winter wind of the Atlantic from penetrating his coat.

It was dark and cold and he didn't remember ever being this miserable. He thought about the countless times he'd duck hunted with his dad through nasty cold storms, but this made those memories seem like a tropical paradise.

He'd been in the regular Navy six months now. Just like most boys with good grades and means, he was given a choice upon graduating high school: ROTC through college and owe the military six years, or go straight into mandatory service right out of high school and get it over with in two.

He'd chosen ROTC because he didn't want to be in the Army, which is where most recruits ended up. He wanted Navy like his father and his father before him. Also, the mere thought of having some dumbass ordering him around made him ill.

Now, he was committed to six glorious years of this bullshit...and there was a war on. At least it was mostly happening on the west coast, thank God. He took the last drag off his cigarette and threw it overboard, quickly losing sight of the glowing ember as the wind caught it and blew it away, "Smoking lamps out, boys."

The six men under his command took their last puffs and flicked the stubs into the sea, "Aye, sir." They came up from below the rim of the four barreled 40mm Bofors gun adjusting their bulky Mae West life jackets. Normally, during the middle of the night there were only three men manning the anti-aircraft guns, but the captain had gotten some intel that spooked him and the order of the day and night, was readiness.

He paced behind the gun trying to stay warm as the crew stomped their feet and rubbed gloved hands together.

"How long you reckon we have to stay out here, sir?" Drawled Gunner's Mate Lyle.

Ensign Park shrugged but knew he couldn't see him in the pitch darkness. "Until the captain tells me otherwise, Lyle." Park was annoyed by the question. Wasn't it obvious? "Why don't you sing us one of those southern ballads you're so fond of?"

"You mean the ones about the thieving, murdering Yankees, sir?"

Park grinned and accentuated his New York accent, "That's the one."

"But sah," Lyle drawled, "won't that offend your Yankee sensibilities, sah?"

"I think I can take it, Gunner's Mate."

There was a sudden flash out to sea which drew their attention and ceased all conversation. Another flash, this time lingering long enough to see the outline of one of the cruisers in their formation. Despite the wind, the clap of an explosion washed over them. "What the hell?" exclaimed Park.

The blaring of the battle stations klaxon filled the air and Ensign Park knew it meant only one thing, they were under attack. "Load! Angle the guns to the waterline. No way this is an air attack in this weather."

The crew sprang into action. The guns rotated downward as the gunners spun cranks with practiced ease. The cruiser lit up again and remained visible as fire swept the decks. "That's The Spark, she's on fire," Ensign Park yelled over the din of the klaxon. "Gotta be a sub attack. I didn't see any gun flashes."

The battleship increased speed and slewed to the side as the captain went into evasive maneuvers. The burning cruiser suddenly erupted in a massive explosion and in the sudden light, Ensign Park saw white streaks lancing through the water. He pointed and yelled, "Torpedos incoming!"

Two seconds later, two torpedos impacted the portside stern simultaneously. The brilliant flashes blinded him briefly and he was thrown against the steel wall behind him.

The battleship immediately slewed to port. Park pulled himself off the deck and reached for the gun rail for stability. The fire consuming the stern cut through the darkness. The dual blasts had turned the sleek battleship's stern into twisted steel and wood. He could see the remains of another bofors gun, but saw no sign of the crew. He tried to remember the duty roster, but couldn't remember if it was Ensign Blaine or Rance.

His own crew was reeling from the blast. He yelled, "Look for more, be ready to open fire." His crew settled and tore their eyes from the spreading inferno and focused on the lit-up water.

A frantic voice, "There! Torpedo!"

The gunner saw it too and immediately fired downward. The massive flash from the gun nearly licked the choppy seawater. Great geysers erupted as the 40mm shells impacted.

Ensign Park watched the streaking torpedo slice between the geysers and pass beneath the angle of the gun barrels. He yelled, "Brace for..."

The deck erupted beneath him and he felt a tremendous force compressing his body. There was an instant of intense pain, then he was flying, weightless. Just before his world went black he thought he glimpsed the sliver of the moon.

———

CAPTAIN HEINRICH ONGE watched the carnage through the periscope and a smile spread across his handsome, square-jawed face. "Nice shooting gentlemen. The Watkins looks to be dead in the water. I saw two fish impact the stern and one amidships. She's slewing to port and looks dead in the water." His smile broadened when he heard his men cheer. He kept his eyes to the scope and spun it 360 degrees. No threats.

This close to the surface, the rough sea rocked the boat and the black water sloshed over the periscope obscuring his vision much of the time, but the flames erupting from two burning ships lit up the night.

"Come to heading one-six-one, I want another spread on the Watkins." The orders were repeated and he felt the boat responding to the slight heading change. "It appears U-boat five-oh-three has also hit her target. I see a cruiser already half sunk."

He took his eyes from the scope and looked at his crew. He was proud of them, they'd performed perfectly, he expected nothing less. "Our hunter patrol has fired the first shots into the American Atlantic Fleet, gentleman." There was another raucous cheer.

There was no more need for silence, the Americans certainly knew they were there now.

"Captain, torpedos ready to fire."

"You have a good track?"

"We cannot miss, she's dead in the water. I have torpedos set for deep running."

Onge nodded, "Excellent. Fire at will."

There was a whoosh as three more torpedos launched from the forward tubes.

Captain Ongle put his eyes to the periscope again and easily found the burning battleship. In the darkness, he couldn't see the streaking torpedos but knew they'd impact momentarily. He stepped back and offered the sights to his second in command, Oberleutnant Zimmer, "Take a look, Zimmer."

Zimmer stepped in quickly, relishing the chance to see the torpedos strike. Moments later there was a low rumble as the torpedos lanced into the already wounded battleship. Zimmer said excitedly, "Direct hit, sir. Three direct hits. It's magnificent."

Captain Onge called to sonar, "You still have the other targets, Heinz?"

Sonarman Heinz had one headphone off expecting the question. "Yes sir. Bearing hasn't changed, three-two-zero, speed still twelve knots."

Captain Onge nodded grimly thinking what must be going through the American naval officer's minds. They'd just watched two of their ships erased from the planet in less than five minutes, including one of their impressive battleships.

Zimmer wasn't able to contain his excitement. "Take a look, Captain. The Watkins is going down."

Onge stepped in and focused, immediately seeing the burning ship. It was low in the water and canted over unnaturally. He could see flames being squelched as the ship tipped over with sudden violence. The massive superstructure of the bridge smashed into the sea, sending shockwaves and a massive wave of water. "She's flipped," he exclaimed trying to keep emotion from his voice.

He got back to business. "We'll slip through this mess and take the other two cruisers. Take us down to fifty feet. Coms, inform U- two-oh-three to match us."

"Aye, Captain."

Onge slapped the periscope handles up and the console sunk into the floor mimicking a support beam. He looked around his marvelous ship. He was a veteran submariner. He remembered the days when none of this would have been possible. Ship to ship communications while underway was a fantasy, even the sophisticated sonar system would have been something from a science fiction novel.

The arrival of the Korth in '37 had changed all that. They increased every branch of the military's technology, but none more than the Navy. He had no idea why they seemed to be more partial to his chosen branch of service, perhaps because being on a spaceship was the nearest thing to being on an ocean-going ship. Whatever the reason, he was grateful for the upgrades. He was quite certain they outmatched the enemy by a large margin, certainly in the submarine category.

He'd been appalled to learn that an American submarine had played a large role in sinking the Russian carrier group in the Pacific. He'd felt sure the Korth enhanced sonar would've picked up the submarine easily. He wondered if perhaps the Korth hadn't shared the technology with the Russians. Perhaps they played favorites.

Minutes later the sonar man lifted one side of the headphone, "Targets are changing course, sir. The nearest one is slowing and approaching the sinking ships. The other has increased speed and is weaving and pinging."

"Stay close to the wreckage, all that noise will keep us hidden. Weapons, you have a solution on those targets?"

The two sailors beside the sonar man were hunched over the Torpedo Control Center, adjusting knobs and dials. The senior of the two nodded, "Yes, Captain. Forward tubes one through four are set for the contact moving toward the wreckage. Rear tubes one through four, set for maneuvering contact. Ready to fire on your command, Captain."

The torpedos were also a marvel of technology which he would've never dreamed of before the aliens. They could be programmed to follow the sonar to the contacts, homing in on them as long as the sonar was active. It virtually guaranteed a hit. The only drawback being, as long as the sonar was active, they could be *seen* if someone was searching.

Captain Onge wasn't worried about being seen just yet. His ability to hit targets in any weather at any time of day would have the allies reeling, at least initially. From this day forward his job would become more difficult. He doubted he'd have too many more kills as easy as these unfortunates.

————

UNITED STATES NAVY FLEET ADMIRAL Harold Stine was pulled from a deep sleep by the incessant ringing of his bedside phone. His wife of 26 years mumbled something and rolled away from him, taking the covers with her.

He sat upright on the side of bed and finally found the phone. "Stine here," he grumbled as he slipped on his glasses.

He listened and all his grogginess disappeared as Commodore

Winstrap's voice told him the news. Stine's tone changed, "Put all naval forces on status red-one. I'll be there in a few minutes."

His wife rolled toward him, sensing the change in his attitude. "Trouble?" As a career Navy wife she knew not to pry too much.

He sighed heavily and nodded, "The worst kind, Gracie."

She stroked his back and he leaned over and kissed her forehead, "I may be staying at the office for the duration."

She nodded and the admiral stood and rubbed the sleep from his eyes. Despite his age, he was still in good shape. He exercised every day. Betsy reminded him, "Remember to eat. I know how busy you get. I'll alert Miles."

He nodded, went to the bathroom and shut the door. She heard the shower running. She got up, heated water and by the time he was dressed and heading for the door had a steaming cup of coffee ready for him. He took it and sipped gratefully, "Thanks, darling. I'll check in when I can." She nodded and gave him a peck on the cheek.

He descended the front steps and slid into the backseat of the idling car. "Morning, Miles," he addressed the driver.

Miles looked at him in the rear-view mirror, "Good morning, sir. The Pentagon?"

"Yes, and don't stop for any red-lights."

Miles nodded and depressed the accelerator. "Yes, sir. Should be light traffic this time of the morning."

Stine used the 10 minute car ride to gather his thoughts. He did a mental tally of all the Atlantic US naval forces under his command. They were plentiful, however it sounded as though not as plentiful as they were when he'd gone to bed six hours earlier. The Watkins?

The powerful Cadillac pulled up to the guard shack and Stine was happy to see a squad of stern looking Marines with their weapons off their shoulders, backing up the MPs who inspected their identifications as though they'd never seen the car or Stine before. When they were satisfied, the MP sergeant stepped back and snapped off a brisk salute. The barricades were lifted and the Marines pulled the spiked barriers from the road and stepped back and saluted.

Miles commented, "That's different, Admiral."

"Yes, it' going to be a long day. No need to wait for me. Head back home in case Gracie needs your services."

The Cadillac stopped in front of the building's lit up entrance. More Marines were fanned out and Stine saw a heavy .50 caliber machine gun behind a sandbagged barrier that hadn't been there the day before.

The security of the nation's strategic centers had been increased immediately after the first aggression by the Russians in Alaska months before, but now the threat was off the East Coast only miles away, and security tightened quickly.

Inside, Admiral Stine was whisked through two more security checkpoints. The place was bustling with activity, much more than normal. There was always something going on inside the long hallways, but Stine hadn't seen it like this since the Russian invasion.

Commodore Wallace Winstrap was suddenly by his side. "Morning, Admiral. The staff's still coming in, but I'll show you what we know so far."

They entered a large space with leather chairs placed around an oval bar, which overlooked a sunken room with a huge table in the center. An oversized map of North America, Canada and South America filled the table's surface.

Around the map stood men and women with headphones on, holding long sticks which formed 'Ts' at the end. Occasionally, a worker would lean forward and move a magnetic piece to a new spot as new information streamed in.

Commodore Winstrap pointed at the Eastern Seaboard which was dotted with symbols of known shipping. There was a large red 'X' beneath the symbol denoting Patrol Group Zebra. "That was their location when we received the emergency SOS. It came from the cruiser, Corsican." He lifted one of the many phones placed strategically in front of each leather chair.

Twenty feet away, a Navy lieutenant on the floor surrounding the map table immediately reached for the buzzing phone behind his head and looked up at the Commodore. "Sir?" he asked into the phone.

"Play back the last message from Corsican."

"Aye, sir." They watched as the lieutenant hung up the phone and walked to a console of electronic equipment. He spoke to the operator, a woman with large headphones covering her ears. She nodded and her hands moved so fast they blurred.

The room filled with static then the voice of a harried sounding officer, "This is Patrol Group Zebra. Enemy contact. Suspected submarine attack of unknown origin. The Frost and Watkins…" the voice took on emotion, obviously flustered. "They're going down. Repeat Frost and Watkins are going down." There was more static, then a voice in the background could be heard. "Torpedos incoming, tor..." The transmission was suddenly cut off leaving only a faint buzz of static, which turned off when the operator pulled the switch.

Commodore Winstrap looked at his watch. "That was an hour and half ago. There's been nothing since. We've been trying to raise them, but it's as if they disappeared off the face of the earth."

Fleet Admiral Stine thought about the men serving on the four ships. The captain of The Corsican wasn't a personal friend, but he knew all his senior officers to some degree. He *did* know the captain of The Watkins well, however and he was shocked to hear of its possible demise. The Watkins was one of their newer battleships, huge, displacing nearly 65,000 tons. Losing it was a serious blow to the Atlantic Fleet.

He said a brief silent prayer for his friend's safety then barked, "I want all ships able to muster to do so. I want destroyers and cruisers actively pinging and patrolling the coastline in force. Get the Air Force on the line. I want anti-submarine patrols up whenever possible."

Commodore Winstrap nodded and relayed the order via telephone. "It's done, sir. Who do you think's behind it?"

Stine shook his head and rubbed his chin. "I doubt it's the Russians, their subs have been giving us headaches in the Pacific, can't imagine they're operating out here too. Gotta be Western Europe. Probably came out of the British Isles, but were so damned blind, it could be from anywhere."

He paused and considered something else. "The weather must be worse out there on the water than it is here, how the hell'd those subs attack at night in these kinds of conditions? How'd they find our ships?"

Commodore Winstrap shook his head. "We've had no reports of

Russian subs with that kind of capability. This must be some new alien technology, sir."

Stine nodded and looked worried, "That's what I'm afraid of, Wally." He took a deep breath expanding his chest. "Get me a secure line to the President."

Commodore Winstrap nodded, lifted the phone and talked briefly with the lieutenant who relayed it to the operator. Winstrap handed him the phone, "It's ringing, sir."

Winstrap stepped a few paces to give the admiral space. Stine listened to the ringing and stiffened slightly when he heard his Commander in Chief's groggy voice. "Sorry to wake you sir, but there's a new front in the war…"

5

Rex Crandall was exhausted but that was nothing new. He was four months into the program. It was officially called, The Branch, but everyone in training called it, The Program, as though it was some kind of college class but if he failed this class he wouldn't end up with an 'F,' but a bullet in the back of the head.

His 'class' started with fifty men and women and now they were whittled down to fifteen. Those who'd suffered injury were put back a class or two depending on the severity, but those that simply couldn't cut it, disappeared.

The training cadre didn't hide what happened to them. No one could know of its existence, so they were executed and their bodies burned. There was no family to tell, all the candidates were already assumed dead.

Rex hated the cadre. Everyone did. They were ruthless and unforgiving. Many times Rex had wanted to quit, thinking death would be far easier than the misery he was being put through, but the thought of strangling the sadistic cadre as they slept or slitting their throats or simply filling them full of bullets, kept him going.

The first few weeks they'd been pushed to their physical and mental limits—and beyond. Rex was a good athlete despite being older than most of the others and he re-ignited a competitive spirit he thought he'd left on the basketball court back in high school. Despite his age, or possibly because of it, he worked smarter, making the time cut requirements by a second or two instead of trying to crush the records like the young bucks.

They'd lost many 'recruits' during the physical phase. Rex figured out early, it was mostly a mental game. He could put the pain in a separate compartment and push beyond it, completing whatever task needed completing.

He watched many men, far stronger physically, fail because they simply couldn't get past the pain. When they got to the point where their muscles would no longer work with the normal coaxing, they simply quit. Rex and a few of the others learned it was all mental. Their bodies could be pushed farther than they ever thought possible, as long as they were in the correct mental state.

After the first month of attrition, the physical stressors didn't slack off, however their bodies and minds were attuned to the abuse and built on it, even thrived. Rex had no doubt he was in the best physical shape of his life.

Each new challenge was more difficult than the last. Eventually, the curriculum changed slightly. Instead of constant physical abuse, they spent more time in the classroom. They studied and memorized every weapon the free west had and every known enemy weapon. They could field strip and put them back together quickly and correctly— even blindfolded.

The cadre would isolate each recruit, throw a mass of parts onto a white tarp and shut and lock the door. When they returned in 30 minutes they expected every part to be put back together, and each weapon, Rex had four, was tested with live ammo. If there was a problem, like a weapon didn't fire, the recruit was given one more chance, but instead of 30 minutes, only 20. If they failed—they disappeared.

Along with weapons training, they also learned hand-to-hand combat. The instructors were brutal and relentless, throwing recruits with various Judo, Ju-Jitsu and Tae kwondo moves until they were battered and bruised.

Rex enjoyed the hand-to-hand training. The instructors weren't the normal sadistic cadre members. They were there to teach, not break them down and make them fail.

He absorbed the painful lessons quickly and excelled. The instructors used him more and more for demonstration so he got extra training. Soon, he could hold his own with the instructors. He was motivated to learn, hoping someday he'd have a chance to kick the shit out of the cadre.

Now, after four months, there were 15 recruits left: six women and nine men. During the physical testing, the women were separated, presumably given somewhat lower expectations. Rex hardly noticed when they returned to their ranks. He remembered there being a lot more women at the start. The fact that the cadre would execute women as quickly and easily as a man, made him hate them even more.

"Cadet 520, get up that rope! Now!"

Rex jolted hearing his new name, 520. He jumped as high as he could and gripped the thick rope at the same time lifting his legs and wrapping the rope around his ankle and foot. He pushed with his legs, feeling the crook of rope tightening and forming a half loop for purchase. He reached up and repeated the motion over and over until he was at the top, where the rope was tied to a horizontal, thick wooden pole.

He lunged and gripped the pole, bringing his legs up to wrap around it for more support. Without looking down, he shimmied his way across to the platform and released his legs. An instant later he was airborne and he landed lightly on the wooden platform.

He looked down the 75 feet to the staring faces which seemed so small from his vantage point and gave them a thumbs-up sign. He heard the same harsh voice. "Next!" A young woman, 516, mounted the rope. Rex knew she'd make it no problem. None of the remaining would have a problem with this obstacle, except maybe, 491. He was from an earlier group and had been rolled back due to a broken leg, which had happened on this obstacle. Apparently, he'd fallen midway up and shattered his right tibia.

Rex took his eyes from the young woman shimmying easily up the rope and took in his surroundings. He guessed he was somewhere in the South, based on the heat and humidity, even in winter. He looked over a vast, swampy forest of deciduous trees which he'd become intimately familiar with on countless night operations.

Though it looked beautiful from here, he knew the forest was anything but. It was ugly and wet and full of poisonous snakes and reptiles that would just as soon eat you as swim away. He loathed the forest, but couldn't deny its harsh beauty this evening.

Five-sixteen was suddenly beside him, breathing hard. She ignored him and leaned out to give the thumbs-up. She gasped, "I beat you—I beat your time."

He gave her a crooked grin and shook his head, "It doesn't matter. There wasn't a time element."

"I counted how long it took you, I beat you by 15 seconds." She put her hands on her knees and bent over trying to get control of her breathing.

He reached out gripped her hand and turned her palm over exposing a pink hole where she'd torn off a blister. He ground his grimy finger into it and she pulled back, "Ouch, knock it off."

He showed her his hands, no torn blisters. "It didn't mean anything, but now you're worse off than I am. You're at a disadvantage for whatever they throw at us next."

She spit and it landed between his well-worn boots. "Fuck off, 520."

He tapped his temple, "Gotta think, girl. Gotta be smart if you wanna make it."

She ignored him. The rope was tense and moving, he stepped past her to see who was coming next. "It's 491."

She stood to her full height and leaned over looking down. "Is this where he fell?" she asked.

He could hear the concern in her voice. Despite every recruit being here because of their independent, problematic attitudes, they still pulled for each other. They were careful not to help one another, at least overtly or they'd be singled out for special treatment by the cadre.

When 491 was close enough to hear him, but far enough away from the cadre, Rex urged, "You're doing great. Almost here."

Four-ninety-one looked up and Rex saw pain and fear in his eyes. He whispered to 516, "He's struggling." She gave a curt nod of agreement. He raised his voice. "Don't look down, just one step at a time."

Finally, 491 was at the top of the rope. He looked at them on the platform. He was still clinging to the rope. Rex gestured, "Come on. Just reach up and shimmy across the pole, we'll catch you."

Four-ninety-one looked dubiously at the pole. Rex could see his arms shaking from exhaustion. Four-ninety-one had made it this far because he was made of stern, hard stuff, just like all of them. He took a deep breath and lunged upward and gripped the pole.

For an instant, Rex thought sure he'd fall, but he hung on and tried to lift his feet and legs to wrap around the pole. He failed the first time and when his legs peeled off, he nearly lost his grip again. He didn't have it in him to try to hook his legs again, so he went hand-over-hand until he was halfway between the rope and the platform.

He moved another foot closer and Rex put out his hands indicating he'd catch him. Four-ninety-one swung his legs backward to generate momentum toward the platform. Rex knew he wasn't close enough yet, but it was too late to stop him. Five-sixteen sucked a breath in realizing the same thing.

Four-ninety-one didn't get a good launch. He flailed toward the platform but it was obvious he wasn't going to make it. Rex yelled, "No," and went to his belly and lunged. He clutched the terrified young man's hand and felt himself being pulled off the platform. His momentum was arrested when he felt 516 grab his legs and hold on. She pulled him back until he could hook a foot behind a railing strut.

Once secure, she lunged forward and looked over the edge, "Hold on Dan, hold on."

Rex couldn't help noticing the concern in her voice. It was strictly forbidden to speak names or even to divulge them. He had no idea what anyone's real name was, but now he knew the man dangling beneath him was named, Dan.

Rex strained to pull himself back onto the platform. He needed 516's help. A loudspeaker from the ground belched. "Helping a recruit is forbidden. Release him or be cut from training, 520."

Rex couldn't believe his ears. He couldn't release the man, he'd never be able to look at himself in the mirror again. He'd be a murderer, no better than the cadre sons-of-bitches.

Dan looked up at him and pleaded, "Don't drop me, please."

"No way," he gasped but his grip was slipping and he doubted he could hold him much longer.

The girl was suddenly gripping his feet again, pulling. The loud-speaker again, "That goes for you too, 516."

She lashed out, her voice vicious and full of venom, "Fuck you!" She braced her heels into the slats of the platform and pulled. Rex thought he'd be pulled apart, but slowly she pulled him back until only his arms were over the side, holding the terrified young man. Rex shouted, "Jam my toes into the slats, I'm gonna swing him."

She pushed down on his right foot and he felt it jam and wedge into the floor-slat, painfully. His left foot was still firmly wrapped around the railing. He gasped, "I'm gonna swing him. You need to catch him. Ready?"

She let go of his boot and moved to the edge of the platform and looked down. "Ready," she said. "You can do it, my love," she implored.

"Three swings, Dan." With all his remaining strength Rex swung him: one, two, three. On the third swing, he gave it everything he had. Dan released, flew weightless for an instant and gained the edge of the platform with his fingertips, but it wasn't enough. His muscles were too weakened, he had nothing left.

Five-sixteen reached for his hand, but couldn't hold on. Her finger-nails scraped down the back of his hand leaving bright red scrape marks and deposited curling skin beneath her fingernails. "No!" She wailed as Dan fell.

Dan's eyes never left hers as he silently fell before finally smashing into the ground at the stunned recruit's feet. A pall of dust spread from his body and the recruits turned away from the grisly sight.

———

REX WOKE IN A DARK ROOM. For a moment he didn't remember what happened and he looked around in a panic. There was a heavy steel door with a tiny slat, letting in a sliver of light. Along the wall was a rusted metal bench. In the center of the room there was a hole which appeared to be a drain system. By the smell, he figured it was also the urinal.

Then he remembered. After Dan had fallen to his death, two cadre used the ladder to ascend the tower and forced himself and 516 to descend, where they were met with more sneering cadre holding billy clubs. The rest of the trainees were moved back and the cadre surrounded him and 516. They moved in and beat them. Rex covered himself as best he could but they were relentless and soon his head was bashed and everything went dark.

He had no idea how long he'd been passed out on the dank floor. He shivered uncontrollably. He stood on shaky legs and walked around the small room, looking for some weak point, but there were no windows and the door was stout.

He went to the slat and peered out. The light was coming from a dim, bare bulb hanging from the ceiling. Across the narrow hall he saw another door similar to his own. He strained to see down the narrow hallway, but the slat wasn't big enough.

He put his mouth to the slat and called, "Hey. Is anyone there?" No response. "Hello?" he tried again.

He put his eyes back to the slot. Suddenly the space was filled with bloodshot, angry eyes. "Shut the fuck up, 520."

Rex reeled away, startled. He recovered and asked, "What's going to happen to me? How long have I been in here?"

He was answered with a metal rod jabbing through the slot. It barely missed piercing his eyeball but dug into his cheek. He fell back holding his cheek and cursing. "You son-of-a-bitch, I'll kill you, you asshole." Blood dripped into his mouth.

He saw the eyes peering in. They showed amusement. He sprang from the floor and spit a stream of bloody mucus through the slot and was satisfied to see it splatter on the guard's face. The guard roared and jabbed the rod in again probing for Rex.

Rex reacted instantly. He punched from the side and gripped the metal rod. The sideways force ripped it from the guard's hand and Rex yanked it inside. He heard the guard cussing and screaming in pain.

Rex inspected the end of the rod and saw blood on the squared off metal handle. He must have cut the guard's hand when he tore it from his grasp. He figured it was about three feet long and reminded him of a poker used to stoke a fireplace. He whipped it through the air getting the feel of it. He doubted it would help much, but it felt good to have a weapon. Perhaps he could get one or two licks in before he was taken to the gallows.

———

AFTER THE SCUFFLE with the guard, nothing happened for a long time. He didn't know how long exactly, time seemed to move slower in the cell, but he figured at least two hours passed. He sat on the metal bench and tapped the rod into the ground, thinking how he'd use it to attack whoever entered.

He wondered if perhaps they'd simply leave him there to die. It would be easier than confronting him and the results would be the same. He wondered how it would feel to die of dehydration and starvation. It wouldn't be pleasant.

Finally the light from the slat dimmed as something, or someone, stepped in front. Rex sprang up and pressed himself against the wall beside the door. He wouldn't make this easy for them. He gripped the metal rod like a baseball bat.

The image brought the memory of his son to mind. He was a gifted baseball player. He wondered if he was even alive. What had these sadistic bastards told him? Did his son believe him to be a traitor? What of Miriam? How would she survive without him? He'd been told his official funeral was this week. They'd delayed it, to make it seem like he'd had a fair and thorough trial and was found guilty. The thought made him grip the rod tighter. *I'll make them pay.*

A booming voice through the slat made him jump, "Put the rod through the slot. If you don't comply in ten seconds we'll come back in a month to burn your putrefied bones. The count starts now: One, two, three…"

Rex's mind reeled. Was it a trick? Would they leave him there anyway? The count got to eight. He made his decision. "Okay, okay. Here it is." He thrust the rod through the slot, hoping it skewered someone. He heard it clatter on the stone floor. He put his mouth to the slot, "You gonna let me out of here?"

There was a minute of silence and he wondered if he'd been played. Finally the same monotone voice. "Step to the back wall and stand with your hands on your head, fingers laced. Do it now."

Rex was so used to reacting to the commanding voices of the cadre, he immediately complied. He saw eyes look in, then the latch on the door thunked and the heavy metal door screeched on ancient hinges as it opened outward.

The light from the bare bulb made Rex's eyes burn but he dared not remove his hands from his head to cover them. He squinted and watched a large figure fill the door-space. Rex saw he was aiming a large pistol, the likes of which, he'd never seen. Fear and rage competed in his head. The cadre sneered an evil grin and his eyes were wide with pleasure. The pistol fired and Rex felt needles enter his body. An instant later his world turned to pain as every muscle seemed to contract violently. The world went dark and he crumpled to the floor.

6

Field Marshall Rommel stood on the expansive bridge of the super-carrier, 'Siegfried', and observed the busy flight deck. Sailors dressed in bright colored shirts and helmets hustled around in what seemed like random chaos, but was in fact, orchestrated perfection. The deck was filled with BF 109 Messerschmitts.

Rommel could see the pilots sitting in their cockpits. They paid close attention to the brightly colored sailors as they directed them with lighted sticks and flags. Though the flight deck was immense, it was still small for as many aircraft as it held, so their careful movements were vital to avoid accidents.

Captain Steig, the carrier's commander pointed at the lead Messerschmitt. "The first aircraft is ready to launch, Field Marshall."

Rommel nodded and saw the lead Messerschmitt aimed down the deck. The huge carrier was turned into the wind, which was a substantial 20 knots from the North. A red-clad sailor held two fluttering red flags over his head. They were crossed above his goggled eyes, awaiting the signal from the bridge.

Rommel nodded, "Give the command, Captain. She's your ship."

"Yes, Field Marshall." He couldn't keep the excitement from his voice. He lifted the hand mic and ordered. "Launch, launch, launch."

The sailor saw the signal flag change and immediately dropped the flags, saluted the pilot, ducked to the side and pointed the flags into the wind. The Messerschmitt's engine roared as the pilot went to full power and released the brakes. The lithe fighter shot forward and the 20 knot head-wind combined with the 10 knots from the ship allowed him to lift off within 50 feet.

To Rommel, it appeared the plane was barely moving as it cleared the bow and angled skyward. The next plane was already in place and the process repeated. Soon the flight deck was nearly empty and the broken overcast sky was dotted with planes as they circled above the armada of ships.

Captain Stieg pointed to more dots in the distance. "You can see the other squadrons from 'Von Grif' and 'Faust' forming up, Field Marshall."

Rommel nodded, "When will the bombers launch?"

Captain Stieg pointed at the flight deck, which now had gaping sections dropping to lower levels. "The elevators are bringing them up now, sir."

Rommel watched the huge slabs of flight deck ascending from the lower levels. Each contained two Junkers JU-88s, medium range bombers. He knew each plane carried 1,000 kilograms of bombs, which would be dropped on strategic points along the United States' East Coast. Along with the two other super-carriers, there were 30 bombers, an insignificant amount, however their targets were strategic and their destruction would go a long way toward a successful invasion.

Even with the Korth-enhanced dual engines, the bombers were still heavy for carrier operations. These specially designed JU-88s were lighter and had fewer defensive guns, one in the nose and one in the rear. There were four crew members: a single gunner that spent his time between the nose and rear guns depending on the situation, a pilot, copilot and bombardier/navigator. The aircrews had extensive carrier training and were confident in their ability to complete their mission and return to their floating home.

The carrier increased thrust to 15 knots, as Rommel watched the first bomber line up on the flight line and with the brakes set, push the throttles to full power. Even through the thick glass of the bridge, he could hear the intense thunder of the engines. The red-clad sailor saluted and stepped aside. The bomber shuddered, then rolled forward, seemingly in slow motion. It lifted with plenty of flight deck remaining, and ascended. Compared to the fighters, it looked like a lumbering giant.

Rommel smiled and nodded at Captain Stieg. "They will have the honor of striking the first blow against the East Coast."

Stieg nodded, "Yes, sir. The fighters will keep any allied fighters off them long enough to complete their missions."

Rommel looked to the sky. "The weather is perfect. It's as though God is on our side."

Stieg was momentarily stunned. God, and Religion in general, were frowned upon by the Korth. They found the notion wholly ridiculous and merely a distraction from reality. It wasn't outlawed, but over the years there were less and less churches and places of worship, as the humans tried to stay on the good-side of their Korth overlords. "Yes, sir," he muttered.

Rommel touched the small green button on his neck as if remembering. He nodded, "Everything is moving along perfectly. The Korth's weather forecasts are perfect. The next seven days are forecast to be broken overcast with light winds. For this time of year, that's very unusual. When they predicted this weather and we left the British Isles, I was skeptical, but now I'm a believer. We'll be able to launch our landing crafts, as well as our airborne units and have the luxury of constant air-support."

Stieg was uncomfortable but nodded, "Yes, we couldn't have asked for a better patch of weather. Even with the successful attacks on the US Naval ships yesterday, the Americans won't have enough time to realize the full danger until our airborne units are descending upon their cities."

Rommel nodded and briefly thought of his youngest son who'd be leading a platoon of elite 1st Parachute Division soldiers onto Long Island in a matter of hours. Ricker had always been the defiant one of the family, eschewing the armored corps, which his famous father held so dear. Instead, he'd volunteered for the Fallschirmjäger, the paratroopers.

Despite Rommels initial displeasure, he was proud of him. The Fallschirmjäger were elite troops and despite Ricker's last name, he had to earn the right to be there just as any soldier from the lowest strata had to prove himself. Being an officer was an even tougher task, for he had to not only pass every rigorous test, but also be able to lead hard, tough men into battle. From all accounts, his son had performed marvelously and was a respected lieutenant.

His two older sons, Hans and Sebastian would both be leading a company of Panzers during the invasion, but they would land a full day after their brother. Sebastian, who commanded a company of heavy Tigers, would land in support of his younger brother. Hans would lead a company of light Panzer IIIs further south and would be in support of the main landing forces.

———

CAPTAIN CLANCY MCDERMOTT was reading the paper when the unfamiliar sound of a siren interrupted the article he was reading. He looked around the ready room in annoyance, finally centering his attention on the speaker. When he realized what it meant, he dropped the paper and shot to his feet. "That's the air raid siren," he shouted.

A second later the speaker hissed with an incoming message, "Multiple radar contacts approaching. Scramble, scramble, scramble."

McDermott was out the ready room door, dodging other pilots filtering in from neighboring rooms. He lifted his helmet off the rack, put it on and snapped the chin guard.

Lieutenant Jim Thorpe was beside him. He was five-foot-six and felt like a dwarf beside the six-two, squadron commander. "Is this another drill, Captain?" He asked hopefully.

McDermott shrugged, "It sure wasn't on the docket. You know as much as I do at this point. Mount up, Lieutenant and stay sharp. Hopefully it's just another large flock of Canadian Geese." Thorpe nodded but didn't look convinced. McDermott didn't believe it himself. This felt real.

He trotted to his P-47 Thunderbolt, which was already cranked up and spitting smoke from the exhaust. His flight mechanic, Sergeant

Wifford, hopped out when he saw him coming and stepped onto the wing. He yelled over the roar of engines. "She's running smooth, Captain. We dropped the external tanks, so she'll fly like a dream."

McDermott nodded, climbed into the seat and adjusted his parachute. He crammed in his long legs as Sergeant Wifford clicked him into the six-point restraint system. "Thanks, Sergeant," he grunted as Wifford gave the belt a sharp tug. Wifford stepped back and saluted then dropped off the wing and absorbed the drop with a deep knee bend.

McDermott activated the radio as he checked his instrument panel for any anomalies. "Thalacker Tower, this is flight lead, ready for takeoff on three-two." He caught Sergeant Wifford looking at him expectantly off to the side and slightly in front of the four spinning blades of the propeller.

"Flight lead, Thalacker Tower. You're cleared for take-off on three-two with a right hand turn."

McDermott gave Sergeant Wifford the thumbs-up signal and the sergeant darted in and pulled the wheel chocks. When McDermott saw him safely away, he added throttle and felt the big fighter trundle and bounce forward. He crossed to the active runway, lined up on center line and pushed to full military power. Without wing tanks or bombs and rockets, the fighter was in the air soon after and once the wheels were up and locked, McDermott turned right and climbed.

The radio crackled in his ear, "Flight lead, Flight ops. Climb with all due haste and rendezvous with the rest of the squadron at 15,000 feet. Over."

"Roger, flight ops. Understand all due haste to 15,000." He pushed the throttle past optimum fuel conservation speed and watched the altimeter's dial wind round and round as he shot upward. Despite the P-47 weighing seven tons, its powerful Pratt and Whitney 18 cylinder engine, delivered 2,300 horse power and McDermott could feel himself thrust back into the seat.

He couldn't help grinning. He loved everything about the Thunderbolt. Sure it was unwieldy and was often referred to as a flying tank, but the eight, .50 caliber wing-mounted machine guns packed a whallop and better yet, it could take a beating and keep on flying.

He'd yet to fly a combat mission but he'd heard how well the airframe had performed against the hopped-up fighters the Russians flew. The sexier P-51 Mustangs had more air kills, but only because the Jug, as he liked to refer to it, was used more for ground attacks and close-in infantry support and left most of the dogfighting to the tighter turning Mustangs.

He leveled off at 15,000 feet and started a slow circle. More Jugs entered the airspace and split off into flights of four. When McDermott confirmed all his pilots were airborne and formed up, he squeezed his throat mic. "Flight control, Flight lead. We're formed up and ready for instructions."

"Flight lead, control. Turn to zero-eight-five degrees and climb to 20,000. Contacts are ten miles out."

"Roger. Any idea how many or who they are?"

"Too many contacts to count. Speed indicates bombers mixed with fighters. The signatures aren't Russian, so looks like the rest of Europe's joined the fight." There was a pause and the calm voice broke a little. "You're weapons free. Over."

Captain McDermott took a breath and let it out slow then addressed his squadron. "Alright, men. We've trained for this. Stay with your wingman. Our primary targets are bombers so call 'em out if you see 'em. Let's move to combat spread and get up to 20,000, staggered. Over." No one replied, but planes moved further from one another, some dropped back, and all climbed.

Minutes later someone called out excitedly, "Contact. I see planes," there was a pause, "lots of planes straight ahead."

McDermott's older eyes finally saw the growing dots on the horizon. He felt a burst of adrenaline course through his body and he felt pinpricks of sweat, despite the freezing temperatures outside his cockpit glass. He squinted and was about to call out bombers but someone beat him to it. "Bombers. I see bombers at eleven o'clock."

McDermott keyed his mic, "That's our target. Watch out for fighters. Get in close and let 'em have it."

He pushed the throttles to full power and nosed up, gaining altitude. He turned on the electronic front sight and its orange glow filled the windscreen.

The air around him was suddenly filled with flashing, darting shapes and he realized they were BF-109s. Tracer rounds flashed past his cockpit glass and he instinctively rolled away. He flung his head side-to-side trying to see where it was coming from. He saw the yellow cowling of a 109 settle on his tail.

Forgetting about the bombers, he rolled onto his back and pulled the stick into his belly. He grunted through a high G turn and was now flying 180 degrees the opposite direction.

There was constant radio chatter, but he ignored it as he saw the 109 match his moves easily. He saw the winking of the German's cannon and felt, rather than heard, the impact of a heavy slug. He broke left and moved the stick in unpredictable ways, spoiling the German's aim but he couldn't shake him.

Suddenly there was a flash of yellow to his front and he instinctively squeezed the trigger, at the same time pushing into a steep dive. His airspeed went into the red zone and his much heavier aircraft was pulling away from the pursuing fighter. He watched the 109 pull up and level out, then dart away like a water skipper on a river.

McDermott cut power and gently pulled his Jug out of the dive, careful not to put too much strain on the wings. His body was three times heavier than normal and he grunted and squeezed his abdominal muscles trying to keep from passing out. The Gs finally subsided and he was able to breathe normally again.

He added power and climbed, searching for the enemy. It didn't take long, there were white and black smoke trails crisscrossing the sky above him, as though a naughty child had used markers on a blank wall.

He was still above the ocean. He searched frantically for the bombers but could only see darting fighters. The radio chatter was constant but he noticed it had dropped off a little and judging by some of the panicked calls he'd heard, he guessed he knew why.

He grit his teeth and climbed at full power. As he approached the fur-ball of fighters, he ducked into a cloud bank and his world instantly turned white. He watched his altimeter. He leveled off and banked right until he was 90 degrees from his old course.

He flashed out of the cloud bank at 415 miles-per-hour and his senses reeled as he saw multiple targets. The nearest was flying wingman to a 109 which was trying to line up a shot on a jinking P-47.

McDermott adjusted slightly until his pipper was on the fuselage of the trailing 109. The enemy plane was growing large in his windscreen. He depressed the trigger and all eight .50 caliber machine guns opened up. The 109 sparked and chunks flew off before it rolled onto its back spinning out of control toward the cold Atlantic.

The second 109 was concentrating on the P-47 to his front and didn't notice his wingman's death spiral. McDermott chose half his guns, not wanting to spray his comrade, and when his pipper was lined up on the enemy's tail, he fired and watched in grim fascination as the tail detached from the fuselage and fell away as though cut with an immense scythe. With no rear stabilizer the 109 pitched forward and the engine's torque spun the plane violently.

McDermott got on the mic, "You're clear. You're clear." He kept his speed and was soon beside the other Jug.

The pilot looked his way, gave him a thumbs-up and keyed his mic. "Thanks, Captain."

"That you, Thorpe?"

He nodded, "Yes, sir."

McDermott pulled ahead and looked around the sky but it was suddenly empty. "Where are the others?" He noticed the lack of radio chatter.

"I saw at least three go down, sir. I—I don't know who. My wingman for sure, Greeny. I mean Lieutenant Green, sir. His plane— well it just exploded. I saw some chutes but don't know if they were theirs or ours."

The thought of bailing out over the Atlantic in winter sent a chill up his spine. They wouldn't last long in those icy waters. "There's bound to be more that made it. Come on, let's head back towards land and see if we can sneak up on those bombers." The two silver P-47s turned toward mainland America at full military power.

———

LIEUTENANT BORIS GUTTENBERG piloted the JU-88 medium bomber toward the mainland of the United States of America. In addition to multiple bombers off either wing, there were BF-109s turning lazily back and forth to keep from overtaking the slower aircraft they were tasked with protecting. He'd seen the American fighters climbing toward them earlier and been relieved when they were turned away easily. Now he had more pressing matters.

"Friedrich, update."

Air Sergeant Gren Friedrich, the bombardier/navigator answered immediately. "Maintain heading and speed. Target 20 kilometers." He looked at his watch. "In two minutes descend to 4,000 meters."

Guttenberg smiled, "Remind me."

"Jawohl," came the answer from the no-nonsense sergeant.

Guttenberg got on the intercom again. "Come up to the front gun, Airman Stoltz."

The Airman was barely out of puberty and his voice cracked, "Jawohl, Flight Lieutenant."

Guttenberg pressed the radio, so only his copilot would hear, "So young, that one." There was a sudden shuddering and a loud bang. "Sheisse. Flak." He glanced out the canopy to either side and grimaced at the dark clouds seeming to erupt from thin air. He noticed the fighters climbing to keep out of the deadly shrapnel. *Cowards,* he thought with a grin but he couldn't blame them.

The copilot, 2nd Lieutenant Spiegelman, nodded. "Surprised it took this long."

Another loud bang and the controls jumped in Guttenberg's hands. A near miss off the starboard wing. He noticed a hole in the wing and shredded cloth flapping in the wind. He watched the engine. It seemed to be fine. He went on the intercom, "Everyone okay?"

Sergeant Friedrich's normally stoic voice came over the intercom in quick gasps. "There's a hole. Oh dear God - he's gone. Airman Stolz went out the hole."

Guttenberg shook his head and called on the intercom, "Are you okay? Are you able to navigate?" Despite the gnawing pain of losing one of his men, especially the happy-go-lucky young gunner, the mission was the priority. He'd have time to mourn after he destroyed the target.

Friedrich's voice returned stoic although slower. "Yes, sir. I'm uninjured and my maps and sights are intact." Accurate flak continued to harass the bombers, bouncing them around the air until Friedrich called. "Descend to 4,000 meters on my mark...mark."

Guttenberg pushed the controls forward and gently descended. The flak immediately lessened, not bothering to target one bomber dropping away from the main group. Guttenberg looked through the top of the canopy and watched the bombers grow smaller and smaller as he descended.

The JU-88 broke through a thin layer of clouds and Guttenberg saw endless signs of humanity living in close proximity. The view was awe-inspiring and he was momentarily transfixed. It was his first view of the North American continent and it was beautiful.

Sergeant Friedrich's voice was tight over the intercom, "Turn to heading one-four-zero, and slow to bombing speed." Once the turn was complete, Friedrich continued, "Target should be visible soon. Release point in six kilometers."

Guttenberg and Spiegelman scanned the horizon searching for the building, checking the picture strapped to their legs, trying to match it with the buildings sprawling out before them. The countryside had turned from close packed city to more wide-open spaces.

Guttenberg slapped Spiegelman's shoulder and pointed. "There. There it is."

Spiegelman stared for a moment, looked at his picture one last time and nodded. "Jawohl. I concur. Target sighted."

Sergeant Friedrich's voice, "Jawohl, I'm on the sights. Angle toward target at 30 degrees." The floor tilted forward and Friedrich put his eye to the state-of-the-art bombsight. The forward-looking sight was marvelously clear and the magnification increments perfect. He quickly found the building and gave a curt, "Target identified. I have control."

In the cockpit Guttenberg answered, "You have the aircraft." He reluctantly released the column, keeping his hands hovering centimeters away, ready to take control the instant the bombs were away.

DOCTOR LYLE WAS HUNCHED over the alien body, his steady hands cutting a long precision slice down the Korth's chest. His assistant, Doctor Bartholomew watched in anticipation beside him, ready to assist in pulling back the bizarre, leathery skin.

Dr. Lyle commented for the benefit of the recorder and the other scientists and doctors observing the autopsy from the upper deck. "Skin is tougher than human skin and appears to have four distinct layers. Viscera beneath has a reddish hue. There's no blood, however, the creature has been dead for over 24 hours and I suspect there's been some pooling.

He stopped the cut once he was halfway down the front of the torso. He put the scalpel down and clutched the skin, pulling it back slightly, "The skin is well attached." He looked at Dr. Bartholomew, "Hold the skin. I'll cut it away."

Dr. Bartholomew leaned forward and clutched the section of skin with gloved fingers. Dr. Lyle clutched another, longer scalpel and cut the skin away with slow movements. Once he'd pulled back a few inches he stopped and pushed his glasses up his nose and continued speaking. "It appears there is a layer of," he tapped the area of interest with his knuckles and it sounded like someone knocking on a stout wood door. "What I would call bone, however, there's no sign of ribs. It appears to be a hard casing. I'd assume protecting the vital organs."

He looked to an orderly a couple feet back from the table wearing a long lab coat and surgical mask. "I'll need the rotary saw, please."

The orderly nodded and walked briskly to a shiny chrome table with a power saw on top. Another orderly entered the room and helped him push it to the head of the table holding the Korth. The Korth's unseeing eyes stared at the ceiling and it was all the orderlies could do not to look.

In one motion, they lifted the saw off the table and walked it forward until they hovered above the Korth's chest wall. They carefully brought the four support legs down until they slipped into the holes designed to hold the saw steady. They tightened the wing-nuts beneath the table and gave the saw a tug, making sure it was secure, then stepped away.

Dr. Lyle stepped back onto the step-stool and adjusted the blade until it hovered over where he'd cut the skin. "This is a diamond-cut blade. It might be overkill, but I want to be sure I can get through the bone."

He put earplugs in and flipped the switch. The whirring noise of high-speed rotation filled the room. He adjusted his goggles and glanced back at Dr. Bartholomew who nodded back, obviously excited to see what the cut would reveal.

Dr. Lyle pulled the blade down toward the chest wall, while Dr. Bartholomew held suction, ready to vacuum the bone dust before it filled the room. The spinning blade touched the thin layer of viscera cutting through easily, but when it struck the bone, the sound increased as the blade struggled, as though cutting through hard rock.

Dr. Lyle pulled the blade off and looked at the bone. There was a cut, but much less impressive than it should have been. This same saw cut through human bone as if it were soft butter. He looked at Dr. Bartholomew who shrugged. Lyle pushed down again until he made contact then pushed hard despite the screaming saw. Sweat beaded on his forehead.

Finally the pressure subsided and he felt the saw cut deeper. He quickly stopped pushing and pulled the saw off the cut and shut it off. Dr. Bartholomew ran the suction over the cut, careful not to suck up anything except bone dust, which actually looked more like shards of glass.

Dr. Lyle motioned for the orderlies to take the saw away. They hustled over and quickly unscrewed the smoking saw and placed it back onto the table and wheeled it away. "Chest spreader," mumbled Dr. Lyle.

Dr. Bartholomew stuffed the suction back into its slot and grabbed the archaic looking chest spreader and handed it to Dr. Lyle. Lyle carefully placed the metal edges into the cut, hooking the bones on either side. He made sure it was secure and not pushing against anything he didn't want to crush. Satisfied, he grasped the hand crank and the multiple gears moved smoothly against one another. The spreader pushed outward against the edges, forcing the chest cavity open. The sound of rending flesh and bone sounded like rapid gunfire.

Dr. Lyle stopped cranking and wiped his brow. "The resistance is massive. It's like spreading metal." He leaned over the body, looking into the body cavity. He took in a shallow breath. He quickly pushed his fogging goggles to his forehead and looked again, squinting. "What the hell is that? I need more light."

Every person in the seats above were on their feet peering down, trying to see what caught the attention of the lead physician.

An eardrum-shattering sound suddenly filled the room, making everyone jump and look to the ceiling. The basement shook violently and chunks of concrete fell from the ceiling.

Dr. Lyle instinctively leaned over the Korth body to protect it. An instant later the ceiling exploded downward as two more 500 pound bunker busting bombs pierced through and exploded among the scientists and doctors, turning them instantly to dust.

7

J immy Crandall and his mother, Miriam, departed the train depot, already dreading the return trip scheduled only two days from now. Jimmy was thankful he hadn't traveled across the country by aircraft though. The flight from Anchorage to Portland, Oregon had been terrifying. On two occasions the DC-3 was forced to use clouds for cover as marauding Russian fighters from distant airfields passed nearby. He'd never seen them, nor had the pilots, however, the ever-vigilant West Coast Defense Radar Grid had.

The train ride had taken three days. His mother told him the last time she'd been on a train, before she was married, it took much longer. Since the alien invasion, transportation was seen as a vital part of the nation's defense and there'd been great improvement in all types of transport. Highways, as well as trains and train tracks, were all new and cutting-edge technology, and there were far more of them.

Despite that, it was still three days sitting in a cramped train car. The topic of why they were taking the trip never came up. Instead, his mother talked about her new job, the new people she was meeting and the scary time when they had an actual air-raid. He'd listened and nodded at the appropriate spots. He knew she was just as confused as he was over Rex Crandall's death, but they didn't discuss it.

Jimmy blew warm air into his gloved hands, "It's nearly as cold as Anchorage here. Didn't think that was possible."

Miriam nodded and pulled her coat's wool closer to her chin. "Certainly colder than Portland. At least your uniform looks warm."

They walked along, trying to avoid the slush piles on the sidewalk. Jimmy saw a coffee shop, "Wonder if they have real coffee? Come on, I'll buy you a cup, get you warmed up."

"Of course it's real. Why not? After all, we're in the nation's capital."

He nodded, "We didn't have the real stuff on the front. Some kind of substitute that tastes like—well it's not good."

It was the first time he'd mentioned the front and he noticed his mother stiffen. "Sure, let's go in, only I'm buying," she said.

The inside was warm and smelled of brewed coffee. There were a few patrons sitting at the counter, talking to a man in an apron, who kept rubbing down the counter with an off-white rag.

He smiled at them. "Welcome, have a seat anywhere. Coffee?"

Jimmy and Miriam nodded. Jimmy helped his mother out of her coat and hung it on the back of her chair, then scooted her chair in as she sat. "Always the gentleman, Jimmy. Thank you."

He sat down across from her and mumbled, "It's nothing ma."

She pursed her lips and he could tell she wanted to say something but was unsure if she should. He'd noticed it a few times on the train ride too. He hoped it wasn't something about his father.

He looked her in the eye. "What is it, Ma? Seems like you wanna ask me something."

Her mouth upturned slightly and he noticed how much older she looked. "I— well, I guess I want to ask you about your experiences. About the front." He continued staring and she continued. "I mean, you're different." He frowned and she shook her head, "Not in a bad way. I guess—I just notice you don't smile much anymore. I mean, I know there's not much to smile about, but you used to be quick to smile, even when angry."

He averted his eyes and an image of Hank's shattered body lying in the forest filled his mind. He shook his head, trying to clear the image. He took in a breath and blew it out slow, then looked at her concerned eyes. "It was bad. Really bad." He shook his head hard. "I—I don't think I should talk about it. It's—well, it's too ugly."

She leaned forward and put her hands out palm up. Jimmy placed his hands in her palms. She squeezed and he felt her warmth. "I know I've told you how sorry I was to hear about Hank. I can't imagine what you must be going through." She hesitated and bit her lower lip, "If you ever want to talk, I'll listen."

Jimmy nodded and looked her in the eye. His eyes were hard and she nearly pulled her hands away in fright. They were not the eyes of the son she'd watched march off months before. They were dangerous eyes. "I appreciate the sentiment, Mom, but I don't need to talk about it." He forced a smile and it felt awkward and strained. *I need to kill more of the bastards responsible,* he thought.

She shook her head, "First Hank and now Rex—I mean your father." A tear formed in the corner of her eye and she couldn't keep the grief from spilling. "Oh," she put a hand to her mouth but couldn't stifle the tears or wracking breaths.

Jimmy reached for her and placed a hand on her shoulder and squeezed. He realized he might not need to be comforted, but his mother certainly did.

The man in the apron sauntered over with two steaming cups of coffee on a tray. He was concentrating on not spilling them. "Here you go," he said in a jovial voice. "Two hot coff…" he noticed the attractive woman crying and he pulled up short, sloshing coffee onto the table and onto Jimmy's uniform shirt. He looked mortified, "Oh no. I'm so sorry." He finished putting the coffee cups down and whipped his towel off his shoulder, dabbed at his shirt and wiped the spill off the table.

"It's okay. Don't worry about it," Jimmy said. Miriam kept her head down, her shoulders bouncing as the sorrow wracked her body.

The waiter's voice turned low and worried, "Are you okay, ma'am?"

She didn't respond and Jimmy answered for her. "She lost her husband—my father."

"Oh my God. I'm so sorry to hear that." He looked from the top of her head back to Jimmy, "So tragic."

"We're here for his funeral."

The waiter looked at Jimmy's uniform, "You're from the West Coast then? You both are?" Jimmy looked confused for a moment and the waiter explained. "Your uniform. I know the 45th Division's out there in Anchorage, right?"

Jimmy nodded, "You know your insignia." He looked to his mother who seemed to be getting control of herself.

"It's kind of a hobby of mine. Well, and you boys have been in the news a lot. You really put a stop to those damned commies." He looked nervously at the woman then lit up with a beaming smile, "Food's on the house."

That brought Miriam's head up. She dabbed her eyes and shook her head. "That's not necessary, sir. We can pay."

He threw his hand at her, dismissing her suggestion as being ridiculous. "Least I can do." He looked serious for a moment. "Hey, not to be brash, but where's your husband's service. I can arrange a ride for you. Being from the West Coast and all..." he trailed off.

Miriam started to protest but Jimmy spoke first. "Actually, that would be great." He dug into his pants pocket and pulled out a card with the information he'd gotten about the service. "It's at," he read off the card, "St. Luke's On the Estuary?"

The waiter pulled his chin into his neck and scowled, "St. Lukes On the Estuary? You sure it's not Arlington, down in Virginia?" He leaned over trying to get a look at the card. Jimmy turned it so he could see it better. The man's happy face turned to something far different as he read the service notice. He leaned back, crossed his arms across his sizable chest and said, "Get outta my establishment." Miriam and Jimmy looked at him in astonishment and when Jimmy tried to protest, the waiter raised his voice, "Now!"

Jimmy shot to his feet, not knowing what was happening but damned sure he wasn't going to be thrown out of an establishment without earning it. "What's the big idea?"

The waiter scowled, "I'm not gonna tell you again, get your traitorous asses out of here before I throw you out myself."

Jimmy's face turned purple with rage and he pointed a finger, "You watch your mouth in front of my mother, you son-of-a-bitch."

The two men at the counter stood and turned toward the fracas, "What's going on, Carl?" the bigger of the two asked.

"These two are attending a funeral for her husband and his father at St. Lukes On the Estuary." The two men looked at one another and Carl looked annoyed, "You know, where they bury military members after execution… for *treason*." The last word dripped off his tongue.

The color drained from Miriam's face and Jimmy saw the pain Carl's words caused. He didn't hesitate, "My father isn't a traitor!" his left hand was already moving. Carl reeled back as Jimmy's fist smashed into his jaw. Jimmy followed it with a crushing upper-cut, which lifted Carl off his feet and sent him crashing into another table.

Miriam screamed for him to stop, but he was already leaping forward to continue beating him. He never made it. The two stunned men at the counter saw their friend being assaulted and sprang into action.

The first man tackled Jimmy and they both went to the floor. Jimmy pounded on the man's head with balled fists until the second patron kicked Jimmy in the side of the head, sending blood and bits of teeth across the floor. Jimmy roared in rage and pushed himself out of the first man's grip.

He staggered to his feet and gave a half-assed kick, but his head was swimming. He missed and nearly fell. The two men grabbed Jimmy's arms and pinned them behind his back. Carl had recovered and was walking with murder in his eyes toward the struggling Jimmy.

"Stop this!" Miriam screamed and lunged toward Carl.

He saw her coming and put his meaty hand on her face and pushed her down, growling, "You'll get yours. Wait your turn, darling."

Jimmy saw his mother crash to the floor and his vision narrowed. The only sound was the blood rushing in his ears. He focused on Carl's bleeding face. He relaxed his arms and stopped struggling. He felt the men holding him relax their grips slightly and he acted. He yanked his right arm away while stepping on his captor's foot with his heavy combat boot.

The man yowled and reached for his foot. The other man tightened his grip and Jimmy used all his strength to swing the man forward. He forced him into Carl and all three of them fell over a table. Jimmy was free. He rolled away and came up quickly, all grogginess gone, replaced with solid focus.

He gripped the back of a chair and hurled it at Carl, who was just getting to his feet. Carl yelled in pain as the solid wood chair broke over his back, cutting his shirt and the skin beneath.

Jimmy reached for one of the spilled coffee mugs and threw it at the second man. Jimmy hadn't played baseball in a long time, but the muscle memory was still there. The heavy porcelain mug broke on the side of the man's face and he dropped and didn't get up.

Jimmy was about to leap onto the injured men and continue doling out pain, when the world outside the shop suddenly erupted in fire. The ground shook violently sending him to the floor.

Shards of glass, wood and bricks, suddenly became lethal projectiles. Something hit his head and he saw stars. He saw his mother on the floor only feet away watching him. A fountain of blood was squirting from her neck as though a hose had burst and her eyes were filled with fear. He reached for her, but felt something heavy keeping him from moving. Dust filled his lungs and he suddenly couldn't breathe. He yelled, but the only thing he heard was the rushing sound of fire. A moment later his world went black.

———

JIMMY'S EYES fluttered open and the scene before him didn't make sense. He was on his stomach staring at a dusty wood floor. He turned his head and saw the rest of the room in complete shambles. Chairs, thick wood beams, bricks and crushed tables were strewn everywhere. He shook his head trying to figure out where he was. Dust filtered into his eyes and he was forced to squint.

He tried to move, but felt a weight on his back. He looked behind and saw a heavy wood beam across his back. His mind was fuzzy and his head pounded as he tried to remember what happened. Then he saw caked blood only feet from his face. He followed it to its origin, but whatever caused it was behind or beneath the other part of the beam.

Then he remembered. *Mother!* He tried to speak but his mouth felt like he'd fallen asleep beneath a belt sander with his mouth open. He opened and closed his cut lips trying to get a word out, but it was no use. Anger flooded him and he lunged forward. The beam shifted slightly. He dug his boots into the floor, trying to get enough purchase to push himself forward. He strained, but only achieved an inch at most.

He heard distant sirens. He strained, but soon felt exhausted, as though the only possibility was sleep. His eyes drooped, despite trying to keep them open. He heard something. A voice. His eyes shot open and he closed his mouth and tried to wet his throat. He croaked, "Over here. Over here. My Ma's over here."

The voice was closer and he realized it was many voices. "Anyone here?"

"Here," he croaked but this time it had more volume. "Here. I'm here. Please help my Mom."

The voice called to someone else. "Got a live one inside this mess. I heard a voice." The voice got louder as the searcher turned back his way. "Keep talking buddy, we'll get you outta there."

"I'm here."

Jimmy saw a black shape scuttling toward him. He was confused and thought perhaps he was seeing things. Suddenly a warm tongue lapped his face and he realized it was a dog. The dog barked excitedly and spun in circles as though it had found its favorite plaything. Jimmy reached up and touched the black snout. The dog promptly licked the dirt, grime and blood, then turned and barked.

Soon he heard more voices and dust-filled light filtered into the space as beams and boards were moved. The dog continued to wag his tail and bark. Soon Jimmy saw a man's face peer through a hole in the debris. He smiled and reached for the dog, "Good boy, good dog." He leaned away from the hole and the dog shot through it and the man caressed and pet him, then shooed him away.

He poked his head in again and caught Jimmy's eye. "We'll get you out of there in a jiffy. Can you move?"

Jimmy tried again, but couldn't. He shook his head, "No. I'm stuck." He pointed to the blood. "Do you see my mother? She's under here too."

The man shook his head. "We'll get you out first. Is she alive?"

The question stunned Jimmy and he nearly lashed out angrily, but an image flashed through his mind. His mother's terrified eyes and the blood spouting from her neck. Tears filled his eyes as he realized he was alone in the world.

———

JIMMY SAT on the sidewalk in front of what was left of the diner. The train station, the next block over, was a smoldering pile of burning debris. The only part still standing, a brick fireplace connected to a pot-bellied wood stove.

The rescue team had moved on and now he was being attended to by a man with a Red Cross armband over his sleeve. "I'm gonna pull up your shirt and get a look at your back."

Without waiting for a response the medic pulled up his shirt and Jimmy sucked in air as the shirt was peeled away from his bloodied back. He felt the medic run a wet rag, which must've had soap or some kind of antiseptic because it burned like fire. Jimmy bit his lip and took the pain. He'd felt worse, this was nothing. The pain actually felt good, sharpened his mind.

"Sorry," the medic mumbled.

"What the hell happened here? Gas main?"

The medic stopped scrubbing. "You don't know?"

Jimmy shook his head. "Been trapped in there for who knows how long."

"We're at war. There's been attacks all up and down the coast. Bombers and fighters strafing and dropping bombs." He pointed at the destroyed train station. "Targeting train hubs like that one and airfields and barracks. Even factories. And of course, this is the capital."

Jimmy was stunned. He shook his head. "Russians?"

The medic shook his head, "Nah, Germans for sure. I saw one of those yellow nosed Messerschmitts and saw the iron cross with the fucking alien thingy too." He continued scrubbing the dirt and grime from the deep cuts in Jimmy's back. "I've heard about troops too. On the coast, paratroopers and landing craft. They're landing all over."

Jimmy tensed. "Holy shit! Hurry up with that. I need to report in."

"Yeah, you and me both. I was on leave. My parents don't live far from here. When the bombs hit I came running, but it's time to get back to my unit." He placed a large bandage over Jimmy's back and wrapped cloth around his torso to keep it in place. "What unit you in?"

"I'm West Coast. With the 45th Division. I was here to—doesn't matter now." He shook his head. "Can I tag along? I'm orphaned from my unit." He thought, *my parents too.*

"Sure thing." He pulled Jimmy's shirt down and stepped in front of him and thrust his hand out. "Name's Tom Grothing, Corporal. Nice to meetcha."

Jimmy gripped his hand. "Jimmy Crandall, PFC."

Grothing helped him to his feet and held him steady. "You sure you're okay? You were buried quite a while."

Jimmy looked back at the destroyed diner. His mother's remains were still inside. The rescue crew confirmed she was dead, along with everyone else who'd been inside, but she was too deeply buried to extract. They promised she'd be dug out eventually but they had lots more people to help first. Jimmy turned away feeling anger welling in his gut. "Yeah, I'm sure. Let's get to your unit. I need some payback."

8

First Lieutenant Ricker Rommel was in the front of the JU-25 transport at the head of his platoon, ready to lead them out the door and into combat. The weeks of waiting were finally over. He and his Wolf Company, along with the rest of the 1st Parachute Division had been cooped up in the hulls of various surface warships while they waited for the promised break in the weather.

The big Naval ships as well as the troop carriers and small LVTs could be used in rough seas, the Korth had seen to that, but the airplanes were still vulnerable to weather, especially the light JU-25 transports, which the Fallschirmjäger relied on to get them over their targets.

The Korth, with their advanced meteorology, assured the high brass that a break in the weather was coming, so Field Marshal Rommel immediately put to sea with the largest naval force the world had ever seen, screened and protected by hundreds of Hunter Killer Wolfpack submarines.

They'd crashed across the Atlantic in some of the worst weather Ricker had ever experienced. His men were sick and weak by the time the weather passed. Another week of relatively calm seas and the elite force of paratroopers regained their strength and were ready to get off

the ships and into combat. Just as the Korth predicted, the weather broke. Now all the training, all the grueling marches with full packs, all the strains and sprains would all come together in the next few minutes.

Lieutenant Rommel gazed out the open door, which he would jump through once the light above his head turned green. They were low, only 1,000 meters. Despite the greater danger from ground fire, being low allowed them much better success at actually landing on their target. Todays jump had very little wiggle room for pilot error. If they jumped too early, they'd land in the frigid Atlantic, if they jumped too late, they'd land amongst the high buildings of the city and die hanging hundreds of feet above the streets, or worse, their chutes would collapse and they'd fall to their deaths.

He watched the gray waters flash by below. German, British and Norwegian warships stretched as far as the eye could see. The waters were peaked with white caps, telling him the wind had not yet settled down. He hoped it wouldn't be too windy to jump. Their Korth enhanced, state-of-the-art steerable chutes could cut into a 15 knot wind effectively but more than that and they'd be swept away and scattered.

He looked across the short distance to the next plane. He could clearly see the pilot and copilot and the silhouettes of paratroopers in the windows. More Wolf Company boys.

The wind bit against his face as he leaned out and peered forward, but the view was enough to make him take the pain. He could see the mainland. There were plumes of dark smoke rising into the sky everywhere. A booming sound made him look down just in time to see a ship, he thought it was a cruiser, firing its main guns, softening up the target for them. He could see the arcing shells. He lost sight of them, but they soon ignited a section of the island they were streaking towards…Long Island.

The light over his head turned yellow. He pulled his head back in and looked down the aisle. The seats were packed with faces staring back at him. The faces were streaked with camouflage and they wore their non-brimmed style helmets, tight. Their eyes were wide with excitement, some with fear. Their MP-40 submachine guns were secured against their midsections with two sets of straps. They wore thick, wool coats over many layers of long underwear and they were hunched forward by the bulk of their parachutes pushing against the metal skin of the airplane.

Lt. Rommel stood and raised his voice and signaled at the same time. "Stand up." As one unit the men stood and faced forward. "Sound off."

The men sang out, starting from the back, "One okay, two okay…" until it was his turn, "Lead, okay." He unclipped his static-line hook and held it up. The men mimicked his movement. "Hook up," he shouted. He watched carefully, making sure each man hooked up properly. He adjusted his submachine gun.

A flight crew member's voice crackled through his head-set. "Two minutes, Lieutenant."

He nodded and held up two fingers. "Zwei minuten."

Suddenly there was a loud crump and the plane bucked to the left. He felt his safety belt tighten, keeping him from being flung into space. Out the door, he saw little puffs of angry black clouds erupting all around their flight. In his headset he heard, "Hold tight. Flak." The light changed from yellow to red indicating one minute to jump. He unstrapped the belt, which had just saved his life and held on tight with both hands.

Another close explosion above the plane pushed it down and for a sickening instant he felt his feet come off the ground as he went weightless. The plane quickly righted and his feet slammed down hard. He saw men fall in the aisle but were quickly helped up by comrades.

There was a zipping sound and he recognized it from live fire exercises—heavy caliber bullets. The fabric of the starboard wing seemed to spring leaks suddenly and he saw clear liquid streaming out. He pressed his send button on the radio, "Starboard wing leaking fuel."

He didn't wait for a reply. He flung the headset off his ears. His internal countdown told him the one minute was nearly up. His count ended and two seconds later the light turned green. He instantly flung himself out the door and spread his arms over his head. He felt the freezing fuel hit his face and he hoped he didn't ignite. There was an instant of free-fall then his chute was pulled when his chord hit the end of the rope, and his fall immediately arrested. He swung wildly beneath the chute.

He looked up, relieved to see a fully deployed canopy. He grabbed the risers and looked at the ground searching for landmarks. He saw the Idlewild Airport spread out beneath him. There were burning hulks of planes and he could see tiny ant-like men scuttling around, some with fire hoses. He was right on target.

He pulled his right riser and felt the chute cut right and turn. Once directed the way he wanted to go he angled both risers forward and traveled toward a small outbuilding he could use for cover and a rally point. The sudden ripping sound of an anti-aircraft weapon caught his attention. He saw streaks of tracers arcing from behind a building he recognized as Hangar Two.

He'd studied the schematic of the airfield exhaustively and knew it better than he knew his own house. He had no idea how the Korth were able to give them such detailed photographs, but even they hadn't spotted that particular anti-aircraft gun. He internally marked the location, they'd have to take it out along with all the rest.

When he was a few meters from the ground, he pulled on his risers to slow his descent. An enemy soldier rounded the corner right in front of him and their eyes met for an instant. He held a Thompson submachine gun at port arms. His mouth gaped open in astonishment. Ricker pulled his pistol, his Schmeisser was too strapped down, and aimed. The soldier saw the danger and brought his weapon up slightly before Ricker pulled the trigger four-times quickly. Compared to the anti-air gun, it sounded like a toy, but one of his bullets smacked into the GIs shoulder and he fell to one knee and dropped the Thompson.

Ricker hit the ground harder than he wanted. He absorbed the impact and rolled onto his feet, aimed and fired twice more. The stunned GI's head snapped back and he fell backwards.

Ricker holstered his pistol and quickly unsnapped his rigging, letting it fly away in the wind. Normally he'd wrap it up to keep it from fouling another trooper, but with enemy so close he didn't have time. He loosened the straps holding his Schmeisser MP-40 then unsnapped one side and freed the machine gun. With the smoothness that only comes from countless hours of practice, he unsnapped his ammo pouch and pulled and inserted a 30 round magazine with a satisfying, 'click.'

Another soldier rounded the corner and reeled when he saw his dead comrade's brains at his feet. Ricker released the safety and fired a short burst into the soldier's chest. He fell and his blood spattered the wall.

Another soldier nearly came around the corner but arrested his momentum and dove back. Ricker fired and his bullets put gouges in the concrete wall and sent dust and rock chips flying.

Ricker ran forward and pressed his back against the wall, keeping an eye on the corner. Movement from the sky caught his eye and he saw Fallschirmjäger flying their chutes his way. There was a shot from around the corner and he saw one of his men scream and writhe at the end of his lines.

Sheisse. He stepped to the corner and quickly thrust his body around, his machine gun at his shoulder. The GI was lining up another shot. His eyes widened and he tried to shift his aim, but Ricker fired first, emptying his magazine.

Soon, he was surrounded by paratroopers. He reloaded and directed his men. "Heinz, take Zoller and Henrichs and find the heavy weapons container. We'll need Panzerfausts soon enough." The three men hustled off, keeping low. He pointed, "Sergeant Hoch, how many men?"

"Eight so far, but not everyone's down, sir."

Ricker nodded, "Take First Squad to the edge of the runway. Second Squad," he found another soldier with stripes on his sleeves. "Cover First Squad, then join them and take out those AA units. There's more than we thought."

More troopers were joining every second, honing in on their platoon leader's black parachute, which had snagged and was blowing in the wind like a beacon.

Suddenly the sound of heavy machine gun fire filled the air, making them all hunch lower. Lieutenant Rommel recognized the fearful .50 caliber machine gun and cursed under his breath. Great gouges and plumes erupted behind the building they cowered behind.

The fire shifted, spotting the rest of First Platoon sprinting toward cover. Ricker yelled a warning. "Get down! Take cover!"

Six paratroopers instantly dove and tried to make themselves as small as possible. The closest man was ten meters away, laying in the slight depression of an artillery shell's impact. He pointed, "It's coming from the tower."

Ricker saw one of the troopers hopelessly exposed on the concrete tarmac. Heavy slugs marched toward him. He sprang up and was cut nearly in half, great gouts of blood spilled. *Dammit.* He risked leaning out and saw the muzzle flash in the tower. He quickly pulled back. "The tower's Second Platoon's job. Where are they?" There was no answer and the men were looking to him for guidance. He felt the weight of command on his shoulders. He licked his lips. "Our job's the AA and that's what we're going to do."

He grasped Sergeant Hoch's shoulder, "I want fire on that tower while we get the rest of the men in here."

Hoch nodded and shouted, "First Squad prepare to fire on the tower."

Ricker yelled at the remaining pinned-down troopers. "When I tell you, get your asses over here." He looked at Sergeant Hoch who had his men stacked on the wall, waiting for his command to leap out and fire. "Now, Sergeant." He waited a second until he heard firing then yelled, "Now! Get here! Now!"

He watched the remaining five paratroopers leap up and run with their weapons held firmly in front. Seconds later they slid in on their knee-pads. Ricker yelled, "Cease fire, Sergeant."

First Squad immediately found cover. The steady hammering of the .50 caliber shook the building as it slowly tore it apart, piece by piece. The five soldier's, members of Third Squad, slapped backs and shook hands with the others, thankful to be alive.

Ricker got their attention. "We must get across this open ground and take out those AA guns before Stark Company drops," he looked at his watch, "in eight minutes."

There was a flurry of firing coming from the other side of the airfield, near the tower. Hope filled Ricker's eyes, "Those are Schmeissers. It must be Second Platoon."

One of the five men, Ricker recognized him as Private Kleinowitz nodded and said, "I saw chutes way off the landing zone. They looked like they were near the water. It must be them."

The hammering of the .50 continued but it was no longer targeting their building. Ricker nodded. "Okay, let's go. We'll cover First Squad, then Second Squad then Third. Klar?" There were nods all around. "Okay, Second Squad get ready to cover them, but don't fire unless you see enemy, we don't know the status of the assault on the tower." The men nodded and readied themselves. "Go!" Ricker shouted.

Sergeant Hoch was the first around the corner with the rest of First Squad close behind. Ricker's chest swelled as the men automatically spread out, not making easy targets. Thankfully, there was no fire directed their way and Second Squad didn't fire a shot.

Sergeant Hoch slid in beside the next building and when his men piled in beside him, gave a thumbs-up.

"Second Squad, go!" They were up and across quickly. The sound of battle from the tower intensified then there was a whoosh and a loud explosion. Ricker peered around the corner and saw the tower's windows spewing white smoke. "The .50 cal has had it. Let's go." He waved Third Squad forward and they ran hunched over. Ricker saw the three Americans he'd killed. Their faces were gray and little specks of dirt clung to the congealed blood. He didn't feel anything. He'd simply killed them before they killed him.

———

THE SOUND of snapping bullets passing nearby made Lt. Rommel cringe and run faster toward the cover of the edge of the concrete hangar. He'd trained incessantly for this moment for years but now that he was finally in combat, he realized no amount of training could have prepared him for the sheer terror and chaos.

He dove headfirst, imagining he could feel the heat of near misses. Despite his heavily padded arms, he felt the scrape and hardness of the ground and the pain made him suck in his breath. He'd made it across alive and unscathed and the notion filled him with awe.

"You hit, sir?" asked Sergeant Hoch.

Ricker did a quick self-assessment and shook his head. "I'm intact, Sergeant." He got to his feet and adjusted his helmet. "Where's that coming from? The tower?"

Sergeant Hoch shook his head, "No, sir. There's a bunker around the AA gun. Fire's coming from the Americans protecting the gun."

Ricker sidled up to the edge of the wall. He looked at the ground adjacent to his position, there was very little cover. Most of the vegetation had been cut away to keep the land from encroaching on the hangar. The spread-out trees beyond were too far away. "Let's get inside this hangar. Find an entrance," Ricker ordered.

Seconds later Corporal Heinrichs yelled from halfway down the hangar wall, "Over here, there's a door."

Ricker nodded and waved the men forward. "Let's go." The fire coming from the Americans was still raging and Ricker imagined they were targeting other troopers. He glanced at his watch, *four minutes until the next drop.* "Hurry," he urged.

They stacked on either side of the door leading into the hangar and once they were in position, Ricker nodded at Sergeant Hoch, who touched the trooper's shoulder in front of him.

The trooper let his MP-40 submachine gun hang and used both hands to push the door lever down. He whispered, "Unlocked," then flung the door inward and leaned away allowing the rest of the troopers inside. They flowed in like water with their submachine guns at their shoulders.

Ricker was the sixth man through. The inside of the hangar was dimly lit. He couldn't distinguish one shape from another. The sharp controlled burst from a paratrooper's MP-40 told him the hangar was occupied.

"Contact right," came the calm voice from Sergeant Hoch.

More MP-40 fire and Ricker moved right with his own weapon at his shoulder and ready. He moved quickly, sweeping his weapon, searching for a target. He saw movement left and swung his muzzle. An American soldier appeared around the edge of a large piece of machinery. He staggered and held a pistol, unsteadily aiming at him. Ricker squeezed the trigger. The Schmeisser shook in his hand as five rounds knocked the man to his knees with multiple gunshot wounds to his chest. Between adrenaline charged breaths, Ricker managed, "Contact left. Target down," and kept moving, his weapon at his shoulder.

He stepped over the twitching body and ducked behind cover, keeping his weapon at his shoulder. He heard more firing from MP-40s to the right, but kept scanning his own section. He heard Sergeant Hoch, "Clear right."

More paratroopers swept past Ricker's position, leapfrogging forward. They got to the back of the hangar and yelled, "Building's clear."

Ricker got to his feet, letting his weapon dangle from the strap. He trotted forward, finding his men huddled near another door opposite the one they entered. He saw Private Zoller and Heinz trotting forward holding Panzerfaust rocket launchers. He pointed at them, "Get ready. This doorway should give you a good shot at the AA gun."

They nodded and Zoller moved in front of the doorway and crouched. Private Heinz did the same directly behind. Zoller whispered, "I'm ready."

There was a sudden roar of heavy caliber fire outside and Ricker looked at his watch. "That gun's targeting the second wave. Now," he urged.

Sergeant Hoch touched Private First Class Maddow's shoulder. Maddow reached for the door handle and pulled it open. The dim room lit up with the sudden daylight streaming through. Zoller held the Panzerfaust ready at his shoulder, but didn't fire right away. He scooted forward until he could see the gun emplacement, then depressed the bar on top of the tube, completing the electrical circuit which ignited and fired the armor-piercing warhead.

Zoller suddenly pitched backward as bullets slammed into his chest and head. The single use Panzerfaust clattered to the floor. Hands reached out and pulled Zoller's body from the light and into cover. Maddow leaned out and fired a long burst then leaned back as more bullets slammed the side of the hangar, sounding like a heavy hailstorm.

Despite the danger, Pvt. Heinz scooted forward into the light, his Panzerfaust ready. He leaned forward, steadied his aim, depressed the trigger and quickly dove sideways as a hail of bullets missed him by centimeters.

The hammering of the AA gun continued but the incoming small arms fire diminished noticeably. Lieutenant Rommel ordered, "Go, go, go! We have to take that gun out!"

The men didn't hesitate. Sergeant Hoch was the second man out behind PFC Maddow. He moved left and fired his MP-40 from the hip as he ran. Ricker was the last man out. He squinted in the bright daylight but saw his men engaging the AA gun emplacement. Some were crouched firing, while others ran hard directly into the danger. Ricker saw the smoking holes the rockets caused and saw green clad American soldiers writhing on the ground, some missing body parts.

His men flowed over the position like floodwater, firing into the remaining soldiers. The AA gun's lethal fire stopped. Ricker leaped over the leaking sandbags like a high-hurdler and slid in beside the gun, his weapon at the ready, but there were no enemy soldiers left alive. He looked at the carnage they'd wrought. Men with gaping wounds and torn limbs were everywhere. He was relieved to see none wore the gray camouflage of his Fallschirmjager's.

Sergeant Hoch slapped his shoulder and Ricker followed his pointing finger. He saw the second wave passing over, the sky was filling with parachutes some dangling men, some holding large containers full of weapons and ammo. He saw a dark track which he figured had been an aircraft and wondered if the men inside had made it out or ridden it into the ground.

There was a smattering of gunfire, but the incessant and intense firefight seemed to be over. The neat, orderly airfield was now a battle-field. Structures smoked and there were chunks torn in the runway. The engineers would need to get busy before they could land aircraft, but that was not his mission.

Ricker felt pride swell in his chest. He'd completed his mission. He allowed himself only a second before he barked, "Get the men spread out and dug in for a counterattack, Sergeant. We have to hold out til the armor gets here."

9

Rex Crandall came to his senses. Without opening his eyes, he evaluated his body. One by one he tensed his limbs and found them tethered. He was in a sitting position. He guessed he was tied to a chair. His body ached but his mind was sharp. He remembered the awful feeling when he was shot with whatever he'd been shot with. The feeling of intense pain as every muscle in his body seemed to contract and cramp all at once was still fresh in his mind.

Keeping his head slumped forward he risked cracking an eyelid. He was inside a well-lit room. The floor was gray concrete and he noticed a tiny crack zigzagging beneath his chair. He glanced to the side and saw a white wall. He couldn't help jolting when a loud voice suddenly filled the room.

"Your vitals are being monitored. We know you're awake, 520."

Rex slowly lifted his head, the stiffness in his neck making him nearly gasp. He opened his eyes. He was in the center of a white room with no features. It reminded him of his first introduction to his new life so many months before. He rotated his head, trying to stretch the stiffness out. He knew better than to ask questions but he couldn't help himself, "Where am I?"

There was no answer. A minute passed and he used the time to flex and move his body as best he could. He wanted to be ready to react if he were given the chance. Finally a door opened in front of him. The door seemed to materialize and normally he'd be impressed, but he'd seen these invisible doors before.

He watched a figure step through. He recognized the same man who'd first introduced him to The Branch and the feeling of deja'vu was intense. For an instant, dread filled him as he thought he was in some endless, pain-filled cycle in the pits of hell. "Mr. Black," he muttered.

Mr. Black wore a dark suit with a meticulously tied tie hanging from his thick neck and passing over his meaty chest before disappearing into the V of his suit coat. His expression didn't change. "Ah, you remember. How sweet."

"I'd never forget a prick like you," Rex said in a flat voice edged with hatred.

Mr. Black's face stayed a mask of calmness, but Rex noticed a dangerous fire in his eyes. "You've progressed well through your training. You're ready for the next step."

Rex felt momentary relief as he thought perhaps he wasn't going to be executed. He kept his face a blank mask and asked, "Next step?"

Rex felt the air behind him change slightly, the same way it did when Mr. Black opened the door. He didn't hear anything, but knew another person had entered the room right behind him. He watched Mr. Black's eyes but he gave him no indication there was another person in the room.

Rex saw the slight movement in the reflection of Mr. Black's eyes. The sense of someone close behind him was strong. Rex's legs and feet were tied to the chair. He had just enough leverage to lunge backward. He put everything into the move and he tipped backwards hard. He felt the back of his head slam into something relatively soft and thrust his head backwards with as much force as he could muster and was rewarded with the man grunting as he took the thrust to his crotch.

Rex spun left, pulling the chair with him and balanced on the balls of his feet. The scrunched position was awkward and painful but he was able to hop and spin, thrusting the rear chair legs into the man's shins.

Rex hopped and spun again until he was facing a man dressed identical to Mr. Black. Rex's feeble attack had done little damage. The man stepped back and scowled at Rex, then reared his right fist back and punched him in the face. He was ready for it and moved with the punch a fraction of an instant before it landed, softening the blow and making the man overextend and bring his head too close. Rex thrust his head forward and his forehead smashed into the side of the man's head, knocking him to the ground.

Rex hopped and spun a half turn and landed chair-first onto the man's back. He felt the wooden chair crack and break. His left leg was suddenly free as the chair leg detached from the base. He got his free leg beneath him and sprang upward intending to put the other three chair legs into the man's back, hoping to puncture his muscled body but a sudden force slammed into his chest and he was flung into the wall. He hit his head and saw stars.

Mr. Black was suddenly above him aiming the same odd pistol which had delivered the shocking pain earlier. It was aimed at his face and Rex could see the arcing blue of electricity in the gaping barrel. "Stop," barked Mr. Black. "Now." Rex let his tensed body relax into the floor. He was beat for the moment. He nodded. Mr. Black didn't take his eyes or the barrel off Rex as he spoke to the other man, "Like I said, he's ready."

The other man lifted himself off the floor and strode over to him. Rex expected to be beaten mercilessly, but instead the man grinned, felt the blood running from the side of his head and grinned. "Yes. I agree. With the invasion, it'll be easier to insert him. We'll do it this week."

Rex knew better than to ask questions. They'd tell him what he needed to know, nothing more, but the word 'invasion' focused his gaze. Mr. Black noticed and nodded, "That's right, the East Coast is under attack as we speak. Our country's at risk of being annihilated. You can make a difference but only if you do exactly as we instruct. Understand?"

The news shocked Rex and his mind reeled with questions, mostly concerning the safety of his wife and son. He knew not to ask. Such an inquiry would only put them at risk. He'd been told if he tried to contact them, or find out anything about them, they'd simply be executed. It was The Branch's way of taking his mind off them, by simply removing them from the equation. Rex nodded, "I understand completely."

———

THREE WEEKS LATER, Rex was flying at wave top level in an innocuous, unidentifiable four-seater airplane, over the choppy waves of the South Atlantic Ocean.

The plane had been catapulted off a small ship, whose designation papers marked it as African, but in actuality, was owned by the Brazilian Navy. It had left port from the tiny island of St. Helena, halfway between Brazil and the African coast and flown northeast.

The war raging along the East Coast of the United States hadn't leaked this far south, although no one had any illusions that it was only a matter of time. Brazil, along with every other South American country was at war with the countries allied with the Korth. Although they hadn't been attacked directly, they'd sent troops and supplies north to help defend their reeling allies. Africa, thousands of miles to the East was the nearest threat, but, like the rest of Korth controlled countries, had been silent for the past decade.

As the small plane skimmed the wave tops, Rex felt the dull ache from the implanted Korth translator embedded in his neck. He reached up and felt the small knob sticking from the right side of his neck. The doctors told him the dull pain would go away within a week, but he still felt it after three weeks and wondered if it was infected.

The man beside him, who's unlikely name was, Joe, leaned over and yelled over the din of the engines, "Touching it only makes it worse."

Rex jolted from his thoughts and realized the translator had vibrated and translated Joe's Spanish for him. He dropped his hand and smiled at the man, whose large body barely fit into the confines of the aircraft. Rex spoke Spanish back at him, but knew Joe's translator helped as he butchered the language. "It still burns a little. Wondering if it's infected."

Joe's bright teeth seemed to glow, juxtaposed against his ebony skin. Rex had met many black men, but never one as dark as Joe. "Speak English. Your Spanish is an insult."

Rex smiled and shook his head. He'd met the man a week before and figured his purpose was to watch him. "You mean that tiny shit-hole island you hail from?"

Joe shook his head. "You are a terrible man, 520."

Rex shook his head, "Now we're finally on our way, call me…" he considered as though making up a name. "Call me, Rex."

"Rex? Ha. You don't look like a Rex. How bout something more believable, like…"

Rex interrupted him, "Joe? Something like that? You look as much like a Joe as I do a Jose."

Joe's smile broadened and he nodded, "Okay, *Rex,*" he said it as though tasting something exotic. "Rex it is." He looked at his wrist watch. "We've another two hours until we exit the aircraft. You should get some rest, Rex."

Rex gulped at the flippancy of 'exiting' the aircraft. The insertion promised to be a harrowing experience. The plan was, when they were just outside the envelope of African radar, about ten miles, the aircraft would slow, ascend to 500 feet and they'd hurl themselves from the side door along with a raft and four paddles.

Assuming they and the raft landed intact, they'd paddle the rest of the way through shark infested waters to the hostile coastline of a continent which had gone dark a decade before. They weren't the first operatives to be sent to Africa, but Rex intended to be the first to make it out alive.

———

DESPITE THE FEAR building in his gut, he managed to sleep. He jolted awake when Joe slapped his shoulder and he felt the translator buzz slightly. He instinctively reached for it and Joe frowned and slapped his hand away then wagged a long finger in his face. "You must stop doing that. It's a sure giveaway. No one will even notice their devices anymore and if you continue to touch it, they'll be suspicious."

Rex wiped his eyes and nodded. "You're right. How far out are we?"

Joe held up two fingers, "Two minutes, my friend."

Rex nodded and cinched his parachute tighter. He watched Joe do the same. He didn't know much about Joe and he wasn't happy to be saddled with someone he knew almost nothing about.

Rex had been assured Joe would be helpful once they made it to the African continent. Once he heard about the insertion method, he was glad he wouldn't have to go through it alone and understood Joe would blend in much better than he would. There were plenty of white-skinned people in Africa before the Korth invasion and there was no reason to believe that wasn't still the case, but having a black man beside him would make him less obvious. *But I still don't trust him.*

Rex felt the aircraft slow and tilt upward into a slight right turn. He looked out the window and saw the wave tops getting further away. The green and blue of the sea was beautiful and looked warm and inviting, but he knew this region was famous for sharks and thought of encountering one or several, made him shiver involuntarily.

Joe noticed and touched his shoulder and leaned close to his ear. "Don't worry. This is no problem."

Rex shook his head, "Not worried about the jump but the sharks."

Joe pursed his lips and looked serious. "Yes, get to the raft quickly. Quicker the better."

The plane leveled off at 500 feet and Rex stood and stepped to the open door. He looked out, then back at Joe. He smiled.

Rex gripped the front of the rolled raft and Joe gripped the back. They'd go out at the same time, release the boat, pull their rip cords and float down. The boat would sense when it hit water and a burst of CO_2 would erupt and rapidly inflate it. The method had been thoroughly tested, but at 500 feet, there was very little time to pull their ripcords before hitting the water. Any more elevation, however, could make them visible to a lucky aircraft or nearby boat and their mission would be over before it started.

Rex yelled the countdown, "One, two, three —." He yanked the raft through the door and felt the slipstream slam into him. He immediately released the raft and saw Joe's large body falling alongside, only feet away. Rex clutched his chest and found the ripcord. He steadied, let himself drift a few feet from the boat and pulled. He heard and felt the satisfying snap as the chute deployed. He felt his balls tighten into his gut as the straps yanked hard, but he was happy for the pain. It was much better than spinning into the sea at terminal velocity.

He spotted the raft splash down to his right and shifted his body weight, trying to angle toward it. There was a slight breeze and he felt himself drifting further and further away.

Suddenly the sea was only feet away and he clutched the quick release tabs of his chute. When his boots touched water, he pulled hard and felt the chute's pull vanish. He dropped into the warm South Atlantic and went deep. He spread his arms and legs trying to arrest his descent. The small Mae West-style life jacket around his neck inflated and he felt his descent slow, stop, then he rocketed toward the surface. Fifteen seconds after hitting the water, he was on the surface, panting. He took in large lungfuls of air and lay on his back.

He recovered and searched for the black raft. He caught sight of it when he went up on a swell. It was far away and there was no sign of Joe. He turned onto his side and started using the slow, side-stroke crawl the cadre had taught incessantly.

He'd resented their insistence on perfecting the stroke, after all, he was a decent swimmer and thought he'd be much faster if he just did the normal freestyle stroke. But they'd insisted on the side-crawl and Rex had to admit it was the superior stroke in the open ocean. It wasn't as fast, nor as sexy, but it moved him in the right direction and didn't sap his strength.

He finally reached the raft and pulled himself inside. He untied the ropes securing the paddles, stood and looked for Joe. He squinted in the evening sun, searching sections of ocean by degrees. He'd nearly gone around the compass when he finally spotted him 20 yards away. Rex went to the bow and used the paddle in a forward draw stroke, which allowed him to pull the boat closer to Joe.

When he was ten yards away, he realized Joe wasn't swimming but treading water, staring downward. He yelled, "Joe, over here."

Joe ignored him and pushed himself underwater with a smooth strong motion. Rex continued paddling, sharks very much on his mind. He got to the spot where Joe went under and leaned over the side, searching the clear water. He saw a huge shape which made him shiver. *Shark!*

Behind him there was a sudden flurry of splashing and Rex yelled. He whirled around in time to see Joe coming out of the water as though he could fly, and landed in the center of the boat. He held a knife in his right hand. He lay on his back in the bottom of the raft, panting. "What the hell's going on? Where'd the shark go? Are you bit?"

Joe's chest rose and fell as he caught his breath. Finally, he smiled and shook his head. "I'm okay. Did you know you scream like a woman?"

Rex ignored the jibe. "What happened? I saw a shark."

Joe put himself in a sitting position and sheathed the knife inside his pants pocket. Rex hadn't noticed it before. "There was a shark and there will probably be more." He grasped a paddle and went to the opposite side of the raft.

Rex looked at his compass and pointed, "That way." He pulled the paddle through the water and Joe matched him stroke for stroke. "You gonna tell me what happened?"

Joe answered, "I stabbed it in the nose as he approached. They have sensitive noses. He won't be back soon, but he'll be back."

Rex shook his head, "Damn, you've got balls of steel."

Joe giggled, "That would be a burden my woman would not enjoy nor put up with."

————

THE EVENING TURNED to darkness and Rex had to constantly check the compass to keep them on an easterly course. Their paddle strokes were slow and smooth and they switched sides often to keep fatigue at bay.

They guessed they'd hit land in the middle of the night, which was the plan.

The operation to get him to the island of St. Helena, onto the ship and into the airplane to the proper drop site, had been meticulously planned. However, this part of the operation, paddling to mainland Africa, was a crapshoot. They had no specific idea where they'd actually end up. Heading east at a steady two miles an hour, would put them on the coast, but the various ocean currents were unpredictable.

Rex glanced at the luminescent dials on his wrist watch, "Should be getting close."

Joe grunted, "Assuming you know how to read a compass, yes."

Rex stopped paddling and Joe followed suit to keep them from spinning. "Water break." He untied the supply compartment and lifted a large cylindrical canteen. He took a long drink and handed it to Joe, who took a smaller drink. "Beautiful sky out here." The stars were bright and reached from horizon to horizon. "Glad the weather's held." Joe nodded but didn't answer. Rex murmured, "Man of few words."

Joe screwed the lid on the canteen and placed it back inside the compartment, taking care to retie the laces. He pointed, "That looks like land. You see it?"

Rex looked over the bow and could just make out the outline on the horizon. "I'll be damned. I think you're right."

They kept paddling. The land didn't seem to be getting any closer. Rex knew they were making headway, but it was slow and tedious. Finally the white outline of waves breaking along the coast were visible. They stopped paddling and listened to the welcome sounds of waves breaking on sand.

Rex whispered, "See any signs of life?"

Joe shook his head and whispered back, "No. But the towns might be on light restriction. For all we know, there may be no one left on the continent."

Rex shrugged. "You're right, but we have to assume there are. Let's get closer."

They paddled, making as little noise as possible. They were in a black raft in the middle of a dark night, coming from a black ocean.

Even if someone was looking for them, and there was no reason to think they would be, they'd be nearly impossible to spot. The fact that no operatives had returned from the dark continent kept them careful.

They paddled until they were just outside the breakers. The gentle swell lifted and dropped the raft. They lay on the rubber sides and watched the shore. It was utterly empty. Rex moved to a sitting position and whispered, "Let's get to shore."

Soon they were inside the breaking waves. Rex moved to the stern while Joe stayed on the side and continued paddling. A peaking wave rushed up behind them like a black wall and started to break. Rex whispered, "Hold on." The raft's forward momentum kept them in front of the moderately sized wave and the stern lifted. Rex held his paddle firmly in the rudder position, keeping the raft straight. The raft suddenly rushed forward down the face of the wave and the feeling of speed brought a smile to his face.

Joe looked back and Rex saw his white teeth beaming. The raft bounced along and soon lost speed as the wave's energy dissipated and finally ended on the shore of a sandy beach. Joe launched from the side and waded in calf deep water, pulling the raft along. Rex jumped out and they struggled to lift the raft and move it up the beach, trying not to leave drag marks.

Rex felt the strain on his shoulders as he tried to keep up with Joe's long strides. Rex's breathing was coming in gasps, but Joe barely seemed to be working. They finally reached a large pile of driftwood and stopped.

Rex felt his pulse returning to normal. "We'll bury it here. I'll get the packs." He untied the laced compartment, took out two light packs filled with food, water, and small radios. He placed them on the sand, while Joe moved driftwood and dug in the sand until he'd scraped out a suitable depression.

They stuffed the raft inside, took one last look around, then released the valves. There was a loud gush of air as the tubes deflated. Rex looked around nervously. If there was anyone close, the sound would attract attention. Joe said, "Don't worry. We're alone."

They didn't move for a full five minutes, but the night noises didn't change and he was comfortable that no one was nearby. They placed large rocks onto the raft floor, then rolled it as best they could and buried it under sand and driftwood.

If they hoped to find it again, they needed to figure out where they were. The operational planning was suspiciously thin when it came to the details of returning from the mission. Indeed it was barely talked about at all. Their mission was to blend in and report back using the radios, which were powerful enough to reach St. Helena Island. However, using the radios was considered a last resort as it was assumed the Korth technology could intercept, or even jam the signal.

Rex went to the packs and pulled out his radio. He placed it on a flat rock and picked up another nearby rock. Joe was watching him closely. "What are you doing?" he asked.

Rex didn't answer but lifted the rock over his head as if to crash it down upon the radio. Joe moved like a striking snake to stop him, but Rex was ready. Expecting Rex to be focused on the radio, Joe moved to save it. Instead of crushing the radio, however, Rex shifted his arc and crashed the rock into the side of Joe's exposed head.

He heard the crunch of a cracking skull. Joe went limp and dropped. Rex rushed forward and felt for a pulse. He found one. "Sorry bout this," he uttered. "Can't have you keeping tabs on me." He lifted the rock and was about to bring it down onto Joe's head a final time. The cadre had trained him how to kill and he was one of their best students, but now that he was confronted with actually killing in cold blood—he hesitated. "Dammit," he cursed.

Rex put the rock down, went to other backpack and pulled out a tightly wound length of thin rope. He quickly tied Joe's arms and legs, then wrapped gauze and bandages around his bleeding head. Joe's head lolled and his eyes rolled. He murmured something the translator in his neck couldn't decipher.

He propped Joe up in a protected pocket formed by crisscrossing driftwood pieces. He left him a half-filled canteen and placed the hidden knife beside it. He checked the ropes. The cadre had trained them extensively in escape, particularly how to free oneself from ropes. He knew Joe would be able to escape, assuming his head-wound didn't kill him first, but it would take time. Enough time for Rex to disappear.

He emptied Joe's pack, taking the rest of the food and water. He stood over him and considered killing him. It was the right thing to do. Leaving him alive was an unnecessary risk and he knew the cadre would have killed him without a second thought. The thought made his decision even easier. *I'm not one of them.* "Good luck, Joe." He turned and walked inland.

10

Private Hans Jowitzki was in the sixth LVT to motor its way off the troop-carrying Landing Craft Vehicles and churn toward the East Coast of the United States. They approached a town called, Dover. He was huddled in the armored vehicle beside his fellow comrades, shaking. He wasn't sure if it was from fear or the cold, but either way, he wished he were anywhere else but there.

He glanced to his right and saw Sergeant Kline staring at him with an evil grin. "Don't look so damned glum, Private. It's a good day to die, don't you think?" Jowitzki's blank stare made him laugh uproariously. He slapped his back and Hans flinched. "Fine German soldier," he teased.

Hans ignored him and looked straight ahead, concentrating on the helmeted head in front of him. He gripped his weapon tighter, happy to have the StG-44 submachine gun.

His unit had been issued the weapon just before shipping out and practiced with targets on the open sea while they traveled to their takeoff point. He was impressed with the accuracy and rate of fire. It was a little unwieldy, but worth the extra fire-power it brought to the battlefield. *If I make it that far.*

The boat shuddered as an incoming shell exploded nearby. Hans cringed and looked around the cramped space. He knew there was only one way out, through the massive front gate, but it wouldn't drop until they hit the beach. It took all his resolve to stay calm. He heard someone praying and realized it was his own voice. Another shell landed nearby and he felt the craft list to the side slightly. *Oh God, I'll either burn or drown.* He continued praying, something he hadn't done since he was a boy.

He felt a hand on his right hip squeezing. He turned and in the dim light saw his long-time friend Carl's eyes, barely visible beneath the brim of his helmet. Carl gave him a curt smile, "It'll be okay, right?"

Hans had always been the strong one, always climbing higher, taking chances. Carl was his best friend, timid but always up for some fun. He'd watch Hans and if he were successful in whatever game or feat they were trying at the moment, he'd follow. This was different though. This was beyond skill, they'd die or live based only upon chance and it terrified him. Seeing Carl's eyes though, he realized he had to put on a stoic face, if only to keep Carl from losing it.

Hans took a deep breath and nodded. He even managed a strained smile, "Sure thing, Carl. Sure thing." He immediately felt better having someone to watch over.

They were two of the youngest soldiers in the company. They'd been in high school only the year before. They'd both joined up right out of school, hoping to become pilots, but the Army needed soldiers so they found themselves wearing the mottled gray camouflage of the infantry. A whirlwind of a year passed, full of screaming sergeants and endless training and now here they were churning toward a foreign, hostile shore.

The mounted machine gun on top of the track opened fire, making Hans flinch. He could only see the bottom half of the gunner's body, the rest sticking up from the cupola, leaning into the MG42 and firing short bursts. Hans turned back toward Carl. "Must be getting close," he yelled over the machine gun's din. Carl hunched and nodded. Hans licked his suddenly dry lips, "Wh-when the ramp drops, let's stick together." Carl met his eyes and nodded. The fear coming off him was almost palpable. "We'll be okay if we stick together."

The sudden sound of hammer blows on metal made talking or

hearing impossible. Hans covered his ears. It reminded him of being inside a thin metal shed during an especially brutal hail storm. He remembered his father grinning and holding his shaking body close, calming him. His father wasn't there to protect him now, and it wasn't harmless hail, but enemy bullets smacking the metal skin.

The MG42 gunner lurched and fell inside the compartment. Blood sprayed the walls and dripped from the cupola. "Schiesse," someone yelled.

Sergeant Kline gripped the man nearest the hole and pushed him forward. "Man the gun. Get up there, now!"

The private's eyes were wide as plates but he gulped, nodded, leaned his StG-44 along the blood-spattered wall and stepped onto the metal platform. He reached up, finding the butt of the MG42, then stood. Hans watched him as he worked the bolt, leaned forward and started firing. He wondered what he was seeing. What the hell was going on out there? How close were they? What were they facing?

The MG42 fired longer sustained bursts. Another explosion rocked them and Hans saw sea water enter through the cupola, mixing with the blood and sloshing on his boots. He gripped his weapon and glanced back at Carl who seemed to be muttering a prayer of his own.

The vehicle suddenly lurched and Hans thought sure they'd been hit, but instead the movement of the vehicle changed. The churning treads had found purchase on the rocky bottom and the LVT was transitioning from floating to driving. *Any second now.*

The MG42 kept hammering and he heard the gunner yelling something he couldn't make out. He sounded as though he were either terrified or exultant beyond measure.

The LVT lurched to a halt and rocked on its chassis. *This is it.* Light suddenly filled the compartment as the front door dropped forward and clanged onto the rocky beach. "Go! Go! Go!" he heard Lieutenant Walsh yell.

Hans pushed the man in front who was pushing the next man and they spilled out the doorway. The scene was absolute chaos. Bullets whizzed and zipped past his head, smacking rocks and armor, caroming in every direction making bizarre noises.

Hans kept pushing the man in front—moving forward—his legs

seeming to work on their own. Suddenly the soldiers back exploded in gore and Hans felt warm blood wash over his face. He tripped over the body and went down hard, still clutching his weapon as though it was the only thing keeping him alive.

He felt a boot on his back as a fellow soldier ran over the top of him. His face ground into the rocks and he tasted salt water on his tongue. He looked up and got his first real glimpse of hell.

There were German soldiers everywhere, some crawling, some running, some torn apart. Bullets swept the beach, sending geysers of sand, rock and blood into the air. Mortar shell explosions erupted all around, sending men flying sideways or simply turning them to bits and pieces.

He looked beyond the beach and saw countless muzzle flashes. Someone close yelled, "Move! Move or die!" He didn't know if it was directed at him, but his body responded and he pushed himself forward, keeping as low as possible.

A soldier ran past him screaming and firing his StG-44 from the hip. Hans thought he should get on his feet and join him, but changed his mind when the soldier's gray mottled camouflage suddenly blossomed red and he dropped like his puppet strings had been cut.

He suddenly remembered Carl. He stopped crawling and looked behind. The LVT he'd come from was grinding backwards, the front door now closed, making room for the next wave. The MG42 was still firing and he wondered if the soldier had simply stayed on it, or given the gun up to a member of the crew. He wished he were back on it.

The sounds of bullets hitting flesh snapped him back to the moment at hand. He didn't see Carl anywhere. "Carl!" he yelled, "Carl!" There were mounded bodies between him and water and he wondered if one of them was his friend. He started to shake uncontrollably.

He saw his comrades stacked along a low depression further up and realized he was lagging behind. He didn't want to move, but his training kicked in and he pushed forward on his belly, scraping the front of his helmet along the rocky shore. His vision was fuzzy and he wiped tears from his eyes.

The ground erupted a few feet to his right and he cringed, feeling the heat of shrapnel lancing over his back. He kept pushing until he bumped into someone's boots. He pushed forward working his way between the line of cowering soldiers clinging to the beach.

He rolled to his back staring at the broken overcast sky. He'd made it to relative safety, a slight depression near a seawall. He shut his eyes and murmured a prayer.

He heard Sergeant Kline's voice over the din of enemy fire, "Open fire! Covering fire!"

Forgetting Carl for a moment, Hans rolled back to his stomach and pulled his legs beneath him. He put the StG-44 to his shoulder and rose up. He saw a concrete bunker only meters away spewing fire and he flicked the safety lever up and pulled the trigger. The weapon bucked in his hand and he pulled it tighter into his shoulder. His bullets chipped rock and sparked against metal. He dropped down breathing hard. It felt good to fight back.

A mortar round exploded beside the man to his left, sending a shock wave that stunned him. He rolled on his back, the pounding in his head like nothing he'd ever experienced. The only sound, an intense ringing.

He opened his eyes and saw Sergeant Kline yelling something he couldn't understand. He watched him run forward and Hans rolled back to his belly, intending to follow. He looked left and saw the staring eyes of the soldier he'd rolled in beside. He reached out, gripping his shoulder and his torso came away from his legs, spilling grayish intestines onto the bloody ground.

The scene terrified him and he lurched to his feet and ran forward firing from the hip. He yelled and fired until all 30 rounds were expended and his barrel glowed red. Something caught his ankle and he tripped and rolled sideways into a deep bomb crater. He struggled to get up and continue running but there was suddenly a weight on his chest.

"Get a hold of yourself, Private!" yelled Sergeant Kline. Sanity returned a moment later and he nodded and Kline moved off him. "Reload. We're taking that bunker."

Hans noticed other wide-eyed soldiers in the hole. Some were spread out near the top, others cowered in the bottom. He searched for

Carl but didn't see his friend. "C-Carl? Anyone seen Carl?" No one responded, only stared and gripped their weapons preparing for the next hellish moment.

Sergeant Kline pointed at Hans and three others nearby. "You four cover us. On my command unleash hell. We'll flank right and take it out."

Hans and the rest nodded their understanding. Hans snapped in a fresh magazine and crawled up the side of the wet, sandy hole. He went right up to the lip and peeked over. The bunker was a few meters away, off to the left. It continued to spew fire. He glanced toward the sea and saw more LVTs disgorging troops. He saw men fall, spinning and dropping as the MG cut them to shreds. Anger filled him. "I'm coming with you, Sergeant," he growled.

Sergeant Kline didn't object, only nodded. "On the count of three: one, two, three. Now!" Hans pushed himself down the crater wall as the three soldiers fired on the bunker, then ran up the side wall, right on Sgt. Kline's butt.

Bullets whizzed past him, not from the bunker but the trench-line directly in front. He moved right, spreading out to make a harder target. He saw an enemy soldier only meters away rising up, aiming an M1. Hans didn't have time to aim. He fired from the hip, but at this range, he couldn't miss. The 8mm bullets stitched a line up the GI's chest. He was hurled backwards, hitting the back wall. Hans leaped and landed in the trench. He rolled into the back wall and came up with his weapon ready.

He sensed someone charging his back—he spun and fired. At least one bullet lanced through the GI's head, ending his charge. The soldier's momentum carried his body into Hans and he collapsed under the dead man's weight. He felt his breath leave his lungs as he hit the ground and he gasped like a guppy out of water, desperately trying to breathe.

Another GI was suddenly above him. Hans tried to move but it was useless, he was pinned. He'd die here. Hans closed his eyes, waiting for the shot that would end his short life. *Will I hear it? Will I feel it?* A moment passed and when he opened his eyes the soldier was simply gone.

Hans looked around stunned. The only sound was the ringing in his ears. He felt the dead body weight lighten and suddenly he could breathe again. He rolled to his stomach and threw up violently. He jolted when he felt a hand on his shoulder. He spun and saw his friend, Carl. "What happened to sticking together?" Carl asked.

———

LIEUTENANT FROMKOR GUTH watched the invasion of the United States with fascination and longing. He leaned against the ship railing, his upper arms gripping and releasing in anticipation of combat. He watched the LVTs churning onto the beaches disgorging German and Scandinavian troops. He couldn't help grinning as he watched the human's fickle bodies being torn apart by bullets and bombs. A salvo of heavy shells from a German battleship arced over his head and he watched the explosions demolish buildings inland as though they were made of sand.

His lower arms caressed the heavy MG42 he'd take into battle. It wasn't the trusty laz-blaster he was used to wielding. He wished it were, but without the mother-ship's core operational, he and his Legio troopers were forced to use the human's rudimentary and underpowered weapons. Despite the puny weapons, he and his platoon were ready to enter the fray and do some killing.

Major Korto's voice boomed and clicked from behind, "Is your platoon ready, Lieutenant Guth?"

Guth's head expanded giving the affirmative, "Ready and eager, sir."

Korto's head expanded and changed to a lighter red. "Good. The human's third wave has pushed inland and established a beachhead, finally. It's time to enter the battle."

Lieutenant Guth's head expanded more, displaying his pleasure and excitement. "We'll launch on your command, Major." Guth signaled his platoon and they marched in lockstep to a huge steel platform 80 feet above the water. This particular ship had four such platforms and would be the launching points for the entire company.

Guth was the last to step onto the platform. He looked at his Legio troopers with pride. They'd slung their MG42s on their backs, their chests crisscrossed with bandoliers of ammo. They stood in tight ranks, shoulder to shoulder facing the carnage on the beach only 500 yards distant. Guth slung his own weapon and tightened the straps until it was centered down his back and tight. He barked, "Second Platoon! Prepare for launch." With the precision of professional soldiers the platoon shifted into crouches and waited.

The last booming salvo from the ships quieted and the only sound was the combat on the beach. Lt. Guth glanced from his crouched position at Major Korto, and acknowledged through telepathy that his men were ready. Major Korto's head expanded and he gave the order. "Launch platform one!"

Guth felt the metal platform beneath his feet vibrate slightly as though under immense tension. There was a whoosh as the hydraulics released massive force, sending the platform straight up for 50 feet then abruptly stopping.

Guth relished the intense pressure of the launch on his strong legs. When the platform reached its tether and stopped, the pressure changed to lightness and he felt himself flying through this planet's thin air. It wasn't quite the same as flying on his home planet's heavy air, but it was good to be flying again.

He stretched his four arms, feeling the thin skin between them catching the air and snapping tight. He, and his Second Platoon of the Legio Division troopers angled toward the beach in perfect formation. The wind and lift, although nothing like home, felt good and he relished every second of flight. In his subconscious he heard the other platforms firing as his brothers joined him.

The battle seemed to pause as the humans from both sides marveled at the sight of Korth entering battle. They glided over the sea, passing over stunned, upturned faces of soldiers on landing crafts. They descended quickly, the thin air not able to keep their heavy bodies aloft for long. Guth angled downward, aiming for the cover of the sea wall littered with countless human bodies.

His platoon matched his move and soon they were slicing over the beach, only feet above the human soldiers. Guth's head pulsed with pleasure, changing shades of red. He angled upward, feeling himself slow abruptly and his forked feet touched the sand and rock lightly. He immediately crouched and unsnapped his MG42, bringing the barrel forward. He saw a stunned GI, mouth agape and he fired, stitching the man from head to toe. Triumphantly, he bellowed, "Legios, engage!"

The volume of fire from 50 MG42s was devastating. Guth relished each kill, watching his bullets slice into flesh, tearing men apart. This was what he was born to do.

He stopped firing when he saw no more targets and crouched, reloading the clunky weapon. Their sudden appearance in the midst of the Americans had created a gaping hole in their lines, which was quickly backed up with gleeful German and Scandinavian soldiers. More Korth landed and engaged, opening up with concentrated machine gun fire, creating more breeches.

He saw a pair of streaking enemy fighters flying parallel to the beach and realized they were flying straight toward a still airborne platoon of Legio. He watched a portion of the platoon suddenly pull up, their wings losing lift. As the others flew on, the stalled and quickly falling Korth, unslung their machine guns and engaged the incoming fighters.

Guth's head expanded as both fighters took hits. The lead plane's engine erupted in flame and it plummeted into the sea with a great splash. The second arced upward trailing smoke, stalled and nosed toward the sea. Guth saw the pilot exit the aircraft, the chute barely opened before he splashed into the sea.

The stalled Korth slung their machine-guns with practiced precision, expanded their arms and resumed flight only yards above the sea. They glided to the edge of the water, pulled up and landed perfectly. It had been a long time since the Legios had engaged in combat but Guth was proud to see they hadn't lost their edge.

His platoon spread out, weapons at the ready. Lt. Guth heard Major Korto's voice in his head, "Forward slow, take the town and move inland."

11

The next day Jimmy and Corporal Tom Grothing found Grothing's Army unit. The GIs were sifting through the remains of their smoldering base. The night before, Jimmy and Corporal Grothing had worked their way through the city and throngs of fleeing civilians. More than once, Tom had been forced to pull his pistol to stop looters. It slowed their progress but by morning they finally entered the base.

Tom was devastated to see members of his company dead and wounded. As a medic, he immediately went to work. Jimmy helped for a while, until he noticed soldiers running toward idling trucks.

He slapped Tom's shoulder, "Your unit's about to leave. I wanna join them, get in the fight." Tom nodded, finished bandaging an unconscious soldier's head and pointed to a nearby building, "That's the armory. Get a weapon for me too, I'll meet you at the trucks."

Jimmy nodded and dashed off. He burst through the door and was confronted by an older soldier with a large gut, holding his hand up. "Whoa there. Who are you?"

"I need a weapon for me and Corporal Grothing."

He tried to push past the PFC but a beefy hand stopped him, "Corporal Grothing's on leave and these weapons are Dog Company property. I don't recognize you," he looked him up and down, "Nor your uniform."

Jimmy had enough. "Listen here, fat-ass. In case you haven't noticed there's a battle raging all around us. I need a weapon so I can help fight. Now step aside."

The PFC's face turned bright red and he spluttered, "You pissant little piece of shit, no one talks to me that..."

Jimmy balled his fist and punched the pudgy soldier before he could finish. The man's nose flattened and blood gushed down his face and into his mouth. He sat down heavily, gasping and clutching his nose.

Jimmy stepped around him and pushed the chain-link door to the armory open and helped himself to two M1s, two full ammo pouches, and as many grenades as he could attach to his belt. The soldier sat looking at his bloody hands in disbelief. As Jimmy walked by, he spluttered, spraying blood onto his desk. His nasal voice followed Jimmy out the door, "Get back here! You broke my nose."

Jimmy ignored him and noticed two of the five trucks had already left the compound. He saw Cpl. Grothing standing behind the nearest truck, urging him to hurry. Jimmy sprinted to him and handed him one of the M1s and an ammo pouch. He panted, "Thought medics were non-combatants."

Grothing shook his head, "I think the rules have changed." He pulled back the breech and smoothly slid in an eight-round clip. They mounted the back and Grothing slapped the side of the truck and it lurched forward.

Minutes later, it was apparent they weren't going anywhere. The roads were clogged with panicked and fleeing civilians, tens of thousands of them. Moving forward was like moving against an incredibly strong and unrelenting river current. No amount of honking or weapon wielding mattered. It seemed the entire population was fleeing, moving west.

Finally, the trucks pulled off the road and parked in a large abandoned lot and watched the flow of humanity stream by. Jimmy felt his body stiffening. He'd taken a beating in the bombing and the long hours beneath the rubble hadn't helped. He ran his tongue over the sharp point of a tooth and remembered it being shattered by the Diner owner. That altercation seemed like years earlier but had only been the morning before. *The same morning my mother died.*

He pushed off the ground and stretched his back. He searched the sky for planes and didn't see any. They'd seen enemy and friendly planes all day, but none recently. Every soldier wanted payback and hoped they'd get a chance to shoot at a low flying enemy aircraft. Jimmy listened to them talk, puffing their chests out as though unafraid, but he'd been in combat and knew better. He shook his head, *were Hank and I like that?* Probably.

With night quickly approaching, Jimmy found Cpl. Grothing and sat beside him. "Think the flow will stem with nightfall?" he indicated the throngs of civilians still clogging the roads.

Grothing shrugged, "Sergeant Gooding seems to think so. We're gonna try again in another hour. Even if we only make a mile, it'll be better than sitting here." He handed Jimmy a loaf of bread and block of cheddar cheese.

Jimmy took it gratefully and used his K-bar knife to carve a large chunk off each. Before shoving it in his mouth he asked, "How far we looking at—to the coast I mean."

"As the crow flies less than 100 miles, but that's assuming the bridge is still there. It's a lot less to the shores of Chesapeake Bay, but I haven't heard of any landings there. It may be as far as we get though if the bridge is gone."

"What bridge?"

Grothing looked at him as though he were simple, "The Chesapeake Bay Bridge, of course." He shook his head, "I forget you've never been out here. It crosses Chesapeake Bay, spans about four and a half miles across and connects to the coastal region where the attacks are. If it's gone, we'd have to take the long way around or hitch a ride on a boat."

Jimmy considered, "Crossing a four and half mile bridge over water with enemy fighters around doesn't sound like a good idea at all."

Grothing nodded, "Yeah, that's why the captain wants to cross it at night."

Sergeant Gooding yelled from the center of the lot. "Rally on me."

Jimmy pulled himself off the ground with a grunt and followed Grothing. Their numbers had swelled during the day with more wayward soldiers attaching themselves to the group. The GIs eyeballed one another, sizing each other up. Jimmy leaned close to Grothing's ear, "Feels like a ragtag group we've got here." The edge of Grothing's mouth turned down and he nodded his agreement.

Captain Stewart, was tall and painfully thin. He wore wire rimmed glasses, which he had securely fastened to his head with a tight chord. He waited until the men were gathered then addressed them. "Most of you know me, but I haven't met all of you yet. I'm Captain Stewart," he indicated the beefy sergeant standing beside him eyeballing the men. "And this is Sergeant Gooding." He looked at his watch. "In an hour, at 1600 hours, we'll move out. We'll use an alternate route, one with far less traffic." He pointed over his shoulder at the steady stream of civilians. "As you can see, the damned civilians aren't adhering to the plans the government spent so much time and money drilling into their heads over the past decade. They're using the main roads, which means we'll use the routes they're supposed to be using and hopefully make our way to the Bay Bridge before morning.

"At last count we have 32 soldiers, ranging from cooks to grenadiers. The radios are jammed and confused, but from what I gathered there are large reinforcement columns headed our way. The general order for troops near the front is to hold the line and wait for relief. So, we'll move to the Bay Bridge and add our strength to the bridge unit's defenses. Any questions?" No one spoke, so he wrapped it up. "Stock up on ammunition. Sergeant Gooding will be putting bazooka teams together, so if any of you new men have expertise let him know and he'll match you up with what you need. Dismissed."

The men muttered among themselves and moved off to prepare for departure. Jimmy stayed put then stepped toward Sergeant Gooding and braced. Gooding looked up from his clipboard, "What is it PFC?"

"Just wanted you to know, I'm qualified expert with the Springfield sniper rifle."

Sergeant Gooding looked his filthy uniform up and down and evaluated his swollen and cut lip. "Looks like you've been through the grinder, son."

"Yes, sergeant. I was in a building that crumbled on me during the bombing yesterday."

Sergeant Gooding squinted trying to read his name tape but it was too torn and muck covered. "PFC…"

"Private First Class Crandall."

Gooding nodded. "You came in with Corporal Grothing. You're with the 45th Division boys in Alaska?"

"I was here on leave when the attack happened."

Gooding pulled his chin into his neck. "Leave? From Alaska?"

Jimmy tilted his head and shrugged, "Family emergency." The image of his mother walking alongside him the day before flashed through his mind and he suddenly felt heavy. "Private matter, Sergeant."

Gooding shrugged his shoulders, "Well, guess it doesn't matter." He pointed his thumb over his shoulder. "There's a couple scoped Springfields over there. Pick one out and zero it in, but make it quick, we leave in an hour."

———

THE MOVE EAST WAS SLOW, the trucks barely made it out of first gear. There were fewer civilians on the backroads, even though they were the routes they were supposed to be taking, but not so jammed that they couldn't use them.

Jimmy sat in the back of a truck with his eyes shut. The trucks slow crawled forward, the seeping cold and occasional lurching stops didn't make for great sleeping, but he felt himself slipping into semi-consciousness occasionally. His M1 was under the bench seat, the shiny new Springfield with the 7x scope propped between his knees. He'd fired 15 rounds through it. He would've liked more time, but the weapon felt good in his hands and he was confident he could hit what he aimed at.

Beside him sat the GI he'd been paired with, Private Stan Lodmont.

He was rated a cook. While Jimmy zeroed the weapon, he used the time to give Private Lodmont a crash course in seeing and calling out targets. He listened and tried to pick up the skill, but it was completely new to him. Jimmy wasn't thrilled with his spotter, he was noticeably nervous and they hadn't even been shot at yet. He wondered how he'd hold up once the bullets started flying.

He thought about Hank, he'd been a great spotter. They were a good team. He smiled at the thought, then snapped his eyes open with a jolt when he remembered Hank's dead eyes staring at him.

Lodmont noticed his jolt and asked, "You okay? You were mumbling and twitching a lot."

"Mind your own business, Private." Lodmont didn't answer but said something snide to the soldier to his right. Jimmy closed his eyes again and decided he wasn't going to get to know Stan Lodmont. *Kid won't last long once it starts.* The thought didn't bring him pleasure but he'd seen too much death—too many better men die.

He felt as though only seconds passed when the truck lurched to a stop and Lodmont jabbed him in the ribs and whispered, "Wake up, we're here."

Jimmy looked around, slightly confused then reached for his weapons and asked, "Why you whispering?"

Lodmont shrugged. It was still pitch dark outside. He answered, "Because everyone else is."

Sergeant Gooding appeared at the back of the truck and dropped the tailgate. The hinges squeaked and he cringed and cursed under his breath then waved them to come out.

Jimmy jumped and felt his muscles protest as he landed. He felt like he was 100 years old. He slung the Springfield over his right shoulder and held the M1 at port arms. He moved to the side, making way for the others. He smelled water and the hint of decay.

It wasn't as dark outside the covered truck bed. There was a half-moon darting in and out of broken overcast and he saw the sparkling of water and heard it gently lapping the shoreline. There were a few darkened buildings along the banks, but not many. They looked aban-doned—no lights—but wondered if some were still occupied. He wondered if there were comfortable beds inside. He thought he could sleep for a week if given the chance.

He adjusted his pack and followed the others. They formed into loose lines and marched north for a quarter mile then halted. Jimmy's instinct was to crouch and look for threats but the others stood and looked around, wondering what the hold-up was. Jimmy scanned the area but didn't perceive a threat. Ahead he could see Captain Stewart and Sergeant Gooding talking with someone he didn't recognize, another officer.

After a few minutes, Gooding motioned them to gather round. "Okay men. We've linked up with the 67th Bridge Defense Brigade. They're on both sides, in the bunkers. They haven't seen any action so far. They were ordered to shut the bridge to civilian traffic a few hours ago, which must be why the last hour was less congested. Unfortunately, there are broken down vehicles blocking our trucks. We're crossing the bridge on foot." Jimmy looked at his watch. It was 0500. He figured it would be getting light this time of year around 0700. A four-and-a-half-mile hike shouldn't be a problem if all went well.

———

JIMMY WALKED onto the bridge and walked past members of the Bridge Defense Brigade. Even in the low-light of the half moon, he could see their scowling faces.

As the name suggested, the Brigades had been formed to defend bridges and other vital infrastructure, including railroads and airports. Since they were pulled from the National Guard, they were mostly weekend warriors. The bunkers and defensive outposts were manned 24/7 but it was essentially guard duty and didn't attract the best soldiers. In fact, it was where most of the troublemakers ended up, and because of that, Bridge Brigades had gotten the nickname 'Bridge Babies' and were looked down upon by active duty soldiers.

Jimmy heard a soldier nearby spit toward a Brigade member and mutter, "Don't forget your pacifier." The GIs around him snickered. Jimmy saw the Brigade member start to move, but another soldier clutched his shoulder, holding him back.

Sergeant Gooding noticed the commotion and barked, "Knock it off back there."

Private Lodmont turned back to Jimmy and grinned, "Pissant Bridge Babies."

Jimmy shook his head, "You'll be glad they're there when the shit hits the fan, *cook.*" Lodmont turned quickly away and increased his pace pulling away from Jimmy. Jimmy sighed knowing he should be bonding with his new spotter but, *he's such an asshole.*

The march across the bridge went well at first. The incessant civilian traffic had kept the roads clear and free of ice, but as they neared the middle, the wind kicked up, spraying them with freezing bay water. The bridge iced up in spots making long sections difficult. Normally, there were deicers and gravel trucks keeping the roads passable, but there was no sign of them now.

Their march slowed and Jimmy looked at his watch nervously. He figured they were more than halfway across, but he still couldn't see Kent Island. The only thing he could see was the incessant flashing in the East where the battle was still raging. There was an ever so faint lightening in the sky. He didn't want to be on the bridge when the sun came up.

Finally, after another 45 minutes of marching over ever-more treacherous ice, they were halted by more Bridge Defense Brigade members. Jimmy kneeled near a metal beam, one of hundreds, and looked south over the water. There was a definite lightening in the East. The sun would be up soon and he could feel the temperature dropping. He shivered and tucked his chin into the heavy wool coat. Walking had kept him warm, but it didn't last long once he stopped moving.

Minutes ticked by and he wondered what the hold-up was. Captain Stewart was talking to another officer. *Stop shooting the shit and get us off this deathtrap, dammit.*

Jimmy cocked his head, listening. He'd heard something that made him feel the chill even more. Was he imagining his worst fear? He focused his hearing, listening intently and when he was sure, he yelled, "I hear planes!"

Everyone spun and looked at him. Private Lodmont guffawed and was about to say something snide when he stopped and cocked his head, "I—I hear it too." He suddenly pointed, "There!"

Jimmy saw them at the same time, a line of six aircraft about 2000 feet up, coming straight up Chesapeake Bay. He immediately recognized the yellow cowlings of enemy BF-109s. There was only one possible target, the bridge. Jimmy yelled, "Air raid!" He got onto his belly shifting his body toward the road keeping himself protected behind a thick metal beam.

He pulled the M1 off his shoulder and put it to his shoulder, leaning out and aiming at the lead plane which was arcing down and growing bigger every second. He released the safety and emptied his eight-round clip in seconds. With the 'ping' of an empty clip he pulled himself back behind the beam and pulled his helmet down over his ears and waited.

He didn't have long to wait. The buzzsaw sound of heavy machine guns and the sparking and zinging of bullets hitting metal filled the air. He pulled his legs tight to his chest and cowered. When the first plane passed with a roar, he reloaded the M1. The next plane strafed the section of bridge where it connected with Kent Island.

Jimmy saw the terrified eyes of his spotter, Private Lodmont. He looked ready to break and run. Jimmy held his hand palm out and yelled, "Stay there, don't move! Stay in cover!"

Lodmont looked at him with wild eyes but got the message and nodded. He screamed when the next plane opened up. The span between Jimmy and Lodmont sparked and seemed to come alive with a swarm of buzzing bees. A soldier across the road yelled and fell backwards hitting the guardrail and falling over the side. Jimmy didn't know if he'd been shot or simply tripped, but either way he'd have a hard time getting to shore before freezing and drowning in the icy waters.

When the last aircraft passed, Jimmy got to his feet and ran toward land. Lodmont followed him. When Jimmy passed Sergeant Gooding and Captain Stewart, Gooding yelled, "Stay in cover! Where you think you're going?"

Jimmy paused long enough to say, "Those planes are carrying

bombs, they're lining up on us as we speak. I'm getting off the bridge!"
He didn't wait for permission, but kept running.

Once off the slippery bridge he found his footing and sprinted toward a depression off the road. He slid down the hard ground, stopped at the bottom, and tucked himself against the side of a small concrete tunnel. Lodmont, along with other GIs followed him to cover.

There was a sudden hammering of heavy machine gun fire. The Bridge Defense Brigade's guns were finally joining the fray. Jimmy crawled a few feet up and looked back at the bridge bunkers. They had multiple firing ports, some aiming down the road itself, others pointing skyward. He saw large caliber muzzles aiming upward, sending out streaks of tracer fire, which lit up the early morning sky.

He followed the tracer rounds and saw the six planes flying parallel to the bridge a couple hundred feet up, over the water. They were making micro-adjustments, lining up to drop their bombs.

The Brigade's gunners were off target, shooting too high. Jimmy put his M1 to his shoulder and aimed. He knew he had little chance of hitting anything, but he'd rather do something and feel he were fighting back.

The lead plane got closer and closer and he realized they weren't trying to bomb the bridge but the bridge defenses. He fired four shots then saw the 109 shudder slightly as something dark and small detached from the undercarriage.

He threw himself back down the slope and yelled, "Incoming! Get down!"

The bomb whistled as it dropped. Jimmy pulled himself into a ball and tried to shove himself inside the concrete gutter. The ground shook and he opened his mouth as the air suddenly seemed devoid of oxygen.

Each bomb shook the ground. Jimmy heard screaming all around him as the GIs took the beating. Finally, the last bomb dropped and Jimmy uncurled. Dirt fell off his helmet brim and got in his eyes. He spit, shook himself and squinted through falling debris.

The others were covered in dirt and clumps of grass. Suddenly it started raining hard, but it wasn't rain. It was bay-water coming down after a German bomb fell short. The dirt on his wool coat turned to mud and the coat got heavy.

He climbed the slippery slope and peaked over the side. The bunkers were still intact but were no longer firing. He hoped the soldiers inside were just shaken up and not out of commission permanently. He had a feeling they'd need the firepower soon.

12

T he enemy planes raced away, following the bay water back toward the sea. Jimmy brushed off mud and stepped from the culvert along with the other shaken GIs. He saw a few soldiers in the concrete trenches behind the bridge bunkers. They had dazed looks on their faces.

Jimmy walked to the edge of the trench, "You guys okay?" Off to his right there was a smoking crater, a near miss.

A soldier who'd lost his helmet squinted up at him and nodded, "Guess so. That was close."

The other soldiers pulled themselves together. A sergeant went to the back of the nearest bunker and peeled back the heavy steel door. It squeaked in protest. "You guys okay in there?" he asked.

Jimmy could hear a smattering of replies. A pale face appeared in the doorway. The soldier came into the daylight and peered at the sky as though it might reach out and bite him.

Captain Stewart and Sergeant Gooding walked up evaluating the damage. They stood beside Jimmy. Stewart looked him up and down, "PFC Crandall, right?" Jimmy nodded. "Start digging in. There's only one reason I can think of for that attack: they want this bridge." Jimmy nodded his agreement. Stewart pointed, "Spread out along the road, use the rock outcroppings and whatever cover you can find. Two men per hole."

Sergeant Gooding nodded and barked, "All right men, we're digging in."

The pale faced soldier from the bunker saluted the captain. Before turning to dig foxholes, Jimmy heard him report, "Captain, I'm in command of this unit, First Lieutenant Yance." He hesitated then continued, "We—we took a beating, but we're still operational. Some cuts, bruises and ringing ears, but no casualties."

Stewart replied, "That's good, Lieutenant. I'm not sure what's coming, but we need to hold this bridge. Are you in contact with the other side?"

"Yes, sir."

"Well get 'em on the horn. I want to know their status too."

"Yes, sir."

"My men are digging in along the road. We've got two bazooka teams and a lot of small arms. You got any extra machine guns? If there's a push, it'd be nice to have something heavier than M1s."

Yance answered, "Yeah, I have two reserve Brownings. You need crews too?"

"Yeah. Have 'em report to Sergeant Gooding, he'll make sure they're placed correctly."

———

TWO HOURS LATER, Jimmy put down his shovel and evaluated his hole. Jimmy had done most of the digging. Private Lodmont would start then stop and pick at the blisters forming on his hands. Jimmy browbeat him, making him work but he dragged his feet and complained the entire time.

Despite the cold day, Jimmy wiped his sweaty brow. The hole was 15 yards off the road, tucked into the brush. He'd cut and stacked more brush in front and it was well concealed from the air and ground.

One of the .30 caliber machine gun positions was closer to the road and forward a couple yards from his hole. Sergeant Gooding wanted Jimmy's hole back a little so he could cover their flank and be a fall-back position if need be. Jimmy had made his hole big enough to accommodate the crew, just in case.

Once the hole was finished, Lodmont didn't waste any time getting comfy. He scrunched his back against the dirt wall and hugged himself. "Cold out here."

Jimmy put his wool coat back on, despite his head still steaming from being overheated. He knew his sweat would turn to ice once he stopped working. "You wouldn't be cold if you worked."

Lodmont scowled, "I did work."

Jimmy shook his head, "Bullshit. I don't know how you made it through boot camp. You're a lazy son-of-a-bitch." Lodmont tucked his chin inside his coat and muttered something Jimmy didn't catch. "Look, if the Germans come, it's gonna get dicey out here. You gonna be able to function?"

Through the thick fabric of his wool coat, he answered bitterly, "I'll do what I have to."

Jimmy shook his head, "Yeah, and nothing extra. I think I'll call you, Mini, short for mini-mum." He laughed at his own joke and adjusted the Springfield and M1 rifles.

The sound of distant battle ebbed and flowed from the East, dependent on which way the wind blew. There were still civilians arriving at the bridge and they complained bitterly when told they weren't allowed to cross and were directed north or back the way they'd come.

Jimmy opened a C-rat and cherry picked the crackers and jelly. Suddenly the guns from both bunkers opened up sending tracers nearly straight up. Jimmy heard a terrifying screaming sound and looked up to see black dots overhead, peeling one by one into steep dives. Someone yelled, "Stuka attack!"

Jimmy hunkered into the bottom of the hole and watched them come. The closer they got the louder the scream. They were diving nearly straight down and Jimmy thought they might simply crash, but at the last instant they pulled up and shot over the bridge. There was an explosion, sending up great geysers of water and dirt.

The tracer fire continued and Jimmy saw a plane still in formation suddenly start smoking. It dipped from the organized flight and turned east. Jimmy hoped it crashed.

Another explosion, more screaming planes. The ground shook as the bombs exploded in the hard ground. He looked at Lodmont, he was quivering and shaking, jolting with each new explosion. The Stukas were targeting the bunkers which were a couple hundred yards away. Jimmy felt relatively safe, but Lodmont looked petrified, "Relax, Mini. They're after the bunkers. Don't piss yourself."

Lodmont looked at him with wide eyes. "Fuck—fuck you."

The Stukas disappeared as quickly as they'd arrived. Jimmy poked his head up and looked at the bunkers. The furthest one was smoking. Men were rushing toward it, some staggered away, "Looks like they hit a bunker."

Lodmont got to his feet and lifted his chin to see over the edge. "Holy shit. Thank God I wasn't over there."

Jimmy was about to tell him what a piece of shit he was again, but there was yelling coming from up the road that caught his attention. He saw a group of civilians sprinting on the road, waving their hands and yelling. Jimmy put binoculars to his eyes and quickly adjusted the focus. He watched the civilians running and gesturing behind, like something was chasing them.

Suddenly three of them stumbled and dropped and a second later Jimmy heard the popping of gunfire and saw the ground erupt in geysers, "Shit, something's coming up the road." He put his hand to his mouth and called back to where he knew Captain Stewart and Sergeant Gooding were, "Enemy troops on the road!"

The machine gun crew were already hunkered and Jimmy saw the muzzle lower and aim down the road. Jimmy propped his M1 along the side of the hole and pulled the Springfield to his shoulder and looked through the sniper scope. He found the marker he'd put out beside the road at 50 yards. He clicked and adjusted the scope and watched. "Get the binocs tell me when you see anything." When there was no response he raised his voice in anger. "Do it, Mini. Now." Still nothing. He took his eye from the scope and looked at Lodmont who seemed almost catatonic. Jimmy reached out and shook him, "Snap out of it, damn you. If you want to live, do exactly what I say."

Lodmont shook his head slightly and his eyes came back into focus.

He gave Jimmy a quick nod, leaned against the leading edge of the foxhole and pulled the binoculars to his eyes with shaking hands.

After a tense minute, Lodmont stuttered, "Oh shit. I—I see them. Soldiers. They're coming."

Jimmy swept slowly but still didn't see them. "Where, dammit?"

"Uh—uh, just past those dead civilians. To the right of the road, in the ditch."

Jimmy nodded. "Yes, good. I see them." He adjusted his sights slightly, settled into the stock and slowed his breathing. The lead soldier stopped and the others stacked behind and disappeared into cover. Jimmy kept the reticle on the lead soldier who lifted his head to get a better look. Jimmy squeezed the trigger and the sudden sound was loud in the foxhole. Jimmy saw the soldier's head snap back, spraying blood and he dropped out of sight.

Lodmont's horror was evident. "Oh my God. Oh my God, you—you shot him."

Jimmy kept scanning and grumbled, "That's the idea, asshole." He spotted discoloration further back in the ditch. He centered on it and pressured the trigger until the rifle bucked again. A flash of movement, he adjusted and fired again.

Lodmont's voice was more controlled now. "I—I think you got him. Not sure, but I think so."

"Find me another target," he growled. Before Lodmont could answer, Jimmy saw winking flashes and heard bullets snapping through the air. "They don't see us yet. Just probing fire."

The sound of faint popping made Jimmy pull his eye from the scope and look up. "Shit, mortars. Get down."

They both dropped to the bottom of the hole. There was another pop, but not from a high explosive round. Jimmy knew what it meant. "Smoke. They're firing smoke." He got back into firing position slapping Lodmont's arm, "Come on, Mini. Find me another target before it gets too dense."

The smoke shells landed to their right and slightly behind. The Germans had miscalculated, thinking they were farther back. The air was smoky, but they could still see fine. Lodmont's excited voice, "They're up, coming forward. See 'em?"

Jimmy did. He put the reticle on the nearest man's chest as he ran hunched over. He pulled the trigger and the soldier dropped out of sight. Soldiers near the stricken man dove out of sight. Lodmont touched Jimmy's shoulder, "I see another. 20 yards back from your last shot. See him?"

Jimmy smoothly swung the rifle, keeping his eye in the scope. He stopped when he saw a soldier on his belly looking behind and waving men forward. His mouth was moving but from this distance, Jimmy couldn't hear him. He centered, breathed out smoothly and pulled the trigger. The bullet entered the soldier's neck and Jimmy could see a fountain of blood coming out his back as he fell onto his face, "Target down. That might've been an officer. Good spotting."

There wasn't time for celebration, the Germans opened fire. The air around Jimmy came alive and he dropped into the hole pulling Lodmont with him, "Must've seen my muzzle flash. Stay down."

There were more popping smoke shells, this time in front of their position. Jimmy poked his head up and the smoke was thick and blowing across their hole. He could see the machine gun crew ready to open fire. The sound of small arms fire from the Germans continued, but they were firing blindly hoping to keep heads down. Jimmy said, "Forget the binoculars, they'll be coming through the smoke. Get your rifle ready."

The soft popping of smoke rounds changed to the heavier thud of high explosives. Jimmy swapped rifles, carefully placing the Springfield against the dirt wall. The barrel still smoked. He aimed over the M1's sights. The white smoke was thick. He breathed out a sigh and his white breath mixed seamlessly.

Jimmy noticed the machine gun crew stiffen. They opened fire with a long burst then quickly settled into short bursts. Jimmy still couldn't see any targets. He strained. A slight wind off the bay pushed the smoke and he saw shapes and forms. Lodmont sucked in a quick gasp and fired quickly until his clip pinged. Jimmy saw his target dive for cover. He was on their side of the road along the edge of the swampy field. Jimmy aimed where he'd seen him dive and fired twice.

Another form appeared and Jimmy adjusted and fired three rounds. The German was only 30 yards away. He dropped out of sight.

"They're trying to flank the machine gun." He heard Lodmont cursing. Jimmy urged, "Hurry up and reload, Mini."

Lodmont continued to curse. "I—I can't do it, I can't get it to go. My hands are numb."

Jimmy fired at another shape in the fog then looked at Lodmont in disgust. He had the eight-round clip backwards. "Christ, Mini, you've got it backwards. Pointy end forward." Lodmont cursed and fumbled the clip, dropping it into the bottom of the hole. "Get a fresh one, that'll jam."

Lodmont pulled another clip, shoved it into the receiver and yowled as the breech slammed onto his thumb. Jimmy knew what happened but didn't have time to tease him. Another shape in the smoke. He fired until his clip pinged.

Lodmont was back in action and he fired through his rounds before Jimmy was done reloading. "Slow down, aim carefully. You're burning through ammo too quick."

The other machine gun crew opened up on the other side of the road. The smoke was thinning quickly. The Germans were using cover and bounding forward, but were taking casualties. Jimmy ducked as bullets smacked through the brambles he'd placed in front of his hole. Lodmont did too. "Holy shit, holy shit! That was close."

Jimmy looked at him. He had his back to the wall and was clutching his M1 like it was his momma. "You hit?" Lodmont shook his head and licked his lips. The bullets continued to snap over the edge of the hole. "They're trying to flank the machine gun. I'm gonna throw a few grenades at 'em. When you hear them blow, lay some fire on 'em." Lodmont continued staring straight ahead. "You hear me, Mini?"

Lodmont looked at him angrily but nodded his head. Jimmy pulled two grenades and placed one on the ground at his feet. He pulled the pin on the first, yelled, "Grenade," and hurled it. He grabbed the second and threw it too, then clutched his rifle.

There was a muted explosion then another. Lodmont didn't move. Jimmy kicked him, "Now." They both went up. Jimmy fired at movement in the weeds. He saw a hand fly up and he fired toward it but saw something arcing their way. "Grenade! Down!"

Lodmont had just gotten into firing position. He pulled the trigger twice before the German stick grenade exploded only feet away. His helmet flew off and he was flung backward, slamming into the back wall. Jimmy had his back against the front wall. He saw Lodmont's shocked, white face and thought he was seeing his last moments on Earth.

Jimmy lunged forward and clutched his shoulders and shook him. "Dammit." Lodmont's eyes focused on Jimmy's face and Jimmy saw sudden recognition. "You okay?" he asked while scanning his body for wounds. Lodmont's forehead was bleeding excessively but when Jimmy ran his thumb across the source, he guffawed, "You're one lucky son-of-a-bitch, Mini. Just a scratch."

He heard another explosion and came up with his rifle ready. He saw shapes rushing the side of the machine gun crew, which looked to be reeling from a grenade attack.

Jimmy fired, walking his rounds through the Germans, knocking down all three. The machine gun wasn't firing, the barrel aiming to the sky. "Machine-gun's knocked out. We gotta get up there or they'll roll right through us." Lodmont still looked woozy, his eyes unfocused. Jimmy clutched a wad of his coat and lifted him off the ground, thrusting him toward the lip of the hole. "Move!"

They ran for the machine-gun nest. Bullets snapped and buzzed past them, thick as hornets. Jimmy dove and his shoulder slammed into the dirt berm. He quickly got to his knees and surveyed the scene. Two of the three soldiers from the Bridge Defense Brigade were obviously dead, their bodies torn and their eyes staring. The third was writhing back and forth, his hands covering his face. He grunted and moaned in pain.

Lodmont rolled into the hole, his eyes bugging out. He kept muttering over and over, "holyshit, holyshit, holyshit."

Jimmy dropped his M1 and went to the machine gun. "Check on that guy. I'll check the gun." He reached for the machine gun handle and leaned forward, looking for anything obviously wrong with the .30 caliber Browning. There was still an ammunition belt snaking from a metal ammo can to the machine gun. He pulled the bolt, it felt smooth. "Give me a hand over here, Mini."

Lodmont slithered forward, "That guy's blinded." He looked at the machine gun. "What you want me to do? I've never used one of these."

"Just keep the ammunition coming out of the box smoothly and tell me when I'm almost out."

Bullets smacked the front of the hole. Jimmy sighted down the barrel, seeing targets still trying to flank left. He pulled the trigger and the gun rocked on the tripod. He adjusted his aim, he was firing high, and fired another short burst. German soldiers dove for cover. He swept the area, keeping their heads down, but his firing drew more fire from the road. Jimmy kept his head as low as possible, but the incoming fire was intensifying.

The blinded soldier suddenly screamed, stood up and started running, still clutching his face. Jimmy looked back in time to see his body stitched with bullets and his screaming stopped and he dropped. Lodmont yelled something he couldn't understand. He kept firing in short bursts, but the incoming fire was throwing off his aim. He stopped firing and ducked. "Throw a grenade!" he yelled.

Lodmont looked at him with wide eyes as bullets shredded the cover, sending dirt and debris down on them. He pulled a grenade and handed it to Jimmy with shaking hands. "You—you do it," he stammered.

Cursing, Jimmy took the grenade and without exposing himself lobbed it forward. When it exploded he went back to the gun and fired off a long burst, sweeping back and forth. He'd gained the upper hand and didn't want to give it up. Lodmont assisted, feeding the ammunition to him. Then he said, "Belt's almost done."

Jimmy stopped and looked around the hole. "There's another box, get it."

Lodmont pushed backwards and Jimmy fired the rest of the first box then grabbed his M1 and fired at movement to the right. "They're trying for the other gun. Hurry."

An object flying through the air caught his attention. He watched the German stick grenade sail past and land behind the hole. "Grenade! Down!"

Lodmont had just gotten to the ammo can. He tried to lift it but it was heavier than he thought it would be. He gave a mighty yank and it flung up in front of his face at the same instant the grenade exploded. He was thrown backwards. He lost his grip on the ammo can and it landed on his chest.

Jimmy watched the whole thing, thinking his spotter had bought the farm again from yet another grenade. He yelled, "Mini," and reached for him. Jimmy pushed the ammo can off his chest and noticed it was riddled and smoking with shrapnel. He shook Lodmont, expecting to see a mashed face, but instead he saw his stunned, but very much alive, eyes staring back at him. The dried blood from his head-wound mixed with fresh blood from a new cut.

Jimmy couldn't believe it, "Jesus, Mini, you've got nine lives." He tried to open the ammo can, but the grenade blast had warped it and he couldn't get it open. He threw it in frustration. "We can't stay here without the gun."

He saw Lodmont's eyes go even wider as he looked beyond him. Jimmy reacted, spinning with his M1 in hand and saw a German soldier charging over the lip his submachine gun firing. Bullets snapped past and he felt fire on his cheek and shoulder. He pulled the trigger, firing from the hip and saw his bullets connect, shattering the soldier's pelvis and left leg. He fell, screaming at Jimmy's feet.

Jimmy tripped and fell over the writhing soldier. He was on top of the soldier but on his back. He expected to be shot or stabbed any second. Lodmont screamed and Jimmy rolled away and came to his knees ready to shoot, but Lodmont was lying across the soldier and punching him over and over with his K-bar knife.

Jimmy turned back to the front and fired the rest of his clip. He stepped to Lodmont, grabbed him by the collar and pulled him out the back of the machine gun nest. Lodmont was kicking and screaming and finally Jimmy released him and they ran the rest of the way to their original hole.

Jimmy reload his M1 and steadied the barrel on the lip, aiming at the abandoned MG nest. Two German soldiers came over the lip and fired their submachine guns on full automatic. Jimmy fired at the nearest one and saw him drop. He moved to the next, but he was already lining Jimmy up. Jimmy felt bullets thump into the front of his hole and he dropped down.

"Shit, shit, shit," he cursed. "You got any more grenades?" he asked.

Lodmont nodded and handed him another. "It—it's the last one."

Jimmy nodded, "When this thing goes off, I'm gonna come up firing, I want you to take off back to that stack of boulders back there. Got it?"

Lodmont scowled and shook his head, "No, I'm not leaving you."

"When you get there, cover me and I'll join you. Can you do that?" Lodmont looked back at the boulders 20 yards away. It seemed like an awful long way, but he licked his thin lips and nodded.

Jimmy clutched the grenade and waited for the incoming German fire to stop. He'd have to reload at some point. Finally, there was a pause. "Now!" he yelled and threw the grenade. The MG nest was only yards away, it was an easy throw and he threw a strike. Just as he released, he saw two more gray clad soldiers come over the top. He ducked, picked up his M1 and when he heard the explosion he came up firing.

One soldier was standing, reeling from the grenade blast. Jimmy shot him twice in the chest. From this range he hardly needed to aim. The other two soldiers were down, but he fired until his clip pinged, then took off out the back of the hole. He expected bullets to enter his back any second.

The run seemed to take an eternity. He saw Lodmont firing from the other side of the boulders—slow and methodical. When he was a few feet out, Jimmy dove headfirst like he was sliding into second base, then rolled to cover.

Lodmont's clip pinged and he slid back behind the rocks. Lodmont looked him up and down. "You hit?" he asked.

Jimmy felt his cheek. There was a jagged gash which he only felt when he touched it. He shook his head, "Just a scratch."

Lodmont pointed at his shoulder. "What about that? It's bleeding bad."

Jimmy looked at his right shoulder, it was wet with blood. He lifted his arm, the movement hurt but not bad. "It doesn't seem bad. I barely feel it."

Lodmont leaned his rifle against the rock and fished in his belt for a med-kit. "I'll get you fixed up."

Bullets smacked the rocks and ricocheted making bizarre noises. They both hunkered and Jimmy shook his head. "No time. Get your rifle."

A new sound entered the battle and at first Jimmy was taken back to the Alaskan front and the terrifying artillery barrages he'd endured. He froze, listening to the shrieking incoming shells.

His terror turned to jubilation when the shells landed along the road among the Germans. He yelled out, "It's ours, it's ours!" He laughed as the shells continued to rain down, obliterating the exposed soldiers. "Take that you lousy Krauts," he yelled.

His jubilation was catching and Lodmont yelled, "Yeehaw," and leaned out firing his M1 at the fleeing Germans. "Run you cocksuckers, run!"

His clip pinged and Jimmy pulled him back into cover. "Don't wanna lose you to friendly fire, Mini. I'm gonna need a good spotter."

———

THE ARTILLERY ROUTED the remaining Germans who disappeared back the way they'd come. Minutes passed and Jimmy and Lodmont leaned against the boulders. Jimmy tilted his helmet back and reached for his canteen. He was suddenly as thirsty as he ever remembered being. He drank it dry, his Adam's apple bobbing. He screwed the lid on and let out a mighty burp.

Lodmont grinned and took a long drink from his own canteen. He pointed to the bridge, "Look at that. Hope the German Airforce doesn't come right now."

Jimmy pointed at the sky, "Those are ours. No way the Jerries are getting through those fighters. Looks like the whole US Army's coming across."

The first few vehicles across were mobile AA guns which immediately dispersed along the bay with their barrels pointed skyward. Within minutes the area was a defensive stronghold. Big Pershing tanks rumbled across, mixed with trucks full of troops and equipment.

Nearly every truck towed some kind of anti-tank or anti-aircraft gun. Once across the formidable force spread out and dug in as though they meant to stay awhile.

Sergeant Gooding found them sitting watching the show. He kneeled in front of them and tilted his helmet back, "That was some fight." He looked beyond the rocks to the abandoned machine gun position and their foxhole. "You boys did real good protecting our flank. I saw the MG crew go down and thought we'd had it, but you two charging forward like that made all the difference. The captain..." he hesitated and shook his head, "Well, he wanted to put you two in for medals." They both watched the sergeant struggling. He finally nodded and looked them in the eye. "He got hit right before our artillery. If he'd just kept his fool head down for a couple more seconds —well, he'd still be alive." He stood and shook his head getting back to business. "Our unit's being meshed in with the 54th Regiment." He tilted his head toward the fresh troops. "That's them mostly." He looked at Jimmy remembering where he came from. "If you want I could get you a ticket back to your old unit, although it might be a long trip with the disruption to travel."

Jimmy shook his head, "If it's all the same to you, I'd like to stay here. I've got no one back there."

Sergeant Gooding nodded. "Happy to have you. If we can stand up to Fallschirmjagers, we can stand up to anyone."

They both looked at Gooding with confused expressions. Gooding smiled, "You don't know? Those were German paratroopers, the best of the best, dropped in to take this end of the bridge. We stopped 'em cold."

Jimmy shared a glance with Lodmont, knowing without the help of the artillery, the paratroopers would most likely have been successful. He kept it to himself, nodded and shut his eyes, feeling suddenly overwhelmingly tired.

13

Captain Clancy McDermott wanted payback. His squadron's first sortie had ended with 50 percent losses. He had no idea how many pilots had been able to bail out, but it didn't really matter if they were behind enemy lines and out of the fight.

Now he was leading his men back into the teeth of the tiger, but with far more fighters than before. This time, he hoped they had enough to overwhelm the carrier-based German fighters.

He glanced below and saw the seemingly endless line of bombers and fighters streaking toward the coast. His mission was to make sure the bombers made it to the beachhead and the armada offshore.

His squadron had many new pilots, cobbled together from other shattered units. This was his third mission that day and he was feeling the strain, but this time would be different, this time it would be the invaders that paid.

As they neared the coast the sky was suddenly pockmarked with dark smudges. He heard a calm voice from a nearby bomber pilot. "Here comes the flak. Steady."

McDermott was flying 5,000 feet higher than the bombers, at 15,000 feet AGL. All the flak was directed at the bombers and he felt for them. It was thick and accurate. He saw a flash as a B24 took a direct hit. The wing crumpled in half and the plane seemed to list onto its side in slow motion, then spiral down. He lost sight of it when it passed through the dense layer of black flak smoke but saw no chutes.

He tore his eyes from the scene when someone called, "109s at eleven o'clock."

McDermott scolded himself for not being the first to see them. He saw the tiny dots getting larger, streaking for the bombers. "Let's get in the war. Section two stay high and keep any others off us. Section One let's go get 'em."

He increased power, feeling the Gs in the seat of his pants and angled up slightly. The 109s kept their course and McDermott hoped they wouldn't see them. At their current course and speed, the Thunderbolts would end up on their tails in perfect firing positions. He licked his lips watching the trajectories unfold.

"Now," he ordered, "Break right." The ten silver Thunderbolts turned onto their wings and streaked after the 109s who were wholly focused on the bombers. The heavy P-47 Jugs quickly caught up with the 109s in shallow dives.

McDermott lined up his pipper on an unsuspecting 109's tail. He caressed the trigger getting closer and closer. When the 109 filled his windscreen he fired all eight of his .50 caliber guns. The 109 sparked and chunks flew off, then it simply exploded and bits of it fell like leaves in a fall breeze.

He caught the flash of another 109 erupting in flame to his left and knew his wingman had scored a kill. There was another Hun in front of the first, still diving toward the bombers. McDermott was about to fire, when the German suddenly pulled up sharply. McDermott reacted, pulling power and yanking back the stick. He grunted with the intensity of the Gs and felt himself on the edge of blacking out. He relaxed his pull and felt his vision return. He spun his head, looking for the 109 and caught a glimpse of it behind him trying to turn inside.

He rolled 90 degrees and pulled feeling the Gs again, but this time he kept himself away from the blacking out zone. He increased throttle as the 109 flashed by, seemingly only yards away. McDermott rolled and came up on his tail, but upside down. The pipper showed him in his sights and he squeezed the trigger sending streaking tracer fire into the 109.

He didn't wait to see the final result. He whipped upright and the 109 wasn't there, but the hulking shape of a lumbering B24 was. Instinct took over, he pushed the stick forward and dove beneath its belly, missing a collision by mere yards.

Tracer's the size of tennis balls floated past his windscreen. He felt the hammer blow of a hit. He grit his teeth and yelled at no one in particular, "I'm on your side, dammit." He was inside the bomber's sphere and the jumpy gunners wouldn't be able to distinguish good guys from bad in the heat of the moment. He avoided another bomber, seeing the panicked look of the pilot as he flashed over the top of the cockpit.

He pulled up and cleared the bombers. He glanced over his left shoulder and saw the impressive armada of the entire enemy Navies. There were flashes and rolling plumes of smoke as their main guns continued to rain hell upon America's shores. There were also hundreds of winking lights adding anti-aircraft shots to the flak.

McDermott looked behind and spotted his wingman, Lt. Thorpe bobbing and weaving, but staying on his tail. He refocused forward and saw a small group of four bombers that looked different from the B24s although heading the same direction.

He keyed his mic, "There's a group of German bombers returning from a raid at one o'clock. Let's give 'em a sweep. Anyone else still with us from first group?" There was a smattering of replies. "Stay with the allied bombers. Thorpe and I will just be a minute."

He pushed his throttles to full power and aimed in front of the bombers still 4,000 feet away. He glanced forward and back, but saw no fighter escort. They'd chosen the wrong time to return to their carriers, which would be busy fending off bombers for the next hour at least. "Combat spread, I'll take the lead, you take the next one back."

A tight and excited, "Roger."

The distance closed quickly. McDermott saw the lancing tracer fire from the bellies of the bombers surrounding him, but nothing hit.

He put the pipper where the left wing met the fuselage and mashed the trigger. He yawed the aircraft with the rudder pedals and walked the eight .50 caliber machine guns along the entire length. The bomber sparked and shed skin like bark from a tree, then the left engine ignited and the bomber tipped toward him slowly.

McDermott pushed the stick and flashed beneath the burning plane. He made a hard-right turn and looked behind. He saw a second bomber on fire and falling, Thorpe had scored too. "Nice shooting. Let's get back to the boys."

Thorpe's excited voice came over the air, "Yes, sir. Nice shot. We got two."

He nodded, "There's two more, but they've no place to go. We'll leave 'em, getting too far away from the others."

Thorpe acknowledged with a click of the radio, came up beside his commander and gave him a thumbs up. Their silver steeds flashed upward, angling back toward the black puffs of flak that looked thick enough to walk across.

Minutes later they reformed with their squadron and edged their planes into formation. There were still many bombers but their numbers were thinned, falling victim to the heavy and accurate flak. McDermott heard over the open net, "Starting our bombing run." He imagined the big bomb-bay doors opening and disgorging hundreds of 500 pound explosives.

He swiveled his head, searching for more enemy fighters but for the moment the sky was filled with only friendly forces. He doubted that would last. He checked his gauges, he had plenty of fuel and half his ammunition. He'd added two, possibly three kills, to his two from the first sortie. He was one away from being an ace. He brushed the thought away. It was only the second day of this new war and it wouldn't matter how many planes he knocked down if he didn't survive.

He glanced at the ground, the bombers he was charged to protect were still in the process of dropping their bombs. The leading bombers turned away, back toward base. He watched in fascination as huge plumes rose from the ground, walking forward like some bizarre deadly dominoes set. The bombs continued exploding far out into the sea and he hoped they were sinking and killing many Germans still streaming ashore on their tracked vehicles. He saw a sudden secondary explosion out to sea and saw the heaving of a massive ship taking direct hits. He couldn't help pumping his fist.

His section of bombers were all turned back west. There was still flak, but the volume had died down considerably. His squadron was circling above, but there hadn't been any enemy fighters since the first group. He radioed HQ, "Mother, this is six of flight 23. Over."

There was a moment of static then the tinny voice responded, "Six of 23, read you loud and clear. Over."

"Mother, Six. Requesting permission to expend the rest of our ammunition on ground targets. Over."

There was a brief silence and McDermott imagined the busy controller checking his radar scope. The response came a few seconds later. "Six, Mother. Request granted but be advised there's an alien presence down there. We have multiple accounts of airborne Scalps. Over."

The image made him break radio protocol, "Did you say there's flying aliens down there?"

"Uh, that's affirmative. Be careful. Over."

————

CAPTAIN MCDERMOTT COULDN'T BELIEVE his ears. The rest of the squadron was silent, though they'd all heard the same thing. McDermott felt fear build in his belly. It was one thing to go up against human beings but quite another to fight Korth.

Most of his adult life he'd been fearful of the Korth. Not long before, no one even knew for sure what they looked like. After the battle with the Russians in the Northern Pacific, some Korth bodies had been plucked from the sea. He'd been privy to the information only because he was a ranking officer and had a buddy in intelligence who showed him a snapshot. They were tall with four arms, but he didn't notice any kind of wings. How were they propelled? Did they use external power or simply have the ability to fly like Superman?

He took a deep breath. "Okay boys, let's see what's happening on the surface. We'll attack the beachhead low and fast, south to north. First section followed by Second. Be aware of the ships off the coast, they've got teeth." He paused, "And be on the look-out for flying aliens." The phrase sounded ridiculous even to his own ears and he couldn't help chuckling. "If you see any, swat 'em." There was a series of clicks as the pilots keyed their mics.

He pushed his P-47's nose down and felt his butt lift off the seat. He watched his altitude and made a slow turn to the right, heading south. Soon, instead of fire, smoke and ruin beneath his wings, there were green forests interspersed with farms and small towns tucked along tiny bays and ports, much like the little town he'd grown up in along the edge of the Atlantic. What was it like for those people down there? Were they still huddled inside their houses, hoping the war would pass them by? Or were they gone—evacuated? He thought about his parents, sure they'd still be in their home, probably armed to the teeth, ready to fight.

The thought made him fearful, he hadn't had time to think of them and now that he did, he had the sudden urge to connect and make sure they were okay. It would have to wait.

He turned back north, leveling off at 1,000 feet AGL. Tiny communities flashed beneath his wings. He saw people running this way and that, looking up at his silver plane. He hoped the big blue star on the underside of his wings was visible, letting them know all was not lost. They were still in the fight.

The idyllic greens turned gray and smoky. He saw ships to his right, some on fire, victims of the bombings, but there were far more unscathed, firing and disgorging more and more troop carriers.

The beach was littered with bodies and material. He focused on a group of tanks lumbering from a large boat whose tracks had brought it up the beach, nearly to the headwall. He angled down and lined his pipper on the lead tank. He depressed the trigger, unleashing the .50 caliber machine guns. The tank sparked and he yawed the aircraft, spreading the armor piercing bullets. He pulled up slightly when the lead tank's top hatch lifted and a gout of flame erupted.

He flashed past, seeing more targets, soldiers diving for cover. He angled and fired a quick burst seeing huge geysers of sand and rock erupting in their midst.

His attention was diverted when he felt and heard the hammering of his plane taking hits. The Jug was stoutly made with thick armor on the underside. It wasn't impervious to small arms fire, but it could withstand a lot of abuse. He quickly checked his dials, nothing out of the ordinary.

He looked up in time to see something out of the corner of his eye, something relatively small to his right-front. He focused and couldn't believe his own eyes. A four-armed Scalp, wielding what he thought must be a German MG42, aimed directly at his head. He was airborne, but dropping quickly.

McDermott's instincts took over. He pulled the stick right a fraction and fired a burst. The Korth's body was stitched and flung backward, the MG42 falling from his four hands. McDermott caught sight of its huge sloped skull as his plane shot past. He pulled up, not believing what he'd just seen. He played it over and over in his head. He'd killed one of the ugly bastards.

He was pulled from his revelry when he noticed huge tracer rounds floating beside him like beach balls. He'd been so engrossed in thought, he forgot where he was and had gained too much altitude and lost too much speed. He was an irresistible target for everyone with a weapon. Someone was yelling over the radio, for him to get out of there.

"Shit," he cursed and pushed the throttles to full power and dove back to relative safety. He turned west away from the beachhead and his plane, followed by the rest of the squadron darted past buildings only yards beneath their wings.

Once away from the danger, he gained altitude and leveled off at 3,000 feet. He shook his head and replayed the Korth being eviscerated with his .50 caliber bullets. There was no doubt he'd killed the thing and the thought gave him hope.

14

MaryAnn and the rest of the Fighting 4th Squadron got the news of the East Coast invasion the same way everyone else in the country did—by radio. The news of a new front opening on the other side of the continent was disheartening and made them want to do more, but they were firmly planted in Anchorage for the foreseeable future.

Whenever they could fly, they did because the Russians certainly didn't take breaks and they always seemed to know when a break in the weather was coming. In fact, an outpost had been established on a hill overlooking the nearest Russian airfield and whenever there was flight activity, it was radioed in and the whole squadron was scrambled, even if the weather was dubious. MaryAnn had taken off in near blizzard conditions but every time she thought she'd never find the Anchorage airfield again, it would clear just enough.

Today was cold but the cloud base was at 7,000 feet, well within flight parameters and the short days required takeoffs in near total darkness. The gray clouds spread from horizon to horizon and looked as though they'd never budge.

She was first off the tarmac, her gray and white mottled P-51 purring as it lifted, all twelve cylinders firing perfectly synced. Despite the incessant cold, feeling the plane respond to her touch always warmed her, at least for a moment. She flexed her gloved hands, trying to keep blood flowing to her already frozen fingertips.

She went to full power and circled the airfield just below the cloud base and waited for her flight of eight other pilots to form up. Flying so close to the seemingly solid clouds made her feel as though she were under icy waters, like a fish searching for a fisherman's hole in a Minnesota lake. Finally, with her pilots loosely formed around her she keyed her mic. "Watch for icing. Let's see if the Reds are up for a game of tag."

They knew there were Russians planes aloft, they'd gotten reports from the forward observation teams, but they had no idea if they were above or below the cloud layer. MaryAnn decided she'd rather not risk losing pilots and planes to icing and disorientation by passing through the cloud layer. If an opening presented itself, which seemed unlikely, she'd decide whether or not to take it, depending on how things unfolded.

An hour later, her flight of eight was approaching the stalemated front-line. The scene never failed to pull her heart strings for the men and women struggling in the bitter cold below with little more than the clothes on their backs. It looked like a cold version of hell.

Sometimes soldiers were flown out from Anchorage and she'd listened to their stories—terrifying artillery attacks, strafing and bombing runs, and the constant enemy that was the long freezing nights. One soldier said the only good thing about the cold was it kept the countless mounds of corpses from stinking.

She turned her flight away from the approaching Russian line, not wanting to draw anti-aircraft fire. The Russian AA guns were accurate and deadly and had accounted for most of the squadron's losses since they'd arrived. She was ready to dart into the clouds at the first hint of enemy fire, despite the danger of icing.

The ground was still dark beneath them, but there was still the occasional plume of fire from an artillery piece or something on fire. This was the third day in a row she'd flown over this section of the front. She hoped it would be another fruitless mission where they didn't clash with the Russians, but it was not to be. Her radio crackled in her ear, "Bandits on our six, closing fast."

MaryAnn craned her neck but couldn't see the danger. "Group One, break right. Group Two, break left. If you get in trouble use the clouds."

She didn't wait for responses but turned hard right, knowing the other three pilots would match her. She grunted into her face-mask as the Gs pushed her into her seat. She felt the color draining from her vision and snapped her wings upright and level and the feeling of blood returning made her blink away tears.

The Russians were suddenly the only things she could see. They were closing fast at a combined speed of nearly 1,000 miles per hour. This was instinct flying and shooting. She twitched her stick slightly and mashed the trigger, then threw the plane sideways and prayed the Russian pilot went the opposite direction.

She opened her eyes an instant later and was relieved to still be alive. She swiveled her head and saw a black smoke trail. She'd scored a lucky hit. She saw her wingman still on her tail and hoped Second Lieutenant Flaherty would remember her training and stick on her like glue. She'd come a long way since arriving in Anchorage and had become a good stick, but her forte was ground attack, not dogfighting and she'd told MaryAnn in a moment of confidence one cold night in her country-girl slang, 'dogfighting scares the holy hell outta me.'

MaryAnn didn't coddle any of her pilots. There was no time. They'd either survive or die and sometimes it had more to do with luck than skill. So far, Flaherty had been lucky, scoring a confirmed kill her first week. MaryAnn hoped she'd survive the next five-minutes.

"Stay with me, Flaherty." She cranked back on the stick and her *Tigress* reacted instantly, arcing upward toward the clouds. She kept her loop tight, but she knew it would take her into the clouds briefly. She was counting on it.

The loop topped out and her world was suddenly gray and white. She continued the loop but righted the plane once back beneath the clouds. She quickly scanned the area, seeing a few dots intertwined in combat to her right. The trail of black smoke from her victim disappeared into the clouds. *See you another day, Ivan.*

Her radio crackled with the panicked voice of her wingman, Flaherty, "Got one on my tail."

MaryAnn craned her neck and knew this wasn't going to end well. Propped behind and slightly above Flaherty's six o'clock perched two Russian fighters, "Pull into the clouds now!" It was too late, the nearest fighter's wing's flashed as it unleashed a hail of .50 caliber bullets. MaryAnn watched in horror as Flaherty's windscreen shattered and the engine erupted in flame sweeping into the now open cockpit. Flaherty's screams were crystal clear in her headphones, until they suddenly ceased and were replaced with static.

MaryAnn lost sight of the doomed P-51. She wanted to scream and cry all at once but a cold fury came over her and instead of pulling into the safety of the clouds, pushed her plane into a dive. The Russians followed and fired sending tracers slicing past her wings, barely missing.

She rolled onto her back and yanked the stick straight into her belly. She glanced at her altimeter unwinding at a horrific rate and calculated that she might make it before plowing into the frozen ground. She cut power and watched the ground quickly approaching. She grit her teeth and fought to stay conscious. Later, an eyewitness would describe *The Tigress* as being only inches off the ground at the bottom of the dive.

The thundering explosion behind her told her at least one of the Russian's hadn't been so lucky. A quick backwards glance told her the first Russian, the one who'd killed Flaherty was still with her. More tracer fire bracketed her and she yawed and twitched her stick throwing the enemy pilot's aim off. The battle-scarred ground flashed beneath her like a high-speed movie. She saw dug in tanks, bunkers and burnt-out vehicles. At one point her plane lined up perfectly and she briefly saw the stark faces of soldiers lined up in trenches.

The Russian fighter's fire was incessant. He matched her every move, and felt the hammer blows of hits. She knew if she tried to climb, she'd present a perfect target. Her only chance was to stay low and fly him into something, but there was nothing but flat, burned out tundra. She hoped one of the soldiers shivering down there would get lucky and put a round through the Russian bastard's ass, but knew they were streaking so fast and close, they'd have as much chance of hitting her, as him.

She cringed as she felt her controls mush slightly. She glanced right and saw gaping holes along the trailing edge of her aileron. She had to do something quick, or she'd be dead. She put the plane on edge, her left wing inches above the frozen ground. She pulled into a tight turn, careful to keep from dipping and becoming a rolling fireball.

She stole a quick glance, the Russian hadn't matched her move, he didn't have to. He simply went 100 feet up, matched her turn and cut his power to turn inside. MaryAnn saw the fighter getting ready to pounce. In another second he'd have the perfect angle and shot. She slammed the stick right and despite her holed aileron, *Tigress* turned, sending MaryAnn's body tight against the plane's left side. She felt like she was in an out-of-control ride at the county fair. The ripping sound of bullets impacting the ground where she'd just been told her she'd made her move in the nick of time, but it was only a brief respite from the inevitable.

She pushed to full throttle and pulled the stick back, rocketing nearly straight up, streaking for the safety of the clouds. The Russian's slower speed in the turn allowed her to increase the distance, but the Russian still had her. She swiveled, watching the Russian dart up after her. Her airspeed decreased despite redlining the engine and she wondered if she'd taken engine damage.

She looked longingly at the clouds knowing she wouldn't make it. She yanked the stick all the way back pulling herself into a loop. The Russian was waiting. He let loose and MaryAnn felt her *Tigress* shudder with more hammer-like blows. Smoke filled the cockpit and she wondered what it would feel like to burn. The thought terrified her. She couldn't see out the smoke-filled cockpit, but she could feel her stricken aircraft falling like a leaf off a tree. She had to get out, now.

She found the cockpit release and pulled. It flew off and she could suddenly see. She was upside down, in a spin. She tried to yank herself out the open cockpit but her restraints held her tight. She cursed at her stupidity and mashed the quick release. She remembered to disconnect her radio wire and she launched herself with all the strength she could muster.

She felt a sharp pain in her shoulder and then she was falling. The cold air hit her exposed face and she felt as though her skin would tear off. She clutched for the parachute rip-cord and finally found it. She yanked it and felt the snap of the chute open.

She tried to focus, to orient herself. She heard her beloved *Tigress* hit the ground with a rending and tearing of metal. She glimpsed snow, then a burnt tree, then felt her legs buckled and she slammed her helmeted head into the ground. She felt nauseous and wanted to throw up. There was a sound, someone yelling excitedly, perhaps more than one. Just before she passed out, she realized they were speaking Russian.

————

MARYANN WOKE UP SHIVERING UNCONTROLLABLY. Her head pounded as though someone were beating on it with a sledgehammer. She tried to raise her hands but something stopped her. She tried harder and realized in horror that she was bound. She opened her eyes and the pain in her head magnified, but she kept them open. She was in a dim room, seated on a dirt floor. She felt the cold hardness of the wooden beam she was tied to. Fear raced through her, making her forget momentarily, her pounding head.

She struggled to free herself, but she was bound tight and only succeeded in making her hands and wrists ache. She froze when she heard a voice. She was momentarily confused. She knew it was Russian, but she understood it somehow. She felt a slight buzz of irritation in her neck. "You cannot escape, Miss."

The voice was coming from behind her and she tried to turn her head but couldn't move far enough. "Wh-where am I?" she stammered.

"In the care of the Korth-Russo forces." The man's voice was smooth and low, almost calming. She heard his footsteps crunching the bare floor and the first she saw of him was his polished black boots. He crouched in front of her and shined a light onto her face. The pain in her head increased and she shut her eyes tight and turned away. She felt his calloused hand on her cheek and she pulled back and smacked her head on the pole she was bound to. "Relax, you are lucky to be alive. You bailed out at the minimum survivable height after our heroic comrade swatted your plane from the sky."

She felt his rough hands turn her head as though examining her. "Your face is bruised and swollen, but I can tell you're a beauty. Your heavy clothing hides your curves. You *Americans* are too skinny, but I'm sure some of the men would appreciate your warmth during these cold nights."

She froze, the fear making her hold her breath. "I'm—I'm a prisoner of war. You can't—you can't—I'm a soldier."

"Hmm. Yes, a soldier. From all accounts a deadly one at that. Your plane shows many victories, many kills." She squinted her eyes open and he diverted the light from her face but kept it lit. "You keep score like it's a game." He scowled and his stubbled face looked hard as steel. "Is this war a game to you?"

She stared back at him. "No. Not a game. Your pilots do the same. I've seen it." He leaned away and she thought it prudent to change the subject. "How—how am I able to understand you? You're speaking Russian, but I hear it in my head as English."

He nodded and touched the left side of her neck. She flinched, feeling the pressure of his fingers touching something. He moved it back and forth and she realized in horror that something was sticking from the side of her neck—embedded. "A translator. A Korth gift."

She opened her eyes all the way. "Korth? You implanted alien tech into me?"

He grinned and turned his neck and pulled down the heavy wool of his coat, showing her his own neck. She saw some sort of knob. It was a part of his body, with dark neck hair curling around it. "I forget it's even there. You'll find it useful. It translates any language, we even understand our benefactor's language."

She scowled, "Scalps."

He nodded and smiled. "Scalps? Yes, of course."

She looked beyond him when she saw someone else enter. The figure was huge and had to duck low to fit through the doorway. Their wide body filled the entire doorframe and they had to shimmy in sideways. Once inside they stretched to their full height and MaryAnn sucked in a breath when she realized she was witnessing an alien—a Korth—the true enemy. She could only see the silhouette, but though it walked on two thick legs, it was obviously *not* human.

There was a clicking sound, which made her skin crawl, and she heard the words form in her head, "She's awake, good."

The Russian stood and backed away from her, still holding the flashlight. He braced as though in the presence of an officer. "Yes, sir. Just a moment ago."

"Cut her loose." The Russian soldier reacted immediately, crouching behind her and using a knife to slice the cords.

MaryAnn felt immediate relief, but the blood returning to her hands made her wince in pain. It was not enough, however, to pull her eyes from the beast in front of her. Her entire life, the Korth were an unknown. There had been sketches, guesses, but light from the flashlight showed her what they actually looked like and she couldn't tear her eyes away. The creature's huge sloped head, the black eyes which never wavered, four thick arms, and the most distinctive and fearful part, the mandible like mouth which seemed to be in constant motion, like the legs of a chirping cricket. It was so—*alien*.

"Oh my God," she whispered.

The Korth's head expanded and changed a lighter shade of red. It spoke and she thought she detected a hint of mirth in the voice. "No. I'm not your puny *god*. I'm a Korth warrior."

The Russian was at her side and he yanked her to her feet. She couldn't keep from yelping as the pain and stiffness made her lightheaded. She swooned and he gripped her arm tighter, holding her upright. The pain from his grip made her pull away and she freed herself momentarily. He quickly stepped behind her and grasped both arms and pulled them behind her, stretching her shoulders painfully. She stopped struggling.

The Korth clicked and hummed and again she shivered with disgust, like coming across something foul and writhing in a garbage dump. "This one has spirit." It paused and she felt a dull twinge in the back of her neck. She had the distinct feeling something was inside her brain, digging and probing. She closed her eyes, fighting the dull force.

The feeling disappeared quickly and the Korth clicked, "Yes. This one's special. This is what the TRs requested."

MaryAnn had no idea what the thing was talking about. She felt a slight pinprick and suddenly had an overwhelming and unstoppable desire to sleep. She retreated into darkness.

15

TR Cinter was poised over the top of yet another human subject. She thought this one might be different. It showed some promise, with its brain's capacity to withstand the probing. Indeed, the bridging was nearly complete and the brain's function, though not optimal, was still within what was considered normal.

The human was completely still, held fast by blue arcs of energy emitting from a dull-gray slab of metal it lay upon. TR Cinter knew the stillness was deceiving, for without the restraints shutting down muscular response, the human would be uncontrollably writhing in agony. Every nerve ending in its body was on fire with excruciating impulses of energy.

This species' sensitive nerve endings, so intimately connected to their brains, had confounded previous attempts at bridging. They'd had some success, but their brains, once unleashed, were wild and wholly insane and had to be exterminated immediately.

This subject was handling the bridging better than any others but the hardest part was yet to come. TR Cinter looked at the assistant, Private Trokon, standing by, with one arm on the control panel, the other three gripping the blue glowing rod which would keep the next step from frying him.

Cinter watched Trokon. He, like all other male Korth were growing needful. The TRs hadn't turned female since landing on Earth. This had never happened. Cinter and the other TRs could feel there was something emitting from these lowly humans which was blocking the process, some kind of pheromone. The humans being such lowly, un-evolved creatures had no control over the emission and the TRs were committed to bridging their brains, making them hyper-aware so they could control and extract the mysterious substance.

"Ready, Trokon?" Cinter clicked.

Trokon signaled he was and Cinter took over. His three long fingers connected to Cinter and tapped the monitor so fast his fingers blurred. He was a conduit for the TR's thoughts, a vessel to be used.

Cinter pushed into the human's brain, pushing past the pain recep-tors and hovering where the impulses pounded against what felt like a wall. The wall was chipping, falling away from the bombardment of water and proteins which were so prevalent in their systems. The barrier was coming down and the brain was still within normal limits. This would be a successful bridge. But would the nerves, which were nearly on fire with energy, turn the brain to mush and insanity before the human could take control of the pain and switch it off?

Cinter felt the wall break; the way was open. This was the moment of truth. The crossing. The connection was excruciating and the limit of this brains' capacity to withstand it while keeping sane was close at hand.

Cinter added Kroton's energy waves to his own in an effort to buffer the nerve's signals but it was impossible to stop the majority of them. Human brains were hard-wired to the pain, it drove them and indeed, kept them alive. The process—the bridging—would happen naturally over millennia, assuming their warlike natures didn't lead to their own extinction, but the TRs wanted to understand what was blocking their own reproduction cycles. It could be weaponized and could possibly be their empire's salvation.

Then it was done. Cinter released Private Trokon and he dropped the glowing rod and stepped away from the controls, his mandibles clacking and his head deflated and dark. Cinter pulled herself from the human's consciousness and stepped away from the table. There was only one way to know if the bridging had damaged their mind and that was simply to observe.

———

HUMAN ORDERLIES ENTERED at Cinter's beckoning and pushed the floating metal table toward a wall, which suddenly vanished, opening into a stark, white room. Every inch of it was padded, a lesson learned from the first few bridging attempts. The table was pushed to the center of the room and they pushed the foot of it down, putting the human upright, but still locked into place with the blue energy arcs.

Three of the four orderlies walked away. The fourth was frozen in place as Cinter made her stay behind. The human, a female was wide-eyed, obviously petrified. Many past patients had displayed normal behavior until they were around other beings, at which time they went berserk and tore them apart.

Cinter and the rest of the TRs weren't interested in wasting time. Either the human was strong enough to sustain the change, or they weren't and the fastest way to find out was leaving someone in the room when they were released. So far, none had been successful. Cinter thought this one might be different.

Once out of the room, the three human orderlies filed past, keeping their eyes down and disappeared through another wall. Cinter strode toward the now transparent wall and observed the bridged human. His eyes were open but there was no way to tell if they were those of an insane man or not. Cinter didn't probe his consciousness, it might put them over the edge. TR Gruncy entered and stood beside Cinter and clicked and hummed. "This one looks far more stable than the last."

Cinter's head expanded slightly, "Yes, but only slightly. They were at the edge when I had to leave. We'll know in the next few par-uns."

Cinter released the grip he held on the female orderly and she seemed to physically droop. She immediately looked at the naked man beside her, fear obvious on her face. Cinter directed her to touch the recessed button beneath the table which would release him. She resisted and Cinter sent a painful jolt and she quickly complied.

The blue arcs disappeared and the naked man slid off the vertical slab of metal. His feet hit the floor with an athletic softness. He was an American soldier, captured in Alaska. He'd been 'interviewed' by the local Korth warrior, who'd been told what to look for. He was by far the best specimen thus far.

Of course, they'd tried the procedure countless times on every human variation within the borders of the Korth occupation, but the human brains had weakened since their arrival and that was by design. A slightly impaired mind was easier to control. The Americans and others from the West were not so impaired and the process worked much better, although none had been successful.

Cinter and Gruncy watched the human stand to full height. He looked around the room, not being able to see the Korth watching. He ignored the woman, who stood stock still, breathing fast and staring at her feet. This was a good start.

The man walked around the edge of the room taking in the environment as though searching for a way out. His right hand slid along the padding as he walked.

He stepped to the vertical table and pushed it, but it didn't budge. He looked to the woman standing in fear, only feet away and Cinter saw the first indication there was something wrong: his male parts became erect.

Gruncy clicked in displeasure, "The human can't control his primal mating urge."

Cinter's head turned a slightly darker shade of red. "We'll know soon enough." He'd seen this happen before and hoped he wouldn't witness it again.

The human approached the woman and circled her like a beast evaluating its next meal. Cinter could see the hunger just beneath the surface, the danger, the insanity. "There's still a chance. It needs to know it's wrong. I'm going to try to persuade it."

Gruncy's arms reached out, "No," but it was too late.

Cinter entered the bridged being's mind and felt the power there. This one was unleashed and the impulses were like a lightning storm.

Cinter applied pressure and the lightning was instantly directed back at him. He repulsed it, but it was strong. He pulled back but the door was closing fast.

Cinter dropped to the ground and Gruncy called Private Trokon to help. He did so immediately and lifted Cinter off the ground and placed him on another floating metal slab. Gruncy was beside him and probed his mind cautiously. His head deflated but then inflated and colored pink. "He's okay, he's still in there and intact."

Trokon pointed, "The same cannot be said for the human." Gruncy looked into the room and his head deflated and blackened. "Animals."

The male soldier had the woman pinned to the wall and was thrusting into her, his face twisted with anger, lust, and a ferociousness, which made even the Korth, nervous.

The woman's face was agony, her screams of pain and horror unheard through the soundproofing. Another few seconds and the male, incensed with rage, reached for her neck and brought his mouth down hard. Blood spurted from her and covered the man's face and body. He tore flesh as he threw his head back and consumed the flesh. Her face went slack and she slid down the wall, her neck pulsing gouts of blood, which slowed with each dying heartbeat. Her dead eyes seemed to look through the wall, seeing the Korth watching, but that was impossible.

"Disgusting creatures," hissed Private Trokon.

———

TR CINTER AWOKE on the metal table and knew he'd failed yet again. Perhaps the humans were just not ready for the unleashing. Perhaps his dream to harness the pheromone and use it to eradicate their enemies was fantasy. But the last one was close, he could feel it. All they needed was to find the correct host, the correct brain.

He sat up and hopped off the table. TR Gruncy was gone, but Private Trokon was ready to assist. "Another failure, TR Cinter."

Cinter's head darkened. He looked into the room and saw the bloody mess that had been a human female. The disgusting male, covered in blood was flinging her body around painting the walls with her blood. His mouth was open as though howling like the wolves of the North.

He went to the viewing wall and watched the spectacle. He didn't dare try to enter the human's brain now, he'd nearly been trapped inside before. He'd postulated the possibility, that once unleashed, the human mind would be difficult, if not impossible, to control and the brief foray into this diseased mongrel's mind proved the theory correct.

"Exterminate it, please."

Private Trokon's color lightened, "My pleasure, TR Cinter."

The inert table inside the room, suddenly started spinning and the blue arcs of energy shot out and struck the gyrating, howling human who was now violating the corpse. The energy split him open like an exploding water balloon and his body turned to red dust. It was over in a split second.

Cinter turned from the grisly scene. "Get it cleaned, we'll need the room again."

Moments later the same three orderlies and a replacement, entered the room and approached the bloody scene. They held mops and buckets, not being trusted with the Korth technology, which could've cleaned it thoroughly, in seconds. They'd cleaned many similar scenes and seemed resigned to their fate, each knowing they'd eventually be the body they were cleaning up.

TR Cinter turned away and left the room, leaving through the same door the orderlies had entered.

In the blue-lit hallways of the mother-ship, Cinter passed Korth warriors who braced and eyed him suspiciously as they passed. Every Korth on the ship and on the world below wondered why the TRs hadn't turned female. They tried to hide it, but Cinter could feel they blamed the TRs as if they were doing it on purpose. Nothing, of course, could be further from the truth. Their role was to continue breeding, continue populating the stars with Korth warriors, ships and TRs until all their many enemies were vanquished forever.

TR Gruncy came around the corner and his head turned pink in pleasure. "Another has arrived. An American female fighter pilot and this one may be the one. She is very strong and there is depth I've not yet seen in any of the prior subjects."

Cinter's mood changed and his head inflated but only a little. He'd had his hopes up before. "A female? How unusual. Take me to her."

Gruncy bowed slightly and led Cinter through the maze of halls until they entered a blue and red lit loading dock. Korth workers darted around, giving the TRs space. Gruncy said, "She's in the box over there. See for yourself. She *resists.*"

TR Cinter went to the box, more like a squat rectangular cage, and peered down on the diminutive female. She was naked, but despite that didn't try to cover up like all the prior humans. Cinter could feel her rage and indignation even without entering her consciousness. "Human," he said and the female looked up, showing off a bruised and swollen face. Cinter reared back in surprise. The female human had given his brain a slight twitch with just a look.

Cinter held the human's gaze and reached out to her mind. Access was normally easy—child's play, but this one's 'door' was more difficult to find. He finally did, but it was more like trying to enter a bolted and locked door. He pushed until he was finally inside, but only just. Advancing was hard, like advancing against a resistive Korth warrior.

Cinter left the human's consciousness and his own head swelled bright red. "This one *is* strong. What is your name, human?"

The naked female stared, and Cinter delighted in *feeling* her anger. Finally, as though making a decision, the human proclaimed, "MaryAnn Larkin, you ugly piece of Scalp shit-for-brains freak."

16

Rex didn't know what to expect on the African continent. No previous agents had reported back, which made everyone in The Branch think there might be some alien tech that was able to detect their presence, but so far, the week had been quite uneventful.

Perhaps part of the reason was because they'd come ashore in a super-remote area. He'd pushed inland and found a little-used dirt road paralleling the coast. He moved north, hoping to come across signs which would tell him where he was. There were none.

The first two days he'd walked without coming across anyone. The days were sweltering hot, the nights cold, so he moved mostly at night. The sounds of animals in the dark kept him on his toes. No one knew for sure what the Korth invasion had done to the animal population. Rex could unequivocally say, there were still plenty of wild animals about.

The third night, after walking for hours, he noticed distant lights on the horizon. It was the first indication of civilization he'd seen and he hoped there'd be a road sign before he entered the town, but as he neared, there was nothing.

When he figured he was a mile from the town, he moved off the road and found cover in an outcropping of rocks, rising from the desert. He sipped off his diminishing supply of water and gazed at the flickering lights. The sound of clomping hooves and murmuring voices made him sink lower. Someone, or something, was coming his way on the road. He was 50 yards from the track. He felt a surge of excitement to finally get a glimpse of something besides wild animals. He was beginning to wonder if he were the only one on the continent.

There was a half-moon, which lit up the desert like a flashlight. He saw movement and focused his eyes to the side, using his superior peripheral vision. There were four camels approaching. He could discern people riding them. They'd pass right by him. He wondered where they could possibly be going in the middle of the night.

When they were nearly abreast of his position between the rocks, they turned off the road and came directly at him. They were following a well-used trail that he hadn't noticed before. It led to the rocks where he was hiding. He silently cursed himself for not doing a better reconnaissance of the area.

Rex was well-hidden between a jumble of boulders but once the sun came up—if they lingered—they'd see him. What would he do then? Fight them? Kill them? It would be better to try to talk his way through it. He had the translator and he assumed they did too, but they'd still know him to be a foreigner, simply by his skin color. Before the Korth invasion, there'd been plenty of white people here, but now —no one knew.

He wore a ragged scarf that hung around his neck. He pulled it over his face and secured it. If he had to fight or run, the less they saw the better.

The camels sauntered around the boulders and the riders stopped and dropped off their steeds. There was a smattering of words spoken and Rex was relieved they were human. They were 30 yards away. He couldn't make out what they were saying. They pulled large containers from the sides of the camels. The sound they made when they clacked together sounded like clay pottery. The four riders left the camels and walked along another path he hadn't noticed and soon dropped out of sight.

If he wanted to get away, this was his chance, but where would he go? The land was virtually flat in all directions. Once the sun came up he'd be spotted for sure. Besides, his mission was to blend in. Before he could do that, he had to figure out where the hell he was. A local, or even semi-local, would at least know the area.

The riders were gone for 30 long minutes. The camels barely moved and he wondered if their noses were as good as horses. Did they know there was a stranger lurking? Probably.

The sky was lightening in the East when the riders returned, laughing and talking and hauling the clay pots, only now they looked much heavier. Each rider assisted the other in lifting and mounting the pots back onto the camel's sides. The camels grunted and groaned with the extra weight. The riders continued talking in low murmurs. Rex wished he were closer, so he could hear what they were saying. Finally, the riders mounted the camels and reversed their course, heading back toward the distant lights.

Rex waited until he was sure they were gone then climbed down the rocks and followed the trail they'd disappeared over. He was dumbfounded to see a large oasis of water. He wondered how he could have possibly missed it. There was a well-used trail winding down a slope and ending at the water's edge. The water shimmered and sparkled in the moonlight and it looked inviting. He walked down and kneeled beside it, taking a large scoop and drinking it from his palm. It was cool and he savored it as it dripped down his throat.

He pulled the pack from his back and quickly filled his water bottles. He dipped his hand and dripped water over his upturned face and wiped the dust and dirt off.

He walked around the oasis, marveling at its beauty as the colors started to change with the rising of the sun. He glanced at the low ridge and wondered if he had time for a swim. He decided against it, there was bound to be more people in the heat of the day. He was tempted to stay along the water's edge, beneath one of the many palm trees, and act like he belonged there. He could interact with the people and figure out where he was. Perhaps travelers weren't unique and he'd be accepted as one. He shook his head, too risky.

Once he'd circumnavigated the water and was back at the trail, he felt refreshed. He took one more longing look at the oasis, then went up the winding path.

Just before cresting the top, he slowed and listened. Had he heard something? He crouched and listened intently. There it was again, the clomping of a hoof. He looked around for a place to hide, but there was nowhere. He resigned himself, he'd proceed and act normal. Hopefully, he'd be seen as a traveler. Perhaps he could even glean his whereabouts if he played his cards correctly.

His heart sank when he crested the hill and instead of innocuous travelers or townspeople, he was confronted with men in turbans pointing rifles at his chest. He smiled and raised his hands. "Good morning," he said.

———

REX WAS STRIPPED of his possessions. His hands and feet were bound and he was flung over the back of a camel as though he were a shot animal. Despite the slow saunter, every jolt hurt and by the time they were on the outskirts of town, he was sore and dripping sweat. He protested his treatment, but his captors hadn't spoken a word.

He craned his neck as they entered the town. It was small, with squat mud-huts on either side of the main road. Curious townsfolk watched them pass as they scrubbed clothes, swept dirt from small porches or simply sat chewing grass shoots. There wasn't a signpost anywhere. He dropped his head and watched the road, wondering if he'd set a new record for mission fail.

Soon he was yanked from the camel and pushed to the ground. He moaned, exaggerating his pain. "This is how you treat a traveler? A guest?" he said in his most indignant voice. Their necks were covered where the translators would be embedded, so he didn't know if they had them. He was hoping for some kind of facial tell, letting him know they understood, but they were unreadable.

Weathered, sandaled feet were suddenly in front of his face. Rex tried to crane his neck, but couldn't arch enough. Rough hands grabbed his arms and yanked him to his feet. He cursed and yelped in pain which was only half-faked.

Before him stood a tall man with deep inset eyes. Despite the wrinkles from a lifetime spent in the withering desert sun, Rex couldn't decide if he were ancient or young. He seemed ageless somehow, exuding youth but displaying age.

The man's piercing eyes looked him up and down. Finally, he nodded as though deciding and pointed to a mud and thatch building. The men on either side roughly hauled him through the low door. The transition from light to dark made it impossible to see, but he could discern he was in a large room, probably some kind of local meeting hall. Perhaps a dining hall.

The two men pulled him further inside and pushed him to the ground. He was still bound and now on his knees. Was this where he'd die? He tested his bindings, they were tight, no way he was getting out of this one. He conserved his strength using the breathing exercises he'd learned to still his mind, preparing himself for violent action. There was no way he would die on his knees without a fight. He wouldn't make it easy for them.

The two men stepped away half a step. Rex kept track of them, formulating how he'd strike and when, while pretending to be cowed, docile, and weak.

His eyes adjusted. He kneeled at one end of a long hall. In the center there was a long table with benches lined on either side. He noticed a sculpture at the front of the table. It was a sculpture of a warrior on watch. He held a spear. The warrior looked to be carved from wood, but the spear was real, with a metal point.

He thought his guess of a chow hall accurate. Perhaps they intended to eat him. He'd heard of cannibal communities in remote areas of Africa. The thought made him grin, *what a way to go.*

From the far side a door opened and in strode the tall, inscrutable man from outside. He approached and stood before him. Rex glanced up at him, keeping his actions as meek as possible. The man's baritone voice startled him. "What's your name, spy?" The man's language came through the translator. Rex didn't answer right away, but lifted his head judging what he'd have to do to kill the man. "Answer me!" He barked.

The sudden outburst nearly sent Rex into action, but he wanted to be put on his feet first. He wasn't being executed just yet. He spoke in a soft voice. "My name—my name is, Rex."

The man leaned forward slightly, obviously having a hard time hearing him. "Get him on his feet." Rex felt hands grip his arms and yank him upright. He yelped and whimpered a little, keeping his eyes down. "Repeat," he barked.

"Rex, sir. Rex is my name, but I'm not a spy. I'm—I'm a traveler from the South." The man scowled and the lines at the crease of his mouth and cheeks deepened into caverns. He reached for something in a fold of his flowing robe. He pushed it into the side of his neck.

"You don't speak the language. Repeat."

Rex was momentarily stunned. He was under the impression the translators were surgically implanted, yet this man had just inserted it as though he could remove it at will. "My name is, Rex. I'm not a spy," he repeated.

The man's scowl deepened and the crease at the junction of his mouth and cheek deepened into a fissure. "Rex," he said and even through the translator it sounded clunky and foreign.

Rex cursed himself silently. He should have used a more appropriate name for the region, although he had no idea what that would be at the moment. He nodded and tried to look as small and meek as possible.

"Rex," he tried again. He worked his mouth as though tasting something new, "Rex." He put his hands behind his back and paced in front of him, "You are a spy. There's no doubt of that."

Rex shook his head and lowered his eyes, but kept the man's feet in view. If he could get a few steps closer, he could pounce and see what happened. "I'm just a traveler."

The man stopped, "Yes, you've traveled, of that I have no doubt. You are not from this land. I can smell it on you. I always can." He stepped closer, "You are not the first, you know."

It was the opportunity Rex had been waiting for. He bent his knees dropping from the grip of the guards, then sprang forward. His head connected with the leader's chin and the tall man toppled backwards hard. Rex somersaulted and rolled over the man's bleeding face. He rolled to his feet then launched again, but this time toward the warrior sculpture. He had one chance and it was a slim one.

He tumbled into the sculpture. It toppled and sent up a dust plume when it hit the floor. Rex pulled his legs tight to his chest and extended his arms until they were in front of his body. He leaped where the spear landed and gripped it between his bound hands. The guards recovered, bellowing curses and charged him. Rex pushed the spear-head down and sliced at the leather cords binding his feet. He'd nearly sawed through when both guards crashed into him. He lost his grip on the spear and it clattered away. He tried to roll to it, but was held fast by strong hands.

The tall man grunted and got to his feet, holding and testing his jaw. He strode to him and laughed his deep baritone laugh, then said. "You fight well, *Rex*. But what have you done with Joe?"

Rex stopped struggling and looked at the man as though he'd seen a ghost. "Joe," he stammered between labored breaths. "You—you know Joe?"

The man scowled. "Of course. He is my son."

"Oh, shit."

––––––––––

THE TALL MAN, whose name was Talib, was not happy when Rex told him the fate of his son. After dispatching men on camels, he pointed a long gnarly finger at his nose. "If my son is dead, you will beg to follow him but I will make your pain linger as long as I can…years."

Rex was put into an abandoned hut with four guards along each wall. He used the time to sleep. The huts were cool, even in the midday heat. He hadn't slept much, or well, since leaving St. Helena Island and he figured he may as well catch up now. If Joe had somehow survived, he'd be pissed and probably have him killed. If he were dead, he'd be tortured until he eventually died. He just hoped, if Joe was found alive, he'd have the decency to kill him outright, but he doubted it. Either way, he didn't see a way out that didn't include a shallow grave.

A full day and night passed before there was a commotion outside.

He peered out the mud slit, which acted as a window. It was early morning and he was expecting breakfast soon. They'd given him plenty of food and water, which he appreciated immensely. He saw the camels trotting in and the men returning.

He looked for a body, but instead saw a man slide off the middle camel with help from the rider in front and wobble on his feet. Women rushed forward and surrounded him. Before he was hidden from view, Rex saw his head was covered in a thick white bandage with pink splotches bleeding through.

Talib stood, talking to the lead camel rider but Rex couldn't hear what was being said. Talib watched his son being helped to another mud hut. He turned toward Rex, who involuntarily pulled away from the window, as though he were breaking a rule by looking outside. He shook his head, and put his eye back to the slit.

Talib approached, stood outside the closed thatch door and crossed his arms across his broad dark chest. "My son is alive. That is good for you, but not too good. Your life hangs on his word, *Rex.*"

Rex put his mouth to the slit and answered, "I understand, Talib." He knew there was no way out. Even if he were able to escape, where would he go? He didn't know the area and as far as he could see in either direction it was flat desert wasteland. In fact, he'd been wondering why the village was there in the first place. Perhaps there'd once been vegetation. There was a nearby water supply, but why not build the town closer?

The other question baffling him was how it was possible for Joe to be Talib's son? He'd been told no operatives ever came out of Africa, ever. Yet Joe, an operative, was family and the way Talib talked, didn't seem to be a stranger. That odd circumstance was the only thing which might just keep him alive.

———

THE REST OF THE DAY, Rex spent pacing and thinking. By the time the thatch door was pulled open, he was no closer to answering the questions. The guards stood to either side and called to him, "Come out, Rex."

Rex nodded and did as he was told. He came out and they immediately grabbed his arms with vice-like grips. He walked between them and he felt the prick of a spear at his back, not a good sign.

He was escorted to the long mess hall hut. His guards kept hold of him the entire way, only releasing him when he stood before the long table. The benches were filled with what must have been the entire adult population, men and women both. He noticed the warrior sculpture was gone. He grimaced when the guard with the spear kicked the back of his legs, forcing him to his knees, painfully.

He wanted to lash out, throttle the man, but instead remained meek and alert. He took in a deep breath and let it out slow. The next few minutes would decide his fate.

A side-door opened and in walked Talib wearing ceremonial garb with brightly colored feathers and a colorful chest plate stitched intricately to look like an eagle's head. Following him, also in colorful feathers and stitchery was Joe. He still wore a bandage on his head. He was thinner than the last time he'd seen him, but that was to be expected, he'd taken his food and water. The withering look he leveled at him, made Rex gulp against a suddenly dry throat.

The villagers stood, Talib waved his hand and they all sat again and fidgeted. Rex wondered if he was the only one in the room that didn't know his fate. Probably.

Talib and Joe walked to the front of the table closest to him and sat in gaudy carved chairs, like something a king and queen would sit in, or in this case, king and prince. Who were these people? Did The Branch know Joe's history? Was Joe a traitor? Was that why no one ever returned? The questions fired inside his head like rifle shots.

Talib clutched the arms of the chair and leaned forward. The villagers also leaned forward, not wanting to miss a word. In his baritone voice, Talib said, "As you can see, my son survived your cowardly attack. My men found him wandering the road like a crazy man without food or water. You took both after bludgeoning his head with a rock and leaving him to die of his wounds." He looked at his son, who stared back, then redirected his gaze at Rex. "You didn't even have the decency to put him out of his misery!" He yelled the last word and it echoed in the tight confines. He leaned back in his chair, getting control. "I want you to suffer, to die slowly, but..."

He hesitated and looked at his son who leaned forward and put his hand on his father's knee and squeezed. He stood and for the first time, Rex realized he looked a lot like his stately father. "I staid his hand. For the time being, anyway. Your fate is tied to how you answer my questions." Rex nodded. Joe raised his hand indicating he should stand. Rex was glad for it, it felt odd kneeling as though he were royalty when only days before, Rex had been considered his superior officer. He got to his feet and glanced back at the guard with the spear. Joe shook his head, "Any attempt to flee will be met with 'extreme violence', as the cadre says."

Rex nodded, "Sorry. Habit you know."

Joe smiled and nodded. "Yes, I do know. The first question I have: Are you loyal to The Branch?"

Rex didn't expect it. Answers flashed through his mind and he finally decided the truth was his best option. If it was the wrong answer, well that's life. "I'm loyal to my country," he shook his head, "but not to The Branch. No." The silence hung in the air, so he continued. "The Branch, and the sadistic cadre, took everything from me. Everyone I ever knew or loved, my wife and son—everyone thinks I'm a traitor—a coward. I've been biding my time, waiting for an assignment. I never intended to carry out their missions. I planned to drop off the face of the earth and make my way, somehow, back to my wife and son. I don't even know if they're alive."

He looked at the dirt floor then back up into Joe's eyes. "When they saddled me with you, I assumed it was to watch me, to make sure I followed through with their orders. When I went to smash the radio and you tried to stop me, I knew I was right. I didn't want to kill you." Rex looked Joe in the eye and the tension in the room was palpable. "I could've." He nodded, remembering holding the bloody rock. "I nearly did. It was what the cadre would've expected, what they trained me to be, decisive and deadly." He shook his head and pursed his lips. "And that's why I didn't do it. Because it would've brought me closer to being what they want me to be. I'll kill. I'm good at it. But I'm not a murderer."

Joe nodded then said, "You leaving me out there with no food, a little water and a head wound could be considered murder. If my father hadn't picked you up, if he hadn't sent help…"

Rex grinned, "You had a fighting chance. I could've taken that away with one swing of my arm. I'm not asking for forgiveness, I'm just telling you the truth." He shrugged, "Your father can fillet me now, or stake me to an anthill or whatever diabolical scenario he can think of, but I'll die with a clean conscience."

Joe stood and leaned toward his father. His father's lips tightened and his jaw flexed, then he nodded as though resigned to his son's decision. Joe nodded and grinned. "We're not going to kill you, although my father would like nothing more." He glanced at his father who nodded slightly. Joe said, "Welcome to my home." He spread his arms wide, "and the resistance."

17

Lieutenant Ricker Rommel and the rest of 1st Platoon of Wolf Company didn't waste time after taking the airfield. Two more companys of Fallschirmjäger had landed and they'd pushed out 100 yards from Idlewild Airport and dug in waiting for the inevitable counter attack.

Ricker crouched in a sandbagged bunker left over from the defending American Bridge Defense Brigade soldiers. His men had reinforced it and placed an MG42 facing outward.

He watched the skies nervously. They'd tried to keep the American AA guns intact during the attack but three of the six had been damaged and were unusable. The remaining ammunition had been dispersed and his men now manned the three guns, but as of yet the only aircraft they'd seen were friendly. Ricker doubted that would last. In the confusion of the invasion, the Americans might not even know the airport had been taken. He hoped that would last a few more hours.

He looked at his watch. The daylight was fading and the temperature dropping. He gazed at the surreal landscape of the nearby cityscape. At first, he'd seen civilians everywhere, some wandering close to see what was happening, others thinking the airport was still open for travel. The paratroopers had orders to shoot anything outside their defensive ring and there'd been a lot of firing over the past few hours. Ricker hoped they'd shot over the civilian's heads but knew some of the more sadistic soldiers relished killing and it didn't matter if they were noncombatants.

"Sergeant Hoch, make a final sweep before dark. Make sure the men are in place and ready. Two-hour guard shifts. The tanks arrive in the morning, just need to hold out until then."

Hoch nodded, "Yes, sir." He sprang over the sandbags and trotted to the other positions, keeping low.

Ricker and his men held the center position, straddling the main road leading into the airport from the city. If there was a concerted counterattack it would most likely come down that road, particularly if it was armor. He visualized his defenses. They had plenty of anti-armor Panzerfausts and Panzerschreks distributed among the foxholes dug along the road, as well as MG42s strung out in overlapping fields of fire. Two of the twenty-millimeter AA guns were aimed horizontally to be used as anti-armor and anti-personnel. If there was a night air-raid, the men would need to scramble to re-adjust, but they knew what they were doing.

A shot rang out and Ricker ducked, then brought his head up searching the buildings. There had been a few sniper attacks from the buildings which had caused no casualties so far. He was sure they were overzealous civilians trying to get in on the action. Another shot and he saw the telltale puff of white smoke coming from the 5th floor of a building 100 yards away. There was an immediate response from his men. He watched the window explode with hits and the building's bricks shattered, obscuring the target with red dust. There were no more shots from the building.

———

FIVE HOURS LATER, Ricker was nudged from a restless sleep. Sergeant Hoch whispered, "HQ on the radio, sir."

Corporal Hinkler was beside the sergeant extending the radio handset. Ricker rubbed his eyes, adjusted himself then took the hand-set. "Six of First, go ahead. Over."

The tinny voice of his commanding officer, Major Spitz made him stiffen slightly. He listened, nodding occasionally. Finally he signed off, "Understood. Six of First, out." He handed the headset back to Hinkler who hung around hoping for news.

Ricker addressed Platoon Sergeant Hoch. "The Scout Platoon says something's coming up the road. Sounds like tanks and troops. Get word to the men, everyone on high alert." Sergeant Hoch passed the info to a nearby Sergeant who disappeared into the night. Ricker continued. "The major wants the buildings brought down once we make contact. Wants to cause confusion and pen them in so we can kill the tanks one at a time."

Platoon Sergeant Hoch nodded. "They're wired and ready to go. Sergeant Faulk and second squad have the plunger. They checked the wiring an hour ago. They know what to do, sir."

Ricker nodded and slapped his platoon sergeant's shoulder. "I know they do, Sergeant. Let's hope the enemy is as unorganized as the Bridge Defense Brigades were."

Thirty minutes later, Ricker could clearly hear the rumbling of heavy motors and clanking treads coming from the city. He glanced at his watch. They only had to hold for another six or seven hours.

He heard what he'd been dreading, the distant thumping of artillery pieces. There were no other German troops nearby, so he knew they were the target. "Cover!" He yelled. He pushed himself inside the covered bunker and looked up at the sandbagged ceiling, wondering how effective it would be against a direct hit from a 105mm Howitzer shell. He thought of his men cowering in foxholes with no overhead cover, and said a prayer for them.

The screeching shells impacted and he felt the ground shudder. Dust and bits of debris rained down from the ceiling. He saw the brilliant flashes of explosions landing behind him; walking down the airfield toward the tower. It was an obvious target and had been abandoned as soon as the air traffic controllers had been cleaned out.

Shells crashed into the airport terminal sending great chunks of concrete and bricks flying in every direction. The bombardment concentrated on the airport buildings. Ricker grinned, knowing they were wasting ammo, the buildings were empty. The paratroopers were forward along the edges of the airport, dug in deep. Despite that, the barrage was still terrifying. When the Americans realized where they were, those guns would adjust and Ricker wasn't looking forward to that.

Finally the bombardment ended. He dusted himself off and left the confines of the covered portion of the bunker. He went to the edge of the wall and gazed into the night. The small fires from the artillery barrage allowed him to see a few meters into the gloom but he still couldn't easily see his men. That was good, the Americans wouldn't be able to see them either.

The sound of clanking tank treads and revving motors increased. They sounded close. Ricker tried to slow his breathing. He called inside the bunker, "Stay near me, Hinkler. I may need the radio in a hurry."

As if in answer, Hinkler put his hand to his ear, steadying the earpiece. "Sir, Sergeant Faulk reports a large force of enemy armor and troops advancing toward his position. He wants to blow the buildings."

Ricker moved quickly inside the bunker and took the headset and mic, "Fire when ready, Sergeant."

The reply came with a flash in the night. The sound was muted, much different from the artillery explosions. Ricker could see the outline of at least two tanks against the backdrop of the flashes. The sound intensified as a building on this side of the road crumbled and all ten stories fell like a large tree in the forest. Even though it was dark, Ricker could see the dust spreading toward the airport. It would overtake and consume the enemy troops, choking them with dust and debris, blocking their advance. His men would be hunkered low, waiting.

The rumble swept over their lines, shaking the ground. Ricker smelled the dust, but it settled before reaching the airport. Some of his men, Sergeant Faulk's squad, were certainly within the dust cloud.

The night grew silent as the dust settled. Then there was yelling, followed immediately with small arms fire. Ricker heard the whoosh of a Panzerfaust firing its armor piercing grenade. There was a flash of yellow, which lit up the dust and darkness. More mini-explosions as more Panzerfausts fired their deadly projectiles into the stalled armor.

An MG42 fired and Ricker watched the tracers reaching out toward the tanks and troops. Shots ricocheted and shot high into the sky and the light-show was like a fireworks display.

A tank fired, sending orange and yellow gouging flame from its barrel. The flash lit up the road and he saw more tanks and soldiers. Another machine-gun opened up from the other side of the road and Ricker knew it was Fourth Squad getting into the action. The attackers were caught in a crossfire, half their force caught inside the city, forward progress blocked by the destroyed building, unable to help their cut-off comrades. Ricker grinned, the plan was working perfectly.

He yelled to his radioman, "Fire the mortars."

Corporal Hinkler quickly relayed the orders and soon the popping of mortars stationed near the AA guns added to the carnage raining down upon the Americans.

Ricker watched the mortars exploding among the tanks and men. Flashes of light revealed men running, diving and dying. Tracer fire ripped into their ranks, giving no quarter. The return fire stopped a minute later and the well-trained Fallschirmjäger ceased fire all along the line.

Ricker surveyed the battlefield. Three tanks burned, the flames lighting up two smoldering halftracks. Even from this distance he could see men draped over the sides, unmoving. There was the occasional popping as ammunition cooked off inside the burning vehicles. The smell of burnt rubber mixed with flesh wafted over him.

Cpl. Hinkler stiffened, taking a report. He nodded, signed off and relayed the message. "Sir, Sergeant Faulk reports lead enemy element completely destroyed. No friendly casualties."

Ricker was ebullient and couldn't keep the smile off his face. "Tell him job well done and to hold position."

————

THE HIGH FROM beating back the enemy counterattack waned and Ricker felt the day and night's action catching up with him. His eyes felt heavy and he bit his lip until it bled in an effort to stay awake. Major Spitz wanted everyone on high alert, expecting the American force behind the rubble to attack at some point before dawn.

To keep them on their toes, the major ordered the heavy weapons platoon to fire harassing mortar fire beyond the rubble at random intervals.

An hour after the first attack the sound of more artillery shells filled the air and Ricker once again hunkered in his bunker. This time, the shells landed among the foxholes and bunkers of his men.

Ricker curled into the fetal position as the ground shook beneath him. He thought the earth would crack and they'd all fall into a crevasse and never be heard from again. It seemed to go on for hours but when it finally stopped and he wiped the dirt and grime off his watch-face, he was stunned to see only ten minutes had passed.

He shook himself and stumbled out of the bunker. The normally sheer sides of the trench beside the bunker were sloped from the mini-avalanches the barrage caused. In order to see over, Ricker had to crawl his way to the top.

The loamy smell reminded him of trips to the country with his famous father as they drove past fresh-tilled fields. The thought made him wonder how his father and more importantly, his brothers were doing. Hans and Sebastian were tankers and, if all was going according to plan, would lead their Panzer Company's ashore in the morning. He wondered how it would be to see them. Would they look at their grimy little brother with pride or disgust? He was the black sheep of the family, the only Rommel to eschew the Panzer Corps.

His thoughts returned to the present when the night suddenly flared into artificial daylight. Multiple flares floated beneath white parachutes, lighting up the churned-up ground. There were rifle cracks and Ricker felt a hammer blow against his head. He was flung backwards and his helmet flew off, hitting the back wall.

Two paratroopers were immediately upon him. "Sir! Sir, are you all right?" Ricker was dazed and couldn't seem to focus. "Get the medic," he heard one of them say. His vision tunneled and he struggled to stay conscious, unsure what was happening to him. He felt suddenly nauseous and couldn't keep the vomit from coming up. He leaned forward and spewed onto the mud. It helped him focus and he felt the tunnel widening. Sound suddenly returned like a record going from ultra-slow to regular speed.

He felt hands on his shoulders pushing him back. He tried to fight, to stay upright but the hands were persistent and he succumbed and lay on his back. He watched lit-up clouds skittering by overhead and wondered how it was possible for the sun to be up when it should still be night.

Something pungent and strong cleared his head. He pushed whatever he was smelling away and sat up and shook his head. He looked at the concerned faces huddled around him and asked, "Wh—what happened?"

Private Heinz filled him in, "Sniper. They moved snipers up and when the flares ignited, fired. You got your head creased by a near miss." He held up a helmet. There was a long crease just over the ear. "You'll need a new helmet, sir."

Ricker felt sick again, knowing how close he'd come to dying, but managed to keep the bile down. "Did, did anyone else get hit?"

Heinz lowered his eyes and nodded. "Second Squad lost three men. Sergeant Faulk, Privates Ramsey and Clausman."

The news stunned him. Those were his men. He'd put them out there on the outskirts in harm's way. His head suddenly throbbed with an oncoming, crushing headache. He murmured under his breath, "Should've brought them in closer."

The medic, Corporal Steinway touched his head with something wet and cold. Ricker smelled the alcohol and felt the sting but kept still, the pain a reminder of his failure. Steinway finished cleaning the wound, placed a bandage over it and wrapped a strip of gauze to secure it. "You may have a concussion, but your wound's not bad. How do you feel? Remember everything?"

Ricker nodded. "I'm fine. A little fuzzy, but I remember everything, yes." He looked around the trench. "Get me Sergeant Hoch. I need a report."

Thirty seconds later Sergeant Hoch appeared and looked concerned. "You all right, sir?"

Ricker waved his hand like shooing a fly. "It's nothing. What's happening?"

Hoch looked to the medic who gave him a nod, telling him Ricker wasn't lying. "Those snipers hit us hard. Three men from the second squad including Sergeant Faulk, were killed. Private Loski took one in the shoulder, he's out of it, on morphine." He licked his lips and pushed his helmet brim up. "Nothing since, but I'll wager they'll attack before dawn." He looked at his wrist watch, "Which is only an hour away."

Ricker nodded. "Pull the rest of Second Squad back to the main-line. Move the MG42s to their alternate positions. Make sure everyone has plenty of ammo and water."

Hoch nodded, "Yes, sir. Already done."

Ricker focused on his Platoon Sergeant and realized he must've passed out for a bit. "Thank you, Sergeant."

Hoch grinned, "If they come again, we'll be ready, sir."

———

THE SKY WAS JUST BEGINNING to lighten when the morning calm and cold was broken with the thumps then crashes of accurate mortar fire.

Ricker, still a little hazy, leaped up and pushed himself to the lip of the embankment and pressed binoculars to his eyes. Private Heinz tugged at his coat, "Careful sir, that's where they got you from last time."

Ricker nodded and slid down. Corporal Hinkler called from the bunker. "Sir, the major says there's motorized units coming around the sides of the rubble. Not tanks but smaller halftracks and jeeps with mounted machine guns."

Ricker ignored Heinz' advice and went up on the lip again. He saw exhaust plumes coming from the alleys and narrow roads. The Americans were trying to displace them with an end-around run with light, fast armored troops while the mortars kept their heads down. He shouted, "Get word to shift fire right."

He heard Hinkler relaying the message over the finicky handheld radios. He glanced behind at the 20mm AA guns, their ominous four barrels aiming down the main road. They hadn't been needed yet, but that was about to change. "Heinz, get back to the AA guns. Tell them to slew right, the American armor's coming from the right. Hurry!" He shoved him and Heinz ran over the back wall and disappeared into the gloom of early morning. Four paratroopers, all privates, looked at him waiting for orders. He waved them to follow. "Come on, we'll move right. Bring those Panzerfausts." As he ran past the radioman. He tapped his shoulder, "Come on and grab your weapon, we'll need everyone on this one."

Hinkler got to his feet, slung his rifle and grabbed two of the hand-held radios. He hustled after the others, his Mauser rifle banging painfully against his back with every stride.

Ricker ran over open ground, his MP-40 at the ready. Mortar shells erupted along the main road where most of his platoon was dug-in, but he stayed as low as possible and kept running. He glanced right and could see the outlines of the AA gun against the lightening eastern horizon. He stopped when he was halfway between two of them. There was ditch and partially destroyed chain-link fence, which separated the airport property from a frontage road.

He slid into the ditch and the five Fallschirmjägers followed suit and spread out. Two men held Panzerfausts. "Get the Panzerfausts to either flank." The men nodded and spread to the ends of the line.

Private Heinz joined them and between breaths said, "I alerted the AA crews. They're ready."

"Good. They're our best chance to knock the armor out, along with the Panzerfausts, but we only have two of those. Let them get close. Fire on my command."

The men hunkered and soon all they heard was the unmistakable sound of revving engines and heavy tracks tearing up ground. The mortar fire stopped and there was a smattering of small arms fire from the road. Ricker wondered if this was a two-pronged attack. If it was, he and his small crew would be badly exposed.

He lifted his head and saw three armored halftracks and two Jeeps coming straight at them. He looked right and got the attention of his

Panzerfaust trooper, who was hunched, ready to go to his knees and fire. He assumed the other soldier would also be looking. Ricker held up his hand slowly. He noticed enemy soldiers on foot, trying to keep up, but the initial targets were the armor.

When they were 30 meters away, he dropped his hand. He watched Private Schmidt rise up onto a knee. He aimed the unwieldy weapon and depressed the top bar. The armor piercing grenade shot out and arced into the grill of the nearest halftrack and exploded. The vehicle slewed hard left and nearly flipped over, sending GIs sprawling out the back and over the side.

The second grenade shot out and slammed into the ground beside another tracked vehicle and sprayed the armor with dirt and shrapnel. The halftrack continued forward, the .50 caliber machine gun poking from the top fired a long burst and before the paratrooper could take cover, was nearly cut in half by the massive shells.

Ricker pushed forward and fired his MP-40 at the nearest Jeep. His bullets sparked and ricocheted off the metal and the driver pulled right and accelerated, kicking up dirt behind the knobby tires. The gunner holding onto the .30 caliber machine gun handles nearly fell out the back but managed to stay in. He fired, but the bouncing Jeep threw his aim off and bullets sprayed everywhere.

Two paratroopers hurled stick grenades, knocking foot soldiers to the ground. Ricker fired the rest of his 30-round magazine, then dove as the .50 caliber half track gunner swept his position. He felt the heat of the heavy bullets passing close and he nearly lost control of his bowels. He admonished himself thinking what a disgrace that would be for his brothers to see.

He rolled right until he came up alongside another paratrooper. He was firing a Mauser rifle and Ricker recognized his radioman. "Raise the AA gunners. Tell them to engage!"

As if in answer the heavy 20mm AA guns opened fire. Ricker knew the heavy shells were firing just over their heads, probably the reason they hadn't fired yet. He yelled at the top of his lungs, "Stay down!" No one needed coaxing; the sizzle of the passing shells were close enough to touch.

The effect was devastating. Even from the bottom of the ditch,

Ricker heard the terrible crash the shells made as they impacted the thin metal of the halftracks and jeeps. An explosion shook the ground only meters away and Ricker imagined either a gas tank or ammunition blowing up. The heat washed over his back and he tried to dig into the hard ground.

Something landed on his back. He had the distinct feeling it was a person. It rolled off his right side and he kicked at it like it was infected with the plague. In the dim, early morning light, he saw the dull olive drab of an enemy soldier. He lunged, pulling the knife from the sheath at the same time. He sank the blade into the soldier's back. There was no reaction. The sickening feel of blood seeping over his hand nearly made him gag. He pushed the soldier and he rolled onto his back. There was a gaping, smoking hole in his chest. He was already dead, his eyes staring and lifeless.

The firing from the AA guns stopped and Ricker pushed himself up slightly and looked over the edge. The scene stunned him. The field was littered with bodies and smoking, burning vehicles. One of the halftracks was on its side. He could see legs and torsos of soldiers sticking from beneath the armor and he hoped they'd been dead before their bodies were crushed, but from some of their facial expressions, he doubted it.

He had his weapon up and ready but he couldn't see anyone alive. The sun's rays hit his back and he looked east. There were clouds making the sunrise a beautiful shade of orange. The smell of blood, burning flesh and burnt gunpowder mixed and he thought the colors in the sunrise would never look the same. They'd always remind him of this day's carnage and death.

More paratroopers got to their knees, their stunned expressions telling him they were as surprised to be alive as he was. He exchanged a glance with Corporal Hinkler. Ricker noticed not everyone was getting up. He walked along the ditch and came across Private Heinz. At first, he thought he was still taking cover. He was curled into a tight ball but when Ricker touched his shoulder, he toppled over and his face was gray. There was a large pool of sticky blood stringing from the ground to his belly, mixed with the pale gray of intestines. Ricker stared, unable to turn away.

Someone yelled and he tore himself from the grisly scene. "Here they come! Here comes the armor." At first, he thought it another enemy attack, but the voice was excited, not fearful.

He turned toward the sea and in the morning light saw large, specially designed LSTs disgorging huge friendly tanks. They hit the ground running and were soon tearing up the asphalt as they churned toward their positions. Ricker no longer cared whether his brothers would be proud of him or not. He only felt the heavy burden of the dead paratrooper at his feet. The question played over and over in his head, *what could I have done differently?*

———

AN HOUR later the tanks were dug into pits, with only their long barrels visible. Along with the armor, a full complement of AA guns were arrayed around the airfield, turning it into a deathtrap for any enemy aircraft venturing into their defensive zone.

Soon after, Stuka dive bombers and fighters with yellow and red painted cowlings landed and were quickly stowed in undamaged bunkers. Engineers driving huge tractors darted here and there repairing tarmac and filling in bomb craters. Within two hours, Idlewild Airport, once a hub of air-traffic for New York City, became a formidable armed German camp.

Ricker smoked a cigarette and watched the airplanes landing in quick succession. They were the mission. Getting aircraft onto the mainland quickly would allow more room on the super-carriers for aircraft shuttling over from England and would keep the Americans from achieving air-superiority once they recovered from the initial blow.

Major Spitz found him and hunched down beside him. Ricker offered him a cigarette and he lit it and took a long drag. "Your men did well today, Lieutenant."

Ricker nodded and said, "Thank you, sir. They're good men. The best."

Spitz nodded his agreement, "This is only the beginning of course, but it's a good start. We'll be a target for a while until our infantry in the South push through. We can expect constant attacks, but we have the might of the fleet at our backs. It's imperative we hold this airfield." He watched a Stuka land softly and taxi off the tarmac. He took another drag and blew it out his nose. "Need anything, Lieutenant?"

Ricker pointed at the remaining buildings of the city. "Can we level those, sir? We get a lot of sniper fire from them, keeps the men jumpy."

Spitz nodded and squinted. "The naval artillery boys have been itching to do just that, but there's still too many other targets. I'll pass along your concerns though, Lieutenant."

"Thank you, sir." Major Spitz stood and hustled away to the next slit trench. Sergeant Hoch emerged and approached. "What'd the major have to say, sir?"

He shrugged, "Just letting us know, now we've taken the airfield we've got a huge bullseye on our chests."

Hoch grinned and spit, "No shit, sir."

18

MaryAnn sat on the floor of a bare, white padded room. She was naked and despite the pleasant temperature, she shivered uncontrollably. She rocked back and forth slightly, her arms draped over her pulled up knees. Despite the lack of windows, she had the distinct feeling she was being watched. She supposed by the alien Korth. She'd seen a number of them since being captured, but the sight still repulsed and terrified her and she was glad she couldn't see them gawking.

As though reading her mind, a door appeared in the wall, and in stepped four humans dressed head-to-toe in white frocks. She couldn't see anything except their eyes. She guessed, by the tight skull caps, they'd had their head's shaved, but despite the lack of features she could tell they were females.

Between them they pushed a slab of thick, chrome metal. It floated between them and they guided it forward. MaryAnn got to her feet and slunk away into the farthest corner. The four humans placed the floating table in the center of the room and pushed it down until it was only a few feet off the ground.

MaryAnn looked at the open door behind and the thought of escape flashed through her mind. As if in response, a thin blue arc lanced out and before MaryAnn could react, touched her. She felt her body stiffen and no matter what she did, she couldn't make her body move. The feeling terrified her and she began to hyperventilate. She felt herself being lifted and pulled toward the table, floating. Her eyes were wide, but she found she still had control over them. She glanced sideways as much as she could, hoping to catch a glance of the humans. Perhaps they'd take pity on her and help her, but they kept their eyes down, not daring to return her gaze.

Once beside the table, she felt her body being tilted backwards, as though she were being rotated on a stiff board. Her mind screamed at her, the sensation so foreign and unnerving, she thought she might wet herself. When she was flat she stared at the white ceiling and felt herself sliding over the top of the metal table, then lowered until she felt tiny pinpricks against her back.

The blue arc, which held her, disappeared and was replaced with hundreds of much smaller arcs. Each felt like a tiny poke of pressure. It wasn't a bad feeling and soon she realized she was very comfortable, as though lying on the most perfect form-fitting bed ever devised. She relaxed slightly until her mind woke and screamed, 'this is what they want you to feel...fight it.' With a great force of will, she tensed her muscles, flexing and feeling each limb. She was still 'strapped' down, but the feeling of helplessness wasn't as intense.

She felt the four women move to each corner and slowly walk forward, pushing the table along smoothly. She concentrated on the backs of the two women's heads she could see. They never looked back, just kept perfect cadence and posture.

Once out the door, she entered a much larger room. The ceiling was covered in glowing tubes and odd disk-like structures, which spun and emitted blue light, similar to the arc she'd been frozen with.

She studied the ceiling hoping to see something which might help her escape or at least resist. The thought of suicide crossed her mind, it might be better to die than to suffer whatever the Korth had in mind for her. But she was helpless and couldn't move. She shunned the thought to the far reaches of her mind, but didn't discount it wholly.

She felt a presence enter the room and the four women noiselessly scattered. MaryAnn's skin crawled as she heard the clicking and humming and the alien words translated in her mind, "Hello again, MaryAnn Larkin." MaryAnn felt something loosen and realized she could talk. She didn't respond, just continued to stare at the ceiling. The clicking and humming continued. "My name is Cinter. I am interested in helping you. Would you like me to help you?"

MaryAnn considered staying silent, perhaps they'd think her mute and do away with her quickly. But instead she spoke, "You can help me by letting me go."

An odd higher pitched humming, which the translator didn't translate. MaryAnn realized she must be hearing the Korth laugh. *If they laugh, perhaps they have empathy,* she thought hopefully.

The clicks changed and MaryAnn listened to Cinter speak. "I and the other TRs see great promise in your species. We have tried on many occasions to unlock, or unleash, that potential but every attempt has ended in failure. That's not to say the process wasn't successful, but the final result was not what we intended." MaryAnn heard a tapping on the floor as though from an eagle's talon. She realized in disgust she must be hearing the tapping of the Korth's feet as it paced. She tried to move her eyes to better see the Korth but she could only see the top of the thing's head. It was smooth, shiny and reminded her of snake skin.

The alien stopped walking and the tapping stopped. The metal slab lowered, allowing MaryAnn to see the Korth's upper torso and face. She couldn't move but her body repulsed at the sight of the mandibles and black eyes. Cinter continued, "Indeed we've had some promising candidates. The last one, a soldier from your Army, made it through the unleashing process and nearly came out unscathed, but in the end, his mind wasn't deep enough and he fell into insanity, just like all the others that made it that far."

MaryAnn cringed at the prospect of whatever this 'unleashing' entailed. She had no doubt she was the next Guinea Pig, the next to go insane. She asked, "What do you do with these 'candidates,' as you call them, once you're done with them?"

Cinter answered quickly, "We exterminate them, of course. They become dangers to themselves and everyone around them."

"You should just kill me now. I don't want to be unleashed." She tried to stay strong, but there was a quavering in her voice.

Cinter paused and her unblinking eyes stared. MaryAnn held their gaze. Finally Cinter replied, "A successful unleashing will make you something outstanding. Something your species may never achieve. Your brains are destined to become unleashed, the base is there, but only if you don't destroy one another first.

"Most species have already achieved it, or if they haven't, are extinct. Yours is the first we've come across who have existed this long without it happening. The long span of time has made your brains highly attune to being unleashed, but instead you're overwhelmed by the desire for procreation."

MaryAnn didn't want to listen, didn't want to hear and feel the disgusting being talk, but she couldn't help herself. "Why are you telling me this? Why not just do it and when it fails and I go insane, kill me?"

"I'm telling you because knowing what I'm trying to achieve might help your brain accept it better. It is my hope. Your brain is by far the deepest I've come across. I want this to work. I want to free you from your leashed mind, MaryAnn Larkin."

"Even if it kills me?"

"Yes, of course."

"Why? Why would you care to unleash me or any other human? You've brought war to my country. You and those that follow you are my enemy. We're at war, so why *help* me as you call it?"

"I'm a scientist." MaryAnn saw the Korth's head deflate slightly and pinkish hue changed to a drab brown. "Now, hold still and accept what is happening to you. The more strength you save the better the outcome."

MaryAnn felt the metal slab rising and soon she couldn't see Cinter anymore. She shut her eyes and tried to prepare herself for whatever was about to happen. Her eyes flashed open when the most intense pain she'd ever experienced coursed through her rigid body.

———

MARYANN LOST all track of time. Her world was one of intense and constant pain. She felt as though her entire life consisted only of pain. There'd never been a happy home in a small town in Oregon. Never been a time she awoke to the smell of fresh baked bread and felt the warmth from the old wood stove on a cold winter morning. Never had been a loving mother and father and good friends. Her entire world was now—only pain.

It sent her mind into a new space, a dark and deep space she never knew existed. She could still feel the pain nibbling at the edges but she'd entered a segment of her mind which buffered the pain and protected her from it. It became like an annoying, barking dog. She could hear it but it was in another backyard locked in a kennel where it couldn't bite her.

She moved through the space and with each new step the depth increased until she felt herself walking through an endless and massive space without borders or end. And then she was floating. She spread her arms and soared. The feeling of flight a thousand times better than anything she'd ever felt. The darkness lightened and she saw a pinprick of light, like a tiny tear in the expanse of nothingness. She angled for it with a tiny twitch of thought and moved toward the beam of light.

There was no airflow, but the feeling of moving through space was real and she knew she was getting closer with every second. She shook her head, not seconds, for there was no time…only space.

The shaft of light held weight, she floated beside it, knowing if she reached for it she'd feel the weight. She looked at its source, the tear hadn't expanded. She followed its cylindrical path, it spread to infinity. In her head a voice implored, 'touch the light.' She looked around not knowing where the voice came from but recognizing it somehow, from somewhere long before, like a memory of birth. *This is death,* she thought.

The voice again, 'no. This is *life.*'

MaryAnn allowed herself to descend into the beam of light and when it touched her she marveled as her skin tingled and sparkled. The feeling was wholly new and her sense of timelessness disappeared and she was flying along the cylinder's path, back toward the hole.

The feeling of speed as colors and shapes flashed by was surreal, but she felt no fear. The barking dog in the kennel was gone. There was no pain, nor a memory of pain. Her body felt as though it were made of pure light.

She rolled and darted through the hole, feeling the edges ripple as she passed. She looked back and the vastness of space closed like a door to another dimension, one she knew she could find simply by thinking of it.

She stopped and floated, looking down on the vessel which was her body. It's nakedness held fast with beams of energy, whose molecular structure scrolled past her mind like an afterthought.

The eyes, the beautiful blue eyes were open and staring up at her own consciousness. There was a glimmer of mischief she delighted in. She leaned forward and entered this body, this vessel which fit so well, so perfectly formed for her unleashed consciousness.

MaryAnn sat up, the energy arcs disabled with a thought. She was inside the bare padded room again. She noticed a quivering presence, another human, shaking and exuding so much fear, it made MaryAnn worry for the poor thing's heart, but a quick thought put her mind at ease. She was a healthy, although leashed human.

MaryAnn hopped off the metal slab and landed lightly on her feet. There was a knocking, as though someone, or something, was trying to enter her mind. She blocked it easily, not wanting the intruder, more interested in quelling the woman's fear.

She walked to her, exuding calmness to the woman like wafting smoke from incense. The woman immediately looked at MaryAnn and smiled. The relief, the fear leaving and being replaced with hope and love, strengthened MaryAnn, as though a drop helping to fill a vast ocean. She touched the woman's arm and she felt her soul. It was beautiful, yet scarred.

The metal slab flipped upright suddenly and started to spin. MaryAnn looked at it, seeing the molecules coalescing to harm her body. Energy lanced out aiming for her heart, but it seemed to happen in slow motion. She easily avoided the sluggish movement, stepping aside and watching the energy miss. More were snaking her way, but like the first she easily avoided the blasts. She saw the human being targeted and moved her out of the way easily. The woman looked star-tled, but her touch calmed her.

MaryAnn deconstructed the arc molecules and reformed them, making them benign. The table stopped spinning and the arcs of energy fizzed and sparked and faded like a child acting out and being put in a corner.

She felt another presence outside the walls. She looked through and saw three Korth. Their heads were flat and black as night. One held a weapon of considerable power. She could sense the weapon was tapped into the power emanating from the ship they were on.

The Korth clicked and hummed and MaryAnn felt the translator in her neck trying to work, she expelled it from her body with a simple thought and answered the Korth, who she could understand perfectly well without it. "Yes, it worked. Thank you."

———

TR CINTER and Gruncy watched in fascination mixed with horror as the human known as MaryAnn Larkin, expelled the embedded trans-lator as though it were a child's toy. The wound in her neck quickly healed and sealed, leaving no sign it had ever been there.

Cinter had activated MaryAnn's termination after he tried to enter the human's consciousness and been summarily rebuffed. If MaryAnn could so easily keep her out, the unleashing had worked too well, making her more powerful than even the TRs.

It was a possibility he knew existed but didn't think would actually happen. Watching MaryAnn move with unimaginable speed as the energy arcs reached for her and missed, told Cinter everything he needed to know. The human was powerful and most definitely a threat that need to be squashed or contained.

Despite the attack though, the human wasn't exhibiting danger or animosity, quite the opposite in fact. She was emitting only goodwill and Cinter wondered if perhaps her memory had been erased and she had no recollection they were enemies.

Cinter returned MaryAnn's steady gaze. The human hadn't tried probing her mind, but he didn't want it to get that far. He needed to get control of the situation before MaryAnn decided the Korth were threats and needed to be eliminated.

The doorway in the wall opened without it being activated and Private Trokon lowered his weapon and aimed at the human who gave him a disarming smirk, as though he were a child holding a bath toy, instead of a hardened Korth warrior holding a laz-blaster.

The TRs signaled each other and meshed their brains into a powerful meld but before they could force control over MaryAnn, she spoke. "Don't." She held up her hand and shook her head slightly.

The TRs kept their minds melded but Cinter halted hostile action. Gruncy wanted to continue but Cinter was more powerful and arrested her aggression. She spoke to MaryAnn. "The unleashing worked. You are the first of your kind. Congratulations, MaryAnn Larkin."

MaryAnn considered her words and shook her head. "I am not the first. There was another unleashing. I can sense it. They left this world millennia ago and I cannot track where they went. Far, far away." She looked wistfully beyond, then her blue eyes refocused on the Korth. "I feel reborn. Although I know there was another life before this, it seems distant and difficult to see, even so near."

Cinter nodded, "We have unleashed you. We are your benefactors responsible for your new life of enlightenment." Two of Cinter's arms extended to Gruncy and Trokon. "Us and every Korth."

MaryAnn nodded and stepped through the doorway, pulling the human orderly along with her. The orderly never took her eyes from MaryAnn as though she were witnessing the coming of the Messiah. It made Cinter wonder, not for the first time, if perhaps the religious figures they fawned over were actually unleashed humans. All the goodwill and light pouring from MaryAnn certainly increased her suspicions.

Cinter said, "We'll get you some clothes."

MaryAnn shrugged, "I've no need, I have control of my body, but it's the norm to be clothed, so yes."

Cinter tweaked Trokon's brain to get him to move. He grunted and reluctantly lowered his weapon and went to gather clothes. The doorway leading to the hall opened and in stepped six more TRs. They moved quickly beside Gruncy and Cinter and their minds were soon melded to one another in a tight, strong mesh.

MaryAnn dressed and looked the new arrivals over. She continued to exude goodwill and light. Cinter clicked and hummed. "We need to study you, MaryAnn. Thank you." All eight reached out and pried into MaryAnn's consciousness.

MaryAnn felt the unwanted presence but was unable to turn them away. They were too powerful together. She pushed back and felt pain. The memory of which assaulted her senses and forced her back. Forced her to retreat. The TRs completed their encirclement and closed her inside her own mind.

MaryAnn didn't like the feeling of being trapped. The memory of pain made her seek her old memories. She accessed them like a movie. The Korth, she used to call them Scalps, her benefactors were actually not her friends, that much was clear.

19

R   ex was stuffed and could hardly move. After his fate was decided, there was a huge feast celebrating Joe's return to the village. Rex danced, ate and drank. It was an awful concoction that burned his throat but made him feel good. The more he drank the better he felt, but now he was suffering. He felt as though a group of tribesmen were pounding his head like the drums they never stopped drumming.

He must've slept, for now it was light. The great hall was littered with other party-goers some sleeping, some cleaning and he was pretty sure there was a couple in the corner, screwing.

He stepped outside and squinted. He covered his eyes. He'd slept much longer than he thought, the sun was straight overhead and the blistering heat nearly sent him to his knees.

He stumbled his way toward the hut he'd been imprisoned in, wanting to lay on the dirt floor and sleep without interruption, but Joe was suddenly beside him slapping his shoulder with his huge hand. He seemed to be fully recovered from the past few days. "You're finally awake! Thought you might sleep the week away. Come, there's much to do. You must have questions."

Rex had no idea how he could be so chipper. He'd drank as much of the vile stuff as he had, yet he didn't seem to be hung over at all. Rex answered haltingly, "Yes, yes of course, only I don't feel well. I need to piss and probably throw up."

Joe laughed uproariously, throwing his head back. He slapped his back again and Rex thought he should've killed him when he had the chance. "Go piss and throw up." He pointed to a likely spot, "Over there. Then I'll accompany you to the oasis for a refreshing swim and bath."

The short ride to the oasis nearly killed him, but he had to admit when he immersed himself in the cool water, he felt one hundred times better. He floated and looked up at the blue sky. The rim of the crater shimmered with heat, but the oasis was 20 degrees cooler, and the water was invigorating and he felt he could stay there forever.

He noticed Talib making his way down the path. Joe greeted him and Rex exited the water and stood naked and dripping. He wrapped himself with his white loose-fitting clothes and joined them beneath a copse of palm trees near the water's edge. He sat on sculpted boulders and leaned into the perfectly shaped rock chairs.

Joe addressed Rex. "You feel better, yes?" Rex nodded emphatically. "Good, good. The waters are said to have healing power, particularly in curing headaches from too much imbibing."

"I would agree with that," said Rex.

Joe opened his arms and said, "Ask your questions, Rex. I'm sure you have many."

Rex nodded, "I guess my first question is: how is it that The Branch doesn't know who you are? As far as they're concerned no one's ever come out of Africa since the aliens. You seem to be a regular here, yet I met you on St. Helena."

Joe grinned, "The Branch doesn't know much and we like to keep it that way. We haven't found them to be overly helpful, so we simply don't tell them things. The Scalps don't pay us much attention down here. They have units placed here and there, but mostly in South Africa. They came through and implanted these, of course," he touched his translator, "but left soon after. As long as we don't cause trouble, they don't bother us. My father sent me away years ago to connect with the outside world, but he didn't want me to tell them where I came from. We didn't want to attract their attention. I lived in St. Helena for many years and was soon considered a local. I met members of The Branch when they'd bring agents through and I'd help them like I helped you.

"Soon they offered to train me in the same way you were and I became an agent myself. That training ended five years ago and as far as The Branch is concerned, I'm strictly used to help with insertions. Yours was the first time I was actually sent onto the continent." He shrugged, "And you are right, I was sent to watch you. They don't trust you completely, but they do respect your skills."

"So this is the first you've been back to your village?"

Joe shook his head and smiled, "No, of course not. I've been back many times but only briefly. I bring weapons mostly, and news."

"And you're not missed? Where do you get the weapons?"

Joe shook his head, "No, I'm careful. They don't know when I leave. As for your second question," he smiled ruefully. "I'll keep that to myself."

"You mentioned a resistance?"

He nodded and looked at his father. Talib nodded slightly giving him the okay to continue. Joe leaned forward, "Our land has changed dramatically since the Korth arrived. This area used to be lush. This oasis was one of many. Wildlife everywhere eating fields of green grass." He shook his head, "Now it's a desert wasteland."

"What happened? What's changed?"

Joe shrugged, "The Korth arrived. My father wanted to know the answers too. He and a group of warriors traveled north. The Korth don't allow open travel, so they were careful and moved slow. Like I said they don't come down here much.

"The further north they went the more changes they found. Once thriving towns were either completely gone, or well on their way to being so. My father described walking ghosts, like they'd had their skin blanched gray. Hair loss, wasting away, sick all the time and death, lots of death. He inquired, asking old friends for information. They told him many people had been taken north by soldiers. None of them returned. He heard about some kind of massive project. He didn't venture farther, but he was convinced there was something going on and it was being caused by the Korth. So, he carefully gathered trusted friends and has put together a resistance of sorts.

"Extracting the translators was the first thing they achieved, making it so they can take them out and insert them when they suspect Korth are nearby. That one act led them to realize something; the translators aren't *only* translators. They also have an effect on the brain. My father and others immediately felt more like themselves, clearer. They were convinced the devices were controlling them, keeping them dumbed down, but it happened so slowly they never noticed until they were removed."

Rex nodded and rubbed his chin. "You mentioned weapons? Are you planning some sort of operation? I mean what can you possibly achieve faced with such an enemy?"

Joe nodded slowly and looked at his father. Talib spoke in his deep baritone, "They are not as invincible as you think. The Korth are strong but they underestimate us."

Rex asked, "And what about the millions of people they command? Armies, Navies, indeed we've seen their ability to wage war first-hand."

Joe looked at his father who nodded allowing him to proceed. Joe said, "The only way we'll succeed in kicking the Korth out and regaining our freedom is to convince the rest of humanity that the Korth are not here to help us. Whatever they are doing is killing the earth. The only way to defeat them is if all humanity rises up to oppose them. There's no other way."

Rex nodded and considered his words. "So your plan is to expose whatever it is they're doing. Do you have a plan for doing so?"

"Before we tell you anymore, we need to know where you stand. You said you wanted to make your way back to America, to your wife and son. If that is what you want to do, we will not stand in your way, but we will part ways here and now."

Rex had a strong sense that if he didn't choose correctly, he might already know too much. Joe was trained the same way he was, if roles were reversed, Rex knew he'd be considering whether or not to kill Joe. He eyed Joe who's bloodshot eyes looked back menacingly. "The cadre didn't teach you this way, Joe."

Joe smiled but it didn't make it to his eyes. "I was trained the same as you, but like you, I still control my own mind. You and I are different from other Branch agents, I think."

"Hmm, I wonder. What became of the other agents sent here? I know of at least five. Did you let them walk away, or are they a part of this?"

"I told you, you were the first I accompanied to shore. The others I helped insert but did not follow."

"You must've warned your father of their coming? Did you kill them then?" he asked Talib.

Rex wondered if he'd offended the old leader, but thought there was no point pussy-footing around the subject. His own life was at stake, he was certain of it. Talib took time to answer and finally said, "No, I did not, but I doubt any are still alive. They went in various directions and have not been heard from since."

Joe chimed in, "None were told of the resistance or the plan to expose the Korth."

"Then why tell me?"

"Like I said, you and I are different. You are the only agent who is not here to mindlessly do the bidding of The Branch. You attacked me, against orders. Not the usual protocol taught by the cadre." He looked hard at Rex. "Now it is time for you to decide, Rex."

Rex looked over the sparkling water. A light breeze rippled the surface and he thought it might be the prettiest spot he'd ever seen. A soon to be wasteland, if these men were to be believed. He pursed his lips and nodded. "The shock of me returning to my doorstep might give poor Miriam a heart-attack. Or she could be shacked up with another guy by now." He tried to grin and chuckle but it was forced.

Joe nodded, "If we survive, there will be time to return home."

Rex shook his head. "It was a pipe-dream. I'll join your resistance. If you'll have me."

Joe smiled and extended his hand. "It will be good to work with you again, Rex."

———

REX STOOD at the bottom of a hidden flight of stairs beneath the floor of a mud-hut. Joe waved him forward and the smell of well-oiled metal wafted from the cellar. Joe hit a switch and a string of lights lit up a long corridor. Along each side was every weapon Rex had ever seen. There was everything from pistols to hand grenades to bazookas.

His mouth fell open and he gasped, "Holy shit." He walked along, running his hands along the smooth, metal barrels and polished wood stocks. He hefted a German StG44. "These are hard to come by. German design. How'd you do it?"

Joe smiled pleased with Rex's stunned reaction. "Like I said before, I'll keep that secret. But rest assured, these weapons are all in perfect working order and my people have been trained how to use them."

Rex nodded but turned toward him, concern on his face. "But this isn't the plan. I mean perhaps these will be useful in an uprising, but not now."

Joe nodded and guided him back up the stairs. "Yes, you're correct. I just wanted you to see them in case you were questioning our resolve or resources."

"So, what is the plan?"

Joe closed the hatch in the floor and latched it. The borders fit perfectly in the grooves making the lines nearly impossible to see. He spread an old ragged rug over the floor and stood to his full height. "Remember how my father told you of all the people transported away, presumably to work on the secret project?"

Rex nodded and when Joe stopped talking, put the rest together. "You and I are going to be on the next transport north?"

Joe grinned and nodded. "Exactly. We'll let them take us to the project. No need to waste time sneaking around looking suspicious. Once we're inside, we'll see what's happening and we can escape, hopefully with evidence, and come back here."

Rex grinned and spread his hands out as if entertaining a child. "Easy." His grin changed and he shook his head. "Thought you said no one's ever been seen again and what about all the sick and dying people? If that's from the project, what makes you think we won't be affected? That's not a plan. That's suicide."

Joe shook his head. "No, we are different. For one thing our translators won't make us docile and subservient. And we're highly trained operatives, they've never seen anything like us. We'll fight our way out if we have to."

"Hmm, wish I shared your optimism."

"You'll see, it'll work out fine."

———

JOE AND REX left the village after a robust send-off party. They rode camels, moving slow, not wanting to draw attention to themselves. Travelers were common in this region, however the practice was shunned. So, they moved slow and avoided the bigger population densities. Rex saw first-hand how the land and the people changed the further north they went. The scrub grass and occasional oases around Joe's village made it seem like the most lush and vibrant place in Africa, compared to land they traveled through now.

There were no more borders per se, but Joe noted after two weeks of riding that they were in the country of Niger. Before the Korth, the area was hard desert and not much else. It was still that way, however the towns and villages were nearly all empty and the people that remained were thin and sickly.

"They suffer not just from hunger, for that has always been a problem here, but from the sickness," Joe said. He sniffed the hot air and scowled, "You can almost smell it."

Rex nodded, but kept his shroud over his head and face. "I've noticed it. I suppose whatever it is will kill us too."

"It's a slow process from what we've seen, but yes, eventually. It's why we must find the roundups soon."

"There aren't many people left here. Perhaps they've already taken everyone."

"The patrols travel far and they all lead to that town." They sat upon a high escarpment of rock and sand looking out over the shimmering expanse of Niger, spreading toward Libya. "See it? It's where the patrols take their charges. We'll go there and await the next caravan."

A few hours later, right at midday, they entered the town. It was far busier than any town they'd seen in days. There were open markets filled with haggling sellers and buyers. The people were dressed similarly in off-white robes and all had their faces mostly covered. Joe and Rex fit in seamlessly and no one gave them a second look.

Rex asked, "Why is this town so vibrant? Why is no one sick? What's the difference?"

Joe shifted his chin forward, "That."

Rex looked beyond the hustle and bustle and saw a large building in the distance. It sat upon the highest point in the area. The severe angles and deep insets of the supposed windows made it look angular and menacing. A long snaking dirt road led to the base. The cobalt black of its walls shimmered with heat. Rex shook his head. "And what, pray tell, is that monstrosity and what dolt decided on black in this part of the world? Surely it'll melt."

"It is Korth built. It's where the Army patrols take their charges. The soldiers leave, but the people they bring there, don't."

"So that's the big project? That's where it's happening?"

"We don't know, but it's where countless people have disappeared. We suspect it's the cause of Africa's death." Joe looked at Rex, his bloodshot eyes the only part of him visible. "And it's where we're going."

20

PFC Jimmy Crandall and the rest of the ragtag group of soldiers from the company were asleep inside a bunker near the bridge. They'd been relieved after the battle with the paratroopers and given hot food as a reward for surviving. The food tasted wonderful and every one of the 16 survivors from the bridge defense fell asleep soon after finishing. There'd been no action since stopping the attack and the few hours of sleep felt wonderful.

Jimmy opened his heavy eyelids, stood and stretched. Corporal Grothing stirred at his feet and turned away, continuing to sleep. Jimmy carefully walked between the slumbering soldiers and found the metal back door. He pushed it and it swung open with an awful squeak. There was grumbling from the men and he quickly stepped through and closed it again shutting the afternoon light out.

He adjusted his M1 on his shoulder and covered his squinting eyes to keep the harsh winter sun out. He felt the chill of the wind coming off Chesapeake Bay. His eyes adjusted and he took a short set of stairs out of the connector trench and surveyed the land. The Chesapeake Bay Bridge met the banks of Kent Island 40 yards away. There were GIs manning formidable defenses everywhere he looked. The ground was churned up and muddy from the constant foot traffic and occasional passing vehicle.

He heard the distant rumble of continuous battle to the East and realized it was such a constant, he barely noticed it anymore. There was still the buzzing of aircraft, but the stout AA defenses surrounding the Bay Bridge had discouraged air attacks, at least for the time being. Vehicles and men continued to trundle across the bridge, but the flow had died down to a trickle compared to earlier in the day.

Jimmy walked to the edge of the water and took a long overdue piss. He gazed across the bay trying to make out the other side, but there was a haze and he couldn't see the low flat scrub he knew was there. He zipped up and was about to head back to the bunker to get more sleep, when something caught his attention. He looked south. There was something on the water. He squinted and held his hand up against the sunlight. The mist swirled on the water, sometimes thick and sometimes wispy and light.

He extended his neck forward, there was definitely something there. Boats, lots of boats churning up the bay toward the bridge. The longer he looked the more he saw until the entire bay was filled almost bank to bank. He pulled his rifle from his shoulder and looked around. Had anyone else seen them? And more importantly were they friendly forces or enemy?

The answer came seconds later. A rippling of fire erupted from the lead boats. Jimmy got on his belly as shells arced over his head and slammed into the completely surprised GIs. Explosions rocked the area and Jimmy watched helplessly as men and material were obliterated. A tank, one of the new Pershings, rotated its turret and got a shot off, but a second later blossomed with fire as a shell slammed into the lightly armored rear compartment. Fire and smoke billowed from the hatches.

Jimmy was frozen to the spot, the gunboats were targeting the defense installations, but the roar of shells passing close was terrifying. A machine gun nest, one of only a few facing the bay water, opened fire and raked a nearby boat. Jimmy saw it was an LVT and could see the tops of helmeted enemy soldiers. The bullets sparked against the metal sides and the water around the boat churned and spouted. The machine gun nest was immediately met with withering fire from other LVTs, armed with mounted MG42s, and was put out of commission.

Jimmy saw the bunker he'd just left erupt in fire and smoke and saw chunks of concrete flying off in every direction. He thought of the men inside. Had any survived? Had his full bladder saved his life?

Anger welled in him and he brought the M1 to his shoulder and aimed. He sighted on an enemy gunner, sweeping the banks with deadly fire. He was sideways to Jimmy, exposed. Jimmy pulled the trigger and watched the soldier's head snap and he fell out of sight. The weapon's barrel aimed at the sky. Another soldier quickly took his place and Jimmy fired the rest of his clip and felt satisfaction as that soldier met a similar fate as the first.

He couldn't stay here. He'd be gunned down as soon as they saw him. He sprang to his feet, ran inland a few yards and launched himself into the irrigation ditch running alongside the bay.

He splashed into the frigid water and bullets whizzed and snapped over his head. His head submerged but he quickly got his feet beneath himself and took off running south. The ditch water was waist deep and the muddy bottom made running difficult. Soon he was overheating and breathing hard but he kept churning his legs until he thought his lungs would burst.

He stopped and threw himself along the edge, hiding himself in the tall grasses trying desperately to get control of his breathing. He shook the mud and dirty water off his M1 as best he could and reloaded, hoping the wet and dirty ammo wouldn't jam his weapon.

The sound of battle was intense and close, but by the sound of it, he thought he'd moved past the main push. He crawled up the embankment until he was on top of the ditch trail and lifted his head. The sight took his breath away and he nearly panicked and ran.

The enemy gunboats were against the bridge struts and continued firing their cannons into the defenders. He saw men being cut down everywhere. A few Pershings had managed to turn and were picking off boats with accurate fire, but there were far too few and too many boats. LVTs ran aground and their fronts flopped down spewing men like deadly spawn. The enemy troops ran forward, guns blazing and were making huge inroads into the defenses, which were mostly turned the wrong way.

Forty yards away the nearest LVT churned to the bank and stopped. The front door opened and soldiers spilled out. Their helmets looked different from the Germans he'd seen and he wondered where these soldiers originated from.

He didn't dwell on it long. He positioned himself, brought his weapon to his shoulder from a prone position. He aimed at the first man he saw, someone waving men forward, perhaps an officer. He fired three times in quick succession and saw the man flinch and drop, holding his leg and screaming.

Jimmy pulled the trigger again but nothing happened. He rolled onto his back and pulled the bolt, trying to release the clip, but it was jammed and he couldn't move it. He could see the bent shell casing firmly stuck. "Dammit," he cursed and dropped the weapon.

He rolled back to his belly and looked up. The LVTs continued to disgorge troops and the gunboats continued firing. The defenses had stiffened and there were multiple machine gun nests coupled with tanks and AA guns that managed to turn and get into the fight. The enemy troops were stalled, taking heavy fire.

Jimmy wished he had his sniper rifle, he could do real damage from this spot, but he'd left it inside the smoldering bunker. He looked right, seeing the road paralleling the bay and the ditch. He saw the closest machine gun nest. It was silent, the crew was dead or wounded, but the machine gun, as far as he could tell from this distance looked intact. If he could make it there, he'd be able to lay down lethal fire into the enemy's right flank.

He looked at the momentarily stalled enemy only 30 yards away. They were focused forward, not worried about the deserted area south. They were firing and maneuvering on the rejuvenated defenses, trying to roll them up once and for all.

Jimmy made his choice. He crawled back to the irrigation ditch, slid into its icy waters and climbed the far bank on his belly. He glanced left but no one was paying any attention to him. The terrain was thigh-high grass all the way to the road. The MG nest was on this side of the road, in a sandbagged foxhole. He pushed his way through the grass quickly until he got to the sandbags. He couldn't see inside the hole but there were no signs of life. The .30 caliber machine-gun was aimed toward the sky but looked intact. A wisp of smoke curled from the barrel.

He lunged and rolled over the two layers of sandbags and fell into the hole. No bullets followed him and he took a deep breath and evaluated the position. There were three Bridge Defense Brigade soldiers. Two were obviously dead with seeping, heavy caliber bullet holes in their chests. The third was faced away, and there was caked blood on his coat.

They were in the way of him manning the machine gun, so he pushed them away. He nearly shit himself when the soldier facing away called out in a panicked, scared voice. Jimmy reeled back, clutching instinctively for the knife at his side. The soldier turned wide-eyed and pushed his way up the side of the hole, trying to get away.

Jimmy relaxed his grip on the knife handle and lunged forward before the soldier's screams drew unwanted attention. "Hey, shut the fuck up!" He seethed. "It's okay, I'm on your side." Finally the soldier's darting, wide eyes settled down and he focused on Jimmy who was inches from his face. "You okay? You hit?" The soldier shook his head and let himself relax into the bottom of the hole. "You able to help me with the gun? I need a loader."

The man's eyes once again widened and he shook his head emphatically. "No—No, don't do that. They—they'll kill us. You'll kill us."

Jimmy's eyes turned hard and he seethed, "You got two choices, go out fighting or run like a coward and leave your buddies to die." The soldier shook his head and without a word crawled out the back of the hole and never looked back. Jimmy watched him snake away and whispered to himself, "That didn't go the way I'd hoped."

He checked the machine gun over, it looked okay to him, but he wasn't an expert machine gunner. He wouldn't know if it worked until he pulled the trigger.

Staying low, he lifted the breech and adjusted the ammunition belt snaking from a tipped over ammo can. Everything looked okay to him. He took one last glance behind him and shook his head at the departed soldier. *Probably should follow him.* He grit his teeth and pulled the bolt back, feeling the satisfying tension. He looked over the barrel, lining up a group of completely unsuspecting and exposed enemy soldiers only 40 yards away, getting ready to rush a position. He lined them up, aiming slightly low and pulled the trigger.

The heavy weapon sent .30 caliber bullets into the men who never knew what hit them. They toppled over like bowling pins. Jimmy adjusted his aim and shot up an LVT whose front end had just dropped. The debarking soldiers were met with withering fire. They dropped and those behind tripped and fell trying to get away but were unsuccessful.

Jimmy stopped firing, remembering how easy it was to burn out one of the finicky machine gun barrels. He fired shorter bursts. A group of exposed soldiers leaped up and ran headlong at him, trying for the safety of the irrigation ditch. He swept right to left and they tripped and fell into the grasses. A thin red mist hung over their bodies. The power of the weapon was intoxicating, but soon he noticed the snapping of return fire.

He'd been seen. An explosion to his right made him cover his head and he felt clumps of grass and dirt clods land on his back and legs. The gunboats were firing on him. He wouldn't last long. He coughed and spit out dirt and aimed at more exposed troops and sent a long burst, not caring about burning up the barrel anymore, more interested in taking as many with him as he could. He yelled in triumph as his stream of fire cut men down, cutting a swath through their right flank.

Another explosion in front of the hole obscured his vision and he ducked, releasing the handle and covering his head. The nearby explosion seemed to rob the air of oxygen and he struggled to get a breath. The sandbags rolled onto him and he knew the next few seconds were his last.

There was a booming roar to his right and through the haze of smoke and debris he caught a glimpse of something large and menacing and very close. There was another blast and the shape rocked back on its chassis then clanked forward. Through his shock-wave-addled mind, Jimmy realized it was a Pershing tank and it wasn't alone.

———

JIMMY MARVELED that he was still alive. He looked behind him, there was a line of Pershing tanks on the road, firing into the enemy troops and boats. The constant chatter of the machine guns poking out the angled front glacis and the booming of the 90mm main guns was deafening and tearing holes in the enemy line.

The return fire was stiffening and Jimmy hunkered low in the hole. A tank hull suddenly appeared behind him and the memory of the Alaskan front and being trapped beneath a Russian tank flashed through his mind. He thought of his best friend, Hank, remembering how scared they both were. He didn't want to repeat the experience.

He grabbed a Thompson submachine gun he'd noticed earlier, propped along the wall and rolled out the side of the hole toward the irrigation ditch. It would provide cover and protection from the onslaught of fire. He stayed on his belly, crawling as fast as he could. The Pershing tank, completely unaware of him rolled over the MG nest. It stopped and fired its cannon and Jimmy felt the shockwave pass over him.

He rolled into the ditch and landed on his feet with a splash. He checked the Thompson, it was loaded with a full magazine and seemed to be in working order. He listened to the battle and watched the ditch, the Thompson leveled. It would be a natural avenue for enemy troops to try to get behind the Pershings. He would keep that from happening, at least until his magazine ran out.

The battle continued to rage around him. The sky never stopped dropping debris as the gunboats continued raining shells around the Pershings. Jimmy felt the cold water seeping into his legs and he involuntarily shivered. He couldn't stay in the water much longer, or he'd be too stiff to move. He could only see ten yards in front, before the irrigation ditch made a slight turn. There was a spot of land sticking into the ditch at the corner. It would provide him a dry place out of the water but still give him cover.

On stiff legs he moved toward it. He had to lunge to get his feet unstuck from the sticky mud. Each step was exhausting, but he finally arrived at the corner. He pulled himself up onto the spot of land and hunched. It would work for a while, but he could feel himself sinking slowly, like he was standing on a huge sponge.

He adjusted his body until he was somewhat comfortable, then leaned out to see around the bend. His eyes locked with a soldier only a few yards away. Jimmy reacted quicker and fired the Thompson from the hip. The big .45 caliber bullets slammed the soldier back and Jimmy kept the trigger depressed hitting the soldiers behind the first. They never knew what hit them. He stopped firing when all six were down, slowly floating in expanding pools of blood.

The Thompson's barrel smoked and hissed as water droplets turned to steam. He knew he must be near the end of the magazine. The shock of seeing the soldiers so close had him hyperventilating. He forced himself to calm down, to take deep breaths. He needed another weapon, or more ammo.

He stepped into the water again and his legs were numb. He didn't feel the cold. He trudged through the water, coming to the first soldier. He was facedown and had a gaping hole in his back. Jimmy felt around for the weapon he must've been holding. His foot bumped something solid. He got his foot beneath it and lifted his leg until the stock appeared.

He dropped the Thompson and clutched the enemy weapon, it was an impressive looking submachine gun. He pulled the dead soldier to the bank and turned him over. His eyes were open and milky. He searched his body, seeing the Union Jack symbol of the British on his lapel. *Limeys,* he thought. He found an ammo belt attached to his waist. He unlatched it and slung the whole sodden mess onto the bank.

There was a whooshing sound overhead followed immediately with an explosion. More followed and Jimmy wondered what was happening. The booming fire from the Pershings dropped considerably. There was constant small arms fire and the booming of the gunboats never ceased. He realized there was another sound and he looked up, hoping he was wrong. He saw an aircraft angled in a steep dive. He didn't recognize the plane, but knew it wasn't friendly when rockets blazed from beneath the wings and sliced into the ground with rippling explosions.

He pulled his attention back to the weapon he'd found and quickly figured out the different mechanisms. He released the magazine, it was big, he figured it held at least 30 rounds. He pulled the bolt, it didn't seem to be worse for wear from its brief stint on the muddy bottom of the ditch. He liked the feel of it.

He took a glance down the canal, he could see 20 yards and there were no more soldiers coming his way at the moment. The ground shook as more rockets exploded. He chanced crawling up the bank to see what was happening.

He saw burning tanks. Some still firing despite being hit. A few of the massive Pershings were still maneuvering, firing their lethal shells. He watched one center punch a gunboat, the explosion lifted it and dropped it violently. The burning boat listed, the bay water filled the hull and it tipped over, exposing its still turning screws. But the planes were still attacking and the rockets were taking their toll.

He watched a wounded Pershing, its left track gone. The forward machine gun continued firing and the cannon sent out another shell with a long tongue of fire. Jimmy ducked when the whooshing of rockets engulfed the tank, shrouding it in fire. When Jimmy looked again the tank was burning. Hatches opened and tankers flung themselves to the ground. They stumbled and looked around in dazed confusion.

Jimmy got to his knees and waved and yelled, "Over here! Over here!"

The nearest tanker saw him waving and called the rest of the men and waved. He staggered toward Jimmy and he saw the others turn his way. Enemy soldiers popped up and fired.

Jimmy aimed and fired a long stream their way. He was impressed with the balance and slight kick. The weapon was steady and easy to control. He didn't know if he hit anything, but the enemy soldiers ducked down and took cover.

The tankers got to him and saw the safety of the ditch. They lunged for the water. The last man was nearly to him, his one-piece tanker suit was smoldering and he looked wounded. He suddenly arched his back and Jimmy saw his body vibrate with multiple bullet impacts. He flopped onto his face, only a foot from Jimmy. He reached for him and pulled him into the ditch, but he knew he was dead or would be soon.

Jimmy joined them in the bottom of the ditch. He noticed the bars of a Lieutenant sewn onto one of the tanker's lapels. "Sir," he said, "you okay?"

The lieutenant wore soot and grease smudged goggles over his eyes and Jimmy wondered how he could see at all. With blackened, shaking hands he removed the goggles exposing white skin and wide blue eyes. Jimmy thought he looked just like a raccoon. The officer nodded and sat on the bank, his legs in the water. He held a pistol. "I— I think so." Another whoosh of rockets followed by explosions made all four of them cringe. "Fucking Luftwaffe," he muttered.

21

K orth Lieutenant FromKor Guth was exuberant. It had been far too long since he'd experienced combat, and he'd almost forgotten the feeling of power. After flying from the launch ships, landing among the hapless North Americans and laying waste to their front lines, the fighting had continued almost nonstop. He'd stopped counting how many Americans he'd cut down with his MG42.

It had come with a cost, however. He'd lost eight warriors to the pathetic human weapons, but it was a small price to pay and the fallen warriors would be honored along with their families for generations to come. Besides, each warrior would rather die fighting than of boredom.

The beachhead was well established in his zone of responsibility. He and the warriors in his platoon wanted nothing more than to push forward, but Major Korto had stopped their advance, reminding him that the purpose of the entire war was to keep the humans occupied and that meant letting them take on most of the fighting and dying.

After two days of fighting, Lt. Guth ordered his warriors to move back, letting the German and Norwegian infantry take over their positions. His warriors resupplied and were jubilant as they replayed the battles and described the killing in vivid detail.

It was the morning of the third day. The humans had pushed further inland against stiff resistance. The Korth had to satisfy themselves firing at low Allied aircraft. Guth and his warriors were getting bored. The battle was tantalizingly close. Moving forward a half mile would put them at the front lines where they could continue doing what Korth warriors did best, kill indigenous beings. But Major Korto had not issued new orders and Lt. Guth wouldn't dare disobey a direct order, no matter how much he wanted to.

He watched a fight break out between two Korth warriors. He had no idea what it was about, but he knew the root cause was frustration. He didn't interfere, knowing the fight would be settled with a winner and loser and the issue would be resolved. It was a joy to watch trained warriors using their craft to try to kill one another. Of course, it wouldn't get that far, one would best the other and that would be the end of it. The Korth had survived too long to throw lives away uselessly, particularly elite warriors.

Major Korto and Captain Krangmut were suddenly upon him. Guth hadn't sensed their proximity, his mind wholly engrossed in the fight. He snapped to attention and gave an order, which stopped the brawling warriors immediately and brought the rest of them to braced positions of readiness.

Major Korto assessed the situation and spoke, "I know your men are restless, Lieutenant. I can see they are finding ways to entertain themselves, but you'll be happy to know we're moving forward." Guth's head expanded and went deeper red with the prospect of coming combat. Gorto continued, "Your warriors fought valiantly and will get more chances. The defenders have repulsed a unit of German Paratroopers at a bridge crossing Field Marshall Rommel feels is vital to the push inland. A large force of gunboats and LVTs are hitting the bridge defenders from the water in two hours. The defenses in front of us here are strong but they continue to be pushed back. Rommel has asked for our assistance to break the line open and ensure the bridge is taken intact."

He looked at Captain Krangmut. Though all Korth were exactly eight feet tall, Krangmut seemed much taller. He was powerfully built with muscles that rippled and flexed with each tiny movement. His upper shoulders were as wide as he was tall.

Krangmut's clicks and hums were deep and had an odd resonance. The massive scar running from his upper chest, across his neck and through his lower mandible was the obvious cause. Rumor had it, he'd gotten the injury from the glorious invasion of TaymanKur over 200 earth years ago, fighting the Kur hordes.

He was an intimidating warrior, one who'd refused any rank increase after captain. He made it clear, he didn't have any interest in upper command, he was a claws on the ground commander. The warrior's revered him. "Lieutenant Guth, I want your platoon to lead the attack." Guth couldn't keep his head from expanding and turning deep red. He noticed his warriors puffing their chests, some looking as though their heads would actually explode with pride.

"It would be my deep honor to do so, Captain. Thank you." He lowered his head in a slight bow, something only done for Premiers, Generals and Captain Krangmut.

Krangmut clicked, "You leave immediately."

"Yes, sir." Krangmut turned and Major Korto followed. Despite the officership hierarchy, Krangmut was the superior officer in every sense except rank. Guth waited until they disappeared over a rise then turned and barked, "You heard him, gather weapons and ammo, we're going to kill more humans!"

There was a roar of approval as they clacked their mandibles and gnashed their needle teeth together like snapping alligators.

————

LIEUTENANT GUTH HAD his platoon in a loose combat spread. They moved forward quickly, their long strides taking them ever-closer to the constant din of battle. Guth watched a string of German Stuka bombers diving and dropping their deadly explosive eggs. It was helpful to see exactly where the frontlines were. When his platoon was within a quarter mile, he ordered, "Pedestals up!"

A segment of Korth gathered quickly and pulled pieces of metal off their backs and soon constructed a series of large metal slabs. They were identical to the ones that had launched them from the ships, only much smaller. After five minutes the sergeant in charge of the pedestal warriors yelled, "Launchers ready, sir."

Guth set a forward guard, standard procedure during launches. The only real threat this far back from the lines would be enemy fighters and bombers. The Luftwaffe had done a good job keeping the skies clear most of the time. Lt. Guth surveyed the sky and saw only friendly aircraft. He held up his upper right and his lower left arms and moved them up and down and ordered, "Mount up!"

He waited they were upon the launchers then mounted the furthest one back. It would be the last one to launch, meaning he wouldn't be the first to land. He hated the thought, but as an officer he needed to be able to direct his troops. He heard Sergeant TurKul click, "On your order, sir."

The Korth warriors crouched on the pedestals, their clawed feet clicking in anticipation. Guth yelled, "Launch in sequence!" He crouched and heard the first compression engine fire with a dull thump. It was followed immediately with another and another. He was on the tenth pedestal. He felt the familiar shimmy then the full compression as the pedestal sprang upward creating eight times earth's normal gravity. The pedestal reached its zenith, stopped and once again Guth felt the exhilaration of flight as he spread his four arms and the thin skin connecting them caught the air and snapped open.

His MG42 was tight on his back and the bandoliers of ammunition strung across his body whistled in the wind. His platoon was spread in front of him; nine lines of flying warriors. The lead element angled into a dive and Guth noted where First Squad's Sergeant YukHan was aiming; a group of enemy tanks backing away slowly. They looked like the older Sherman tanks. From up here, Guth could see the value of the target. The defenders were using them to cover their retreat. If they could destroy them, the orderly retreat would turn into a panicked free-for-all. His head expanded and he communicated with Sgt. YukHan's mind, "Good target, carry on."

He 'listened' into Sgt. YukHan directing the heavy weapons

warriors, the ones carrying Panzerschreks and Panzerfausts, where to land. He was landing them right behind the Shermans. The rest would land and defend them as they took them out.

Lt. Guth stayed airborne as long as possible watching his warriors. There were six heavy weapon's warriors and each landed behind an unsuspecting tank. The American Infantrymen were so engrossed in their retreat they never saw the flying Korth until they were landing amongst them and killing them in scores.

Guth watched as tanks were destroyed. The Panzerschreks and armor-piercing grenades penetrated the thin metal surrounding their engines, and exploded. The Korth ignored the incoming fire, trusting their infantry comrades to protect them while they reloaded Panzerschreks and pulled more disposable grenade launchers from their backs. Soon there were ten burning tanks.

Lieutenant Guth landed lightly and pulled his MG42 from his back and hefted it as though it were a toy. He quickly loaded and fired into a fleeing soldier. He took delight, seeing his bullets walk up the man's back and send him sprawling onto his face as a thin plume of red mist settled over him.

The Germanic forces watched the Korth ripping through the stubborn lines as though they were fighting Kindergarteners. They yelled their approval and ran into the breech, killing any GIs still alive and filling the gap. They pushed outward, expanding the breech steadily, until the lines finally broke and despite the exhortations of their officers, the Americans broke and ran, some dropping their weapons.

Lieutenant Guth walked forward steadily, his organized, lethal platoon killing anything in range. Soon there were no targets and the incoming fire had dropped to a trickle. His Pedestal Troops caught up after dismantling the pedestals and were allowed forward to get some killing in too. He clicked and hummed, sensing the joy and mirth emanating from his warriors. Not a single Korth warrior had been killed or even hit. It was not the most important thing to Guth, completing the mission was, but it was an excellent start.

———

Sergeant YukHan reached out from the front of the lines and connected. "I can see the water. The bridge isn't much farther, sir. It looks like the attack from the water is well under way but they haven't taken it yet."

Lieutenant Guth replied, "I'll be right there." He trotted forward, the warriors around him keeping their intervals but increasing their pace to keep up with their platoon leader.

Guth came up beside YukHan and warriors moved forward to form a buffer. Guth signaled the Pedestal Warriors to move back and ready the pedestals. He doubted he'd need them again, but wanted to be ready just in case. He listened to Sgt. TurKul showing his squad where to build the pedestals.

Guth stopped and considered the battle field. They'd killed many American soldiers as they moved forward but he knew many had probably made it to the bridgehead and warned the defenders that they were coming. It wouldn't do them any good, but he didn't expect to surprise them again.

There was smoke everywhere mostly from burning tanks and bunkers. The bay water was littered with boats in various condition. Some were on fire and sinking, others without a scratch, still firing their main guns. He saw they were targeting a group of Pershing tanks on their right flank. They'd created a pocket and were threatening to roll up the flank.

Guth looked up at the sound of diving aircraft. They weren't Stukas this time but red-nosed fighter/bombers. Their wings bristled with rockets and he watched them unleash them upon the advancing tanks. "That'll slow the tanks. We'll attack them and finish whatever the Luftwaffe leaves for us. Forget the pedestals, we'll attack on foot."

The German and Norwegian soldiers behind them spread out, seeing the battle raging along the water's edge and not wanting to run headlong into it. Guth reached out and tweaked the first human officer he sensed, to move in support of his attack. His head discolored slightly at the thought of their cowardly caution.

By the time the last of the planes unleashed their rockets and disappeared over the horizon, the Korth were 40 yards away. The heavy weapons squad unleashed Panzerschreks and Panzerfaust grenades, killing the remaining American armor. All that was left to do was overrun the remaining bunkers and trench-lines and the bridge would be theirs.

Lieutenant Guth walked forward, his MG42 mowing down anyone who dared show himself. His head swelled and colored red wondering if the enigmatic Captain Krangmut would decorate he and his warriors with a unit citation.

He stepped into the ruins of a bombed-out bunker and surveyed the remains of dust covered humans. Few were intact, missing limbs and heads. He noticed a live one and he leveled his smoking muzzle and was about to squeeze the trigger and end his miserable existence, when the soldier looked up and sent withering pain into his head. Guth's confusion at being assaulted in such a way by a human made his head deflate and blacken.

Sergeant YukHan stepped into the carnage and sensed the human's attack. He darkened and aimed, meaning to fill the human with many holes, but Guth stopped him with a thought, then clicked, "Don't kill him. The TRs told us to watch for such humans." The mention of TRs got YukHan's attention. There was only one thing equal to combat and that was fucking. He lowered his weapon and moved on.

22

Captain Clancy McDermott barely had time to scarf down a sandwich and a glass of water before the buzzer in flight ops lit up and the voice of the mission control blared. "Now hear this, now hear this. Readiness level three. Repeat: readiness level three."

The harried pilots moaned and shoved food and drink into their mouths. Around a mouthful of sandwich, Captain McDermott said, "Don't choke. We've got a few minutes. Don't want anyone having to turn back because of a sour stomach or cramps."

One of his pilots, Lieutenant Whipps swallowed and asked, "That's an option, sir?" The others snorted and laughed. They all had sour stomachs and cramps every time they went up to face possible and likely fiery deaths against the Luftwaffe and Royal Air Force pilots.

McDermott grinned. He'd lost count of how many missions he'd flown over the past three days. He'd gotten some sleep the night before but only a few hours. He was thankful that at least the upcoming mission would be in daylight. The night missions were frankly, terrifying.

He grabbed another half sandwich from the pile stacked in the center of the room and poured himself another cup of coffee. He had to be careful, having to take a piss during a mission made it all the more miserable. The action was close and things happened quick, leaving little time for such trivialities.

The door to the ready room banged open and in walked Colonel Hastrap. The men braced, but he stopped them with a wave, "At ease. As you were." The men continued chewing and chugging coffee. "Intel's been going over the photos and film of the attack on the beachhead and naval units yesterday. The results are good, although we lost a lot of bombers and fighters, we put a crimp in their offensive. You men have done an outstanding job, and you deserve a rest, but that ain't happening." He gave a sideways grin, showing some of his Wyoming upbringing.

His face went serious and he continued, "The Germans have broken through with the help of those damned flying Korth. They knocked out a bunch of armor units and knifed though the lines. There's a general retreat." With his arms behind his back he paced to the large map of the East Coast hanging from the back wall. He picked up the pointer stick and smacked the map hard, indicating the beachhead. "Right now, it's mayhem, but General Thomas has ordered all units to retreat north." He pointed to the narrow point between Delaware Bay and Chesapeake Bay, just south of Wilmington. "He wants to stop them at this bottleneck."

He slid his pointer down to the Chesapeake Bay Bridge and hovered there. "A company of German Paratroopers nearly took this side of the Bay Bridge but reinforcements arrived in the nick of time and beat them back. Soon after, a large amphibious force attacked the bridge from the water, successfully taking the west side and we assume the Kent side too. We've lost contact with the defenders." He let that sink in, then continued. "Now, with this assault from the water and the push by the Korth straight at the bridge, it's clear they want it intact. If they take it, they'll have a direct path to Washington. Our boys are hammering the western span trying to break through to set charges, but so far, the enemy defenses have held. We can't wait. We need to take that bridge down. That's our mission.

"Half of you will be loaded with bombs and half with rockets. Two squadrons of P-51s will fly top-cover. As you can see the bridge is long, over four-miles long, in fact. It's an engineering marvel which took years to complete and we're going to take it down in minutes. It's up to Captain McDermott, but we suggest hitting the bridge mid-span. It'll cut down on any land-based air defenses. In another day, this area will be bristling with AA guns and will be much harder to assault.

"Radar's picked up a large force of enemy aircraft heading straight for the bridge. The Luftwaffe and Royal Air Force will be defending the span until they've had time to secure the airspace with AA guns." He looked the men over. Each pilot a survivor of three days of nearly constant combat. "We *have* to drop the bridge...at any cost."

————

Thirty-minutes later Captain McDermott and the 21 other P-47 pilots had climbed to 10,000 feet and rendezvoused with a squadron of P-51s. The Mustang pilots were staggered at 15,000 and 20,000 feet, ready to pounce. McDermott's radio crackled and he listened to the tinny voice of ground control. "Flight 36, we have multiple enemy contacts. Count 50 over target and 50 more inbound. Take bearing zero-one-four to target. Over."

McDermott keyed the mic. "Understand bearing zero-one-four to target. Over and out."

The voice added, "Good luck, sir."

McDermott didn't answer but turned to the North heading and addressed his pilots. "Keep your eyes peeled for bandits, but don't engage. You can expect small arms fire and possibly cannon from the gunboats down there, so go in fast and get outta there quick. You know the score, that bridge has to come down." He watched the big fighter/bombers turning to follow his lead. The first ten were armed with two, 250 pound bombs hanging from the wings and one 500 pounder from the underbelly. He'd contemplated attacking the bridge parallel to the span, but didn't want to have to fly through land-based anti-aircraft fire. They'd fly up the bay and hit it broadside.

It was early evening and the skies were dotted with orange and yellow clouds as the sun neared the horizon. The view was ruined by multiple ugly plumes of black smoke. There was a battle raging below, one which hadn't abated a second since beginning three days ago. The bay-water looked black and forbidding and he followed its path until he saw the southernmost point of Kent Island.

He pushed the nose down five-degrees. The heavily armed plane felt sluggish. That would change once he rid himself of the bombs. He scanned the sky and saw dots against the clouds. He couldn't tell if they were friendly or not. They grew in his windscreen and he realized they were bandits, RAF Spitfires. He keyed the mic. "Bandits at eleven o'clock high." He craned his neck searching for the P-51s. They'd be bounced in another minute if they didn't do something. "I don't see the Mustangs. Let's put some distance between us." He increased throttle and dove steeper. "We'll skip the bombs into the bridge."

He looked over his shoulder, the attacking planes were dots again and he surmised they'd be at the bridge and away before they caught up to them. The bay-water came up quickly, and he pulled up only feet above its icy surface. He checked his airspeed and pulled the throttle back a bit. There was something ahead. Boats, lots of boats.

He saw winking flashes and soon huge, beach-ball sized tracer rounds were flying past him. The water erupted with geysers, wetting his windscreen. His concentration was supreme, any slight movement of the stick downward and he'd be in the drink. The tracer rounds were close. It took all his willpower not to break away.

The nearest boat loomed large and he fired all eight of his .50 caliber machine guns. The gunboat was broadside and the incredible onslaught of heavy caliber bullets engulfed it and it exploded in a flash of fire. He pulled up slightly and flew through the billowing smoke, praying he didn't run into any flying chunks.

For a terrifying second it was dark, then he flashed back into daylight and he saw boats and beyond them, the bridge span. He ignored the incoming fire and pulled up slightly to 100 feet then angled down slightly and released the 500 pounder.

He felt the plane shudder and rise as it lost the weight and he pulled the nose up to clear the span and girders, then pushed the nose back down and raced up the water. He turned and saw his bomb detonate. A huge mass of water enveloped the bridge, but he couldn't tell if he'd damaged it. Before turning away he saw the next pilot, Lt. Davenport, fly through the gout of water and pull up. Behind him another explosion of water, but he also saw chunks of debris; he'd at least damaged it.

Over the radio he heard chatter from the P-51 pilots. They were heavily engaged. He looked up through his bubble canopy and saw the twisting turning fur-ball of aerial combat. There were multiple streaks of smoke and he hoped they were from Messerschmitts and Spitfires, not Mustangs.

McDermott was flying along the East bank of the bay-water at 100 feet. He craned his neck and saw his squadron mates following. He couldn't see them all. While he searched for the next waypoint, the furthest north point of Kent Island, he keyed his mic. "Flight 36, report in order."

All down the line the men reported in. Of the 22, there were three missing. He didn't dwell on it now, there'd be time once the mission was completed. "Damage assessment?" he asked.

Lieutenant Thorpe, flying tail-end Charlie, keyed in. "Multiple good hits, both rockets and bombs but the span is still up. Repeat, the span is still standing. Over."

McDermott gritted his teeth and mumbled to himself, "Dammit." He keyed the mic. "Roger. Understand. We'll need to do it again." They'd been over what they'd do if they needed a second run at it. "Bombs, let's get some altitude. Rockets, move ahead and lay down fire on those boats."

Lt. Thorpe was quick to respond. "Roger, we know what to do. Don't wanna have to do this again, Captain. Bring it down."

McDermott keyed the mic. "That's the plan, Lieutenant." He led his section of nine, each with two, 250 pounders on the wings, to 5,000 feet and turned back south. At this level, they'd have the optimal glide path for bombing but also be exposed to AA fire and be easily spotted and bounced by enemy fighters. He pushed to full throttle, wanting to get it over with as quickly as possible.

Ground fire from alerted AA guns opened up and black specks of flak erupted in front of them. McDermott ignored it, more concerned with enemy fighters. The radio chatter from the Mustangs was still going on in the background and he couldn't decide how it was going, but he knew there were lots of prowling enemies.

He glanced down and saw the rocket section's lead plane, which he knew to be Lt. Thorpe, racing across the wave-tops. If they timed it right, McDermott's section would come in right after they tore a gap in the boat defenses. They'd have a relatively uncontested couple of seconds to lay their bombs on target. He keyed his mic. "Keep your eyes peeled for bandits."

The flak wasn't heavy, but it was getting more accurate. "Let's not make it easy on 'em. Spread out." He knew it was a risk, it would make them even more vulnerable to air attack, but only for a couple more minutes. He keyed the mic again. "Okay, let's do it."

McDermott pulled power and angled his heavy Jug down, lining up on the bridge. The boats seemed to notice them at that moment and tracer fire reached up like fingers trying to pull them down. An instant later, Lt. Thorpe's group opened fire with machine guns and their remaining rockets. McDermott saw multiple gunboats take direct hits. His chest tightened as a P-47 clipped the bridge and violently hit the water and tore itself apart as it tumbled.

He closed his mind to the tragedy and centered his sights on the bridge. There were men on the span, he could see them aiming and firing at the departing P-47s. There was also an armored vehicle. He touched the trigger and watched the bridge spark and the water splash. He released the trigger and held the bomb release. *Not yet, not yet...Now!* He pulled the release and felt the general purpose AN-M57 bombs drop off his wings. He pulled up and felt the shock wave as his bombs impacted the bridge. *Direct hit!* He exulted.

His glee was cut short when there was a hard hammering beneath his feet. He could feel the impacts through the soles of his boots. He pushed the throttles back to full power and lowered the nose. In front of him, he saw an LVT along the eastern bank, it was offloading troops. He depressed the trigger and his incendiary and armor-piercing rounds engulfed it and it erupted in fire. He saw burning men flinging themselves into the water as he flashed past.

He made a tight right turn until he was flying west. He climbed and looked at the bridge, it was smoking and he could see a hole. He watched the last two Jugs drop their bombs and couldn't help yelling out when two of the four bombs impacted and blew girders and concrete in every direction. The enemy armor he'd seen earlier, was gone and he figured it had dropped into the icy waters. He confirmed the damage, it looked impassable.

"Ground this is 36, lead. Bridge is impassable. I repeat mission accomplished."

"Roger 36 lead. Understand mission accomplished. Be advised multiple bogeys at your six o'clock. Suggest quickest speed west. Over."

McDermott cursed under his breath and craned his neck searching for the incoming fighters. He saw them and knew he wouldn't be able to outrun them before they had at least one pass on them. He keyed the mic, "Bomb section, bandits on our six. Be on us in 30 seconds. Let's get on the deck."

Lieutenant Thorpe's voice, "Lead, rocket section safely away. We'll turn back and assist."

McDermott instantly replied as he put his Jug into a steep dive. "Negative, Lieutenant. Get your section to safety. That's an order." There was a radio click for a reply.

McDermott was once again skimming the wave tops only this time he was running for his life. He chanced a glance back, careful to keep his knees from jostling the controls and putting him in the drink. The enemy fighters—Spitfires—were gaining and would be upon them momentarily. He keyed his mic. "Steady. Break on my command, we'll split them up make it harder on them."

The nearest Spitfire was nearly on the tail-end Charlie. He'd open up any second. "Break right, Whipp! Now!"

He had to look away, the land coming up quickly. He pulled up slightly and saw soldiers diving for cover. He couldn't tell if they were friend or foe. He heard a brief call from the Lt. Whipp, "Can't shake him. Aw, shit, I..." McDermott whipped around and saw Whipp's plane smash into the water, a trail of black smoke rising, marking his path.

There was another call from Lieutenant Montclair, Whipp's wing-man. "He's got me bracketed. I—He's on me."

McDermott watched tracers surround and impact Montclair's plane. It shuddered but the heavily armored Jug kept flying. McDermott couldn't sit back and watch his section be picked apart. "Hold on, Monty." He pulled the stick back into his belly and he suddenly weighed three times his normal body weight.

He struggled to stay conscious, the corners of his vision blurring. When he was flying back east and upside down, he flipped upright and felt the blood rush back into his head, making his eyes bulge.

The Spitfire pilot bearing down on him couldn't believe his luck. He didn't think he'd catch the lead pilot before he was safely inside the AA envelope over his airfield, but here he was delivering himself like a prize pig.

He depressed the trigger at the same instant the big plane went onto its back. He watched with glee as his bullets impacted the bottom of the plane, sparking and sending bits off. He flew past it and turned, not giving the Thunderbolt another thought, but lining up on the next one in line.

McDermott felt the impacts of the Spitfire's bullets and held his breath, waiting for the one that would come through the heavy armor plating and kill him, but it never came. He righted the plane, gave his instruments a quick check, he was losing oil, but not badly. There was a gash in his right wing, but his fuel tank hadn't been hit. He angled down, following the Spitfire as it lined up on another victim.

He quickly closed the gap and when the Spitfire filled his windscreen, he fired all eight guns. It blew up, scattering into fiery chunks. The engine, still connected to the propeller dropped into the sea. McDermott pulled out and flew straight at the next Spitfire, still harassing Lt. Montclair. "Monty! Break left, Now!"

Lieutenant Montclair reacted instantly, turning away an instant before colliding with his flight lead. McDermott fired and the pursuing RAF pilot only had an instant to contemplate his death before he was eviscerated with heavy caliber bullets.

McDermott pulled up but knew he was too close. He felt the sickening impact as the burning Spitfire rammed into his underbelly and sent his P-47 tumbling forward. McDermott struggled to release the canopy, fighting the centrifugal force of his spinning aircraft. He only had seconds before he'd hit the icy waters.

Finally, he clutched the canopy release latch and pulled. The canopy flew off and the wind shocked him, taking his breath away. He clawed at the quick release and finally felt his restraints release.

The next thing he knew he was out and the world spun crazily. He glimpsed his plane, it was in half, the empty cockpit spinning crazily, the rudder section fluttering like a leaf in autumn. There was something he needed to do, something important, but his mind was overloaded. *Oh yeah...pull.*

23

G eneral Thomas, the commander of all US military units east of the Mississippi along with Generals and Admirals from other branches of the armed forces, stood and saluted when President John Franklin stepped into the room and stood at the head of the long mahogany table. At 41, he was the youngest US president, but he looked to have aged considerably since war broke out. There were dark bags under his eyes from lack of sleep, and though he gave the room a warm smile, it didn't translate to his slate gray eyes.

"Please be seated, gentlemen. I hear you have some good news for me."

General Thomas stood again and straightened his already immaculate Army uniform. He nodded, "Yes, sir, that's true." President Franklin nodded wanting him to proceed. "As you know, the invasion has been devastating. They struck as far north as Long Island and as far south as Norfolk. They made gains everywhere, but mostly in the Chesapeake Bay Area. We think they were pushing toward Washington, but we stopped them." He turned to a Lieutenant Colonel who walked to a stand holding large sheets of paper and uncovered the top sheet to show a map of the whole east coast with black lines indicating enemy advances.

General Thomas walked to the map and used a pointer stick to indicate an area near Norfolk. "They landed here and we held them for three days." The Lieutenant colonel turned the next sheet and the map was a closeup of the area from the beach all the way to Chesapeake Bay. "On the third day they dropped a company of elite German Paratroopers from the same division that took and still holds Idlewild Airport on Long Island. The Bridge Defense Brigade soldiers tasked with defending the Bay Bridge fought them off long enough for reinforcements to arrive. A couple hours later the area was hit by British waterborne troops. After a hard fight, they took both the east and west sides of the bridge and obviously wanted to use it to thrust into the heart of Washington. Our Army Air Corps," he indicated General Hampton, who nodded grimly, "bombed and destroyed a large segment of the bridge, here at the halfway point. They've been trying to rebuild, but our artillery and continuing air attacks have hindered their progress. And—I was told only minutes before this meeting—that our forces have destroyed the Germanic forces holding the west end of the bridge, so it would do them no good to repair it any longer."

There was murmuring around the room and even some grins and back slaps. The lieutenant colonel turned the sheet showing a closeup of an area to the north of the Bay Bridge. General Thomas waited for the murmuring to die down then continued, "Once it was clear our forces couldn't hold the beachhead, I ordered all our troops to retreat here." He smacked an area where the points of land pinched to their narrowest. "With the bridge gone and our defenses bolstered on the west side of the bay, the enemy forces have to go the long way, and will have to punch through six divisions to do it. The weather has also taken a turn for the worse, which I'm sure you've noticed."

There were nods all around and the President cleared his throat and said, "Yes, I've never been so happy to see stormy weather."

Thomas nodded and continued, "Their planes are more advanced and can operate in more varied conditions but no one from either side can fly when they can't see their targets or their airfields to land. The playing field, at least in the air, has been leveled somewhat."

President Franklin stood and strode to the map. His fit, six-foot-five frame made him look intimidating, one of the reasons he won the election, a strong, handsome confident leader for difficult times. He studied the map, concentrating on the arrows indicating enemy and friendly force movements. Like every American of military age, he'd served his four years. He led a platoon as an Army second lieutenant and ended his career as a first Lieutenant serving in intelligence. He knew what the markers meant and he nodded, happy with the defense. "Can we hold this line, General Thomas?"

The corners of Thomas's mouth turned down and he rubbed his chin, considering before answering. "For the time being, yes. Through the winter, no doubt, but when spring comes and they're able to use their captured airfields…" He shook his head, "With two fronts, we'll be stretched thin."

He folded a few sheets until he found the photo he wanted. It was a grainy, black and white photo of a company of Korth Warriors crouched on metal hydraulic powered pedestals. "Like the launchers they used on the ships to crack our beach defenses, the aliens take smaller platforms into battle and have used them effectively to fling themselves behind our lines." The next photo showed Korth firing Panzerschreks and Panzerfaust grenade launchers into the backs of American tanks. "They simply wreak havoc and we haven't found a way to defeat them. So far, we've only seen one regiment of Korth, but if they bring more, we'll be hard pressed to stop them."

The President considered the photo. "I wonder why they don't bring more? If they're so effective, why don't we see more of them? They could roll through us much quicker if they committed all their warriors. We've hardly seen any on the Alaskan front, almost like they're in an advisory role. But why?" He looked at the head of the OSS, General Smithers.

General Smither's angular face and long hooked nose was unmistakable. He was recognized as the most experienced officer among them. His ability to keep his job, despite frustratingly low success penetrating Europe and reporting solid intelligence to the many Commander in Chief's he'd served, showed just how much respect he held.

He stood and held his chin up, his dark brown eyes looking down the length of his nose, past the glasses propped precariously at the very tip. "We have wondered the very same thing, sir. One theory: they might be trying to preserve their warriors. Before the war we didn't even know what they looked like, now we not only know that, but know they're vulnerable to our weapons. They can be killed. This could be why we haven't seen them in greater numbers.

"It brings up many questions, though. For instance, we've seen European technology advances in certain areas. Their weapons jam less, their aircraft engines are more powerful and their airframes are stronger, yet lighter. They've also advanced beyond our understanding of Meteorology, and are able to predict weather with startling accuracy. Their paratroopers can fly their parachutes much like gliders. All important and all—except the weather—we are able to reverse engineer once we have the items. They also seem to have some way to see us, without actually having spies on the ground. There's no other explanation for some of the more—sensitive targets they've hit with complete and total accuracy. It's more than them reading our mail. Some of their bombers hit targets that we've been extremely careful to keep as innocuous as possible and completely secret.

"They're impressive." He shook his head and put his thick gnarled hands on the table and leaned forward. "But these creatures came from *space.* That kind of technology must include far more than they're giving the Europeans. If they're trying to keep their warriors alive, then why not send them into battle with their full tech? They must have more advanced weapons than gunpowder and bullets. Why are they being sent into battle with human weapons? There are only two reasons we can think of—either they don't want to win the war, which begs the question—why—or they don't have access to their technology here on earth, which also begs the question—why."

There was a smattering of conversation and President Franklin let it continue for 30 seconds before clearing his throat, instantly bringing order and quiet. He looked General Smithers in the eye and stated, "We need to know what's going on over there, General," there was danger in his voice and the room went deathly quiet.

General Smithers finally nodded, nearly a full minute of silence passing between them. "There has been some progress on that front, sir…"

THE END OF BOOK 2

I hope you enjoyed the second installment of the Korth Chronicles. As always, feel free to reach out via email. I read and respond to every email received.

chrisglatte@gmail.com

Book 3: Strike Force Blue now available!

Please consider leaving a review. Reviews help other readers find quality books like this one.

Want to be notified when the next installment of The Korth Chronicles comes out?
Sign up here!

ABOUT THE AUTHOR

C.T. Glatte lives in southern Oregon in the beautiful Rogue Valley with his wife and two sons. After over 20 years in the medical field, he's now a full-time author.

ALSO BY C.T. GLATTE

Strike Force Red Book 1

Strike Force Blue Book 3

WWII books by Chris Glatte

The Long Patrol

Bloody Bougainville

Bleeding the Sun

Operation Cakewalk

Across the Channel

Tark's Ticks

Made in the USA
Coppell, TX
03 June 2023

17648982R00134